D0364075

QUEEN OF GLORY

QUEEN OF GLORY

Christopher Nicole

This first world edition published 2012
in Great Britain and in the USA by
SEVERN HOUSE PUBLISHERS LTD of
9–15 High Street, Sutton, Surrey, England, SM1 1DF.

British Library Cataloguing in Publication Data

Nicole, Christopher.
  Queen of glory. – (Rani)
  1. India–History–Sepoy Rebellion, 1857-1858–Fiction.
  2. Historical fiction.
  I. Title II. Series
  823.9´14-dc23

ISBN-13: 978-0-7278-8121-2 (cased)

All Severn House titles are printed on acid-free paper.

Severn House Publishers support The Forest Stewardship Council [FSC],
the leading international forest certification organisation. All our titles that
are printed on Greenpeace-approved FSC-certified paper carry the FSC logo.

```
      ®      MIX
             Paper from
             responsible sources
FSC          FSC® C018575
www.fsc.org
```

Typeset by Palimpsest Book Production Ltd.,
Falkirk, Stirlingshire, Scotland.
Printed and bound in Great Britain by
MPG Books Ltd., Bodmin, Cornwall.

'*The old sword flashed once more in 'fifty-seven,*
This is the story we have heard
From the Bundelas who worshipped Shiva
The Rani of Jhansi fought valiantly and well.'

Subadra Kumari Chauhan

At the age of twenty-one, Lakshmi Bai, Rani of Jhansi in Northern India, found herself involved, against her will, in what is known to British historians as the Indian Mutiny; Indian historians regard it as the First War for Indian Independence. Despite her youth and inexperience, the rani personally led her army into battle, time and again, earning from Sir Hugh Rose, commander of the British army opposed to her, the description of being the best general in India.

The Gathering Cloud

Kujula stood in the doorway to the schoolroom, shifting his feet nervously.

Kujula was my manservant, a large Maratha who wore the green and gold uniform and turban of the Jhansi royal guard. He had been 'given' to me by the rajah when I had first arrived in Jhansi seven years ago, and I knew him to be absolutely faithful. But his duties consisted of acting as my bodyguard whenever I left the palace, or doing any heavy work required in my own apartment; he did not usually venture into the royal quarters. Thus I knew the interruption had to be important. 'Yes, Kujula?' After thirteen years in India I spoke Marathi fluently.

'The Major Skene is here, Memsahib. He wishes an audience. He says it is important.'

I felt a sudden tension in my stomach. In the several months that had elapsed since I had rejected his ill-advised 'rescue' of me as I was about to be punished for the crime of adultery, which was the most serious offence, short of murder, with which a Hindu wife could be charged, I had met the East India Company's political agent on several occasions at palace functions, but he had never sought an interview in that time. And even his formal greeting of me on such occasions had been icy.

His coldness towards me was no doubt justified, in his eyes. He had invaded the palace at the head of a squad of Bengal lancers, when I was already suspended on the triangle awaiting my punishment, and demanded my release, producing irrefutable reasons why I could not be punished, on three counts: firstly, because I had been married in a Hindu ceremony and such marriages were not recognized as valid by the Christian Church, and I a Christian. Secondly, while adultery might be socially condemned, it was not a criminal offence under British law. And thirdly, even if I were guilty, under the laws of extraterritoriality, a British citizen could only be tried in a British court.

He had carried me off in triumph, leaving the Rani of Jhansi and her court dumbfounded but angry at this brutal display of British power, only to be dumbfounded himself when, as soon as I had regained my composure, I had chosen to abandon his protection and return to the side of my oldest and dearest friend, the rani, even if, by the laws of her land, she had been the one required to condemn me in the first place, and thus I could expect, as he saw it, nothing but punishment and humiliation. As a result, he had washed his hands of me.

Thus if he now sought an interview with me something fairly dramatic must have happened . . . and I could think of only one event of sufficient importance to bring him to the palace. I therefore closed the book I had been interpreting for my pupil, Prince Damodar, and stood up. 'I am sorry, Highness, but it seems that our lessons must be terminated for this morning. You may join your friends.'

'Yes, Memsahib,' the little boy said, obediently.

He seemed almost disappointed at this unexpected holiday. After the death of their own son, the rajah, Gangadhar Rao and his wife had determined to adopt, an heir being very necessary to the continued royal rule. Prince Damodar, son of a cousin of the rajah, on being picked at the age of five from obscurity to be heir to the throne, to the gratification of his parents, had been a difficult child, but following the rajah's sudden and untimely death, he had come under the sole rule of the rani, and she had made it very clear that he must obey the dictates of his governess without question or hesitation, and was now the most obedient and enthusiastic of pupils. Thus I smiled at him encouragingly, gathered the folds of my dark blue sari, and left the room.

As was the Hindu custom, I arranged the cowl of my sari over my head and half across my face, and led Kujula along the many hallways that filled the palace, past evidences of wealth I could never have dreamed of before coming to India – drapes of inestimable value, gold ornaments and statuettes, which culminated, when we reached the entry hall, in a life-size statue of Lakshmi, the Hindu Aphrodite, whose name had been given to the rani on account of her remarkable beauty.

It was very early on a bright spring morning in the year 1856, and thus pleasantly cool; the kingdom of Jhansi, although situated in the north of the subcontinent, was yet many miles south of the great mountain barriers, and in a month or two would become extremely hot.

On our way we encountered several people, men and women, each of whom gave me the traditional greeting of holding their hands together in front of their breasts and bowing their heads. Last of them was my erstwhile husband, the captain of the royal guard, Abid Kala, a handsome young man wearing the Jhansi uniform of yellow breeches and green tunic. As our separation – there was no provision for divorce in Jhansi law – was not yet a year old, his greeting remained frosty; I was just happy that the whole misguided experience was behind me.

We arrived at the reception room, where Major Skene was moving about restlessly. He was not very tall – I rose some inches above him – and was of slender physique, with crisp black hair. He wore a blue uniform, without any insignia, and lacked a sword, very wisely, as like all Englishmen – and even more, Englishwomen, as I remembered from my own early experiences – he found sitting on cushions, instead of a chair, a difficult business when clad in European clothes.

He placed his peaked cap under his arm and bowed. 'Mrs Hammond.' As the British refused to recognize my second marriage because it had not been a Christian ceremony, he always addressed me by my first married name.

'Major Skene. How good of you to call. I trust you are in good health?'

'Thank you, yes. And . . .' He hesitated, while he studied me without appearing to do so. A sari is actually a most private garment, where it matters, owing to the several folds and pleats of material, but it does reveal the outline of those 'limbs' so sensitively protected by English custom, while the sight of an English gentlewoman with bare feet and a gold bangle on each ankle was positively terrifying, especially as it reminded the prurient onlooker that she was not wearing any of the voluminous underclothing considered so necessary for a memsahib.

All of this was perhaps the more evocative for him because I have been described as a most handsome woman, even in European dress. I am certainly well-endowed physically. My features are well shaped if, I am sure, unremarkable, and if my long auburn hair was concealed he knew it was there: he had once had the privilege of seeing all of me in the nude, a memory which was clearly swirling through his mind at that moment.

I smiled at him. 'I do assure you that I am in possession of both my breasts and, as you can see, my nose. In fact, there is not a mark on my body.' As he seemed to be in a state of shock at my choice of words, I could not resist adding, 'Would you care to examine me?'

He seemed to get his brain working. 'Mrs Hammond! Please! I am here on official business.'

I gestured at the cushions. 'Shall we sit?'

After seven years in Jhansi I sank, gracefully and easily, to the floor. Skene took somewhat longer to arrange himself, but eventually we faced each other, both cross-legged, which he seemed to find more embarrassing than ever.

'I was told you had important news,' I said. If it was the news I sought, I wished to receive it as rapidly as possible, whether it was good or bad.

'Oh, indeed. Firstly, the war in Crimea is over.'

'Good heavens! Would it be possible to ask who won?'

'Oh, we did.' He seemed surprised at my question. 'With the French and the Sardinians, of course.'

'You mean Russia has conceded defeat? After a few battles fought on the perimeter of its empire?'

'Ah, you see, the fall of Sevastopol has convinced them that we mean business. So the tsar has accepted our terms.'

'Which were?'

'A guarantee not to interfere in Turkish domestic affairs, whether secular or religious. And to pay a large indemnity. In return, we will evacuate the Crimea.'

'And this achievement was worth twenty thousand British lives? That is the figure, is it not? Not to mention the countless others.'

'I know it is difficult for women to understand international affairs, but the important point is that the Russians are now banned from any attempt to encroach on Istanbul and the straits, and therefore the Mediterranean. That is what matters.'

'I am sure you are right,' I agreed, without conviction.

'The end of the war also means that our troops will be coming home. Specifically those units withdrawn from the Indian army. That means that they will be able again to take up their garrison duties where it is considered necessary, and this in turn will free the Indian units to return to *their* normal duties. I have no doubt that Colonel Dickinson will be able to regain his old posting in command of the Jhansi garrison.'

'That would be very nice.'

He frowned. 'You *are* still engaged?'

'When last I heard, yes.' Colonel James Dickinson was the man who had rescued me from the thugs who had murdered my first husband, and was therefore my oldest European friend in India. Over the years we had become closer, until he had asked me to marry him. I had accepted his proposal, but the requirements of his profession, and my commitment to the rani, had prevented our immediate marriage, and his absence in the Crimea meant that we had not seen each other for over a year, while the uncertainties of the post had rendered our correspondence very occasional.

'You'll excuse me, but that is a very odd way of putting it.'

'Major Skene, you must know the situation. James and I wish to wed. But the difficulties that lie in the way of such a step are at this moment insurmountable. He is an army officer, sworn to serve queen and country wherever he is sent. Therefore it follows that his wife must be prepared to accompany him, wherever he is sent, unless it is actually to a war zone. I am, I am proud to say, the rani's closest friend, and more importantly, I am her adviser in her relations with the Raj. I am sworn to serve her for as long as she needs me, and she certainly needs me at this moment, and will continue to do so at least until her claim against the governor general's decision to invoke the Doctrine of Lapse with regard to her kingdom has been heard and acted upon by the House of Lords. Now, if you were to bring us news of that . . .'

'I have news of that, at least, indirectly.'

My jaw almost dropped. Why had this idiot taken so long to get to it?

He could see the consternation in my face. 'How is the rani?' he asked.

'The rani is very well.' He was still skirting the subject of his call, so I decided to press matters. 'Would you mind speaking plainly, just for once?'

He drew a deep breath. 'Dhondu Pant, Nana Sahib, has lost his appeal.'

My jaw did drop. 'I hope you are not serious.'

'I'm afraid I am. Their Lordships have determined that as the adopted son of the late peshwa, Baji Rao II, Nana Sahib has no justifiable claim on the late peshwa's pension.'

'Do you expect me to believe that is the real reason?'

'Well, of course, there are other factors involved. Baji Rao bequeathed to Nana Sahib enormous personal wealth. Eighty thousand pounds a year is a huge sum of money, but the absence of it is certainly not going to make him a pauper, or even require him to change his lifestyle in the slightest, and the money can be more usefully applied in other directions.'

'Do you seriously suppose that argument will be acceptable to Nana?'

'Probably not. But he will have no choice. Oh, he will write letters to all his fellow princes, reminding them of the iniquities of British rule, but he has been doing that for years, without accomplishing anything.'

'Which is the nub of the matter, is it not? He is being punished for his criticism of British rule.'

'I am not privy to the opinions of the Company.'

'You only carry out their instructions. I will inform the rani. She, of course, will be interested to know when the axe will fall upon Jhansi.'

'My dear Mrs Hammond, I do not think the rejection of Nana's claim has any bearing on Lakshmi Bai's.'

'You don't?'

I was being sarcastic, but he chose not to take offence. 'The two cases are entirely different, as I am sure you appreciate. The rani is not claiming a pension, which she has already been offered. As you said, she is appealing against the application of the Doctrine of Lapse to Jhansi. Lord Wellesley, when he promulgated the doctrine forty years ago, laid down the rule that any principality where the rajah died without a legitimate male heir should be taken over by the Company. I am sure you understand that this was intended to avoid the possibility of a disputed succession, with the consequent risk of civil war.'

'And was not, of course, ever intended to enlarge the Company's domains and therefore its wealth,' I put in, more sarcastically yet.

'Certainly not. What was never made clear was the interpretation of the word legitimate, and whether it included adoption. The rani, and you, I understand, as well as, I may say, many other people, feel that as Prince Damodar was legitimately adopted by her husband and herself, and the adoption was recognized by the Company at the time, there is no question as to his legitimacy. The Earl of Dalhousie's action is seen by many people as overstepping the mark.'

'But he knows, as do we, that his invocation of the doctrine has nothing whatsoever to do with Prince Damodar's legitimacy.'

He looked embarrassed. 'Well, it is undeniable that since her accession as regent the rani has acted in a somewhat high-handed manner. I mean, riding off to war without referring to the Company garrison commander, or me . . .'

'Major,' I said, 'the rani's people in the north were being ravaged by those Pathans. She conceived, correctly in my opinion, that it was her duty to defend them, as rapidly as possible, not wait while you communicated with Calcutta and received instructions, without which the garrison could not act.'

'But still, an eighteen-year-old girl leading men into battle . . . I understand that she charged at the head of her cavalry. I mean . . .'

'Listen,' I suggested.

The morning had suddenly erupted into sound, drumming hooves, a succession of shots, loud cheers.

'My God!' he cried, scrambling to his feet. 'We are under attack.'

I also rose. 'Come with me.'

'No, no,' he protested. 'By all means take refuge yourself, Mrs Hammond. I must try to get to the cantonments and warn Captain Williams that there is an emergency.'

'There is no emergency. The noise you hear is the rani exercising.'

'What? But the gun shots . . .'

'Come,' I invited again, and led him along the hall, followed by Kujula. 'The rani's daily routine,' I said, 'is well known and greatly admired by the people of Jhansi. I do not know if it is known at all to the European community, nor do I suppose they would find it acceptable to their prurient attitude to life. I must therefore ask you to regard what I am about to show you as confidential, not to be repeated to anyone, and in particular, not to be reported to Calcutta. Will you give me your word as a gentleman on that?'

'Well . . . I suppose . . . if it is not illegal.'

'It is not illegal, in Jhansi. Now, I would not like her to see you. Stand here.' I showed him to a window overlooking the polo field that stretched behind the palace, placing him behind one of the heavy drapes, from where he could look out without being seen. We beheld what to me was the most evocative sight in the world: the Rani of Jhansi, mounted astride a large black stallion, galloping round and round the field, the reins clenched between her teeth, a Colt revolver in each hand, firing at a target every time she passed it, and more often than not hitting it, cheered on by a group of young women, the ladies of her court, and by the officers of her government, her father, Maropant Tambe, who was her chief minister, and several others of her staff, as well as the commander of her army, Risaldar Kala, and his brother, commander of the palace guard and my Indian husband, Abid, from whom I was separated

She was the most perfect of women, small – only five feet one inch tall – but possessed of a mature figure, at once hard muscled and intensely feminine, long black hair that, loose, floated behind her, and exquisitely delicate features, small like the rest of her, flawlessly carved, and dominated by her flashing black eyes. Her complexion was a gentle light brown, and was only slightly marred by a scattering of tiny pits left by the attack of smallpox she had suffered a few years previously, an event that had changed my situation enormously. I had also suffered the dread disease as a young girl, and survived. I was immune for life, and thus I had been able to nurse the queen back to health. From that moment, the hostility she had felt towards the foreigner her husband had foisted on her as a governess had been replaced by a friendship that was very close to love. Well, I loved her, too. To me, she was Manu, the diminutive of her given name, Manikarnika, hitherto allowed only to her husband and her father.

I glanced at the major, who was staring, open-mouthed. 'My God!' he muttered. 'She has nothing on.'

'She is wearing a dhoti, although this is not determined by modesty but to protect her flesh from chafing against the leather of her saddle.'

'And she appears like this before her people?'

'Before her court. But they, and her people, worship her as a reincarnation of the goddess Lakshmi.'

He had actually allowed his gaze to wander, for a moment. 'And that child in the pram. Is it hers?'

'How could it be hers, Major? Her son, as you surely know, died in infancy, and she has no living husband. Prince Damodar, as you also know, is adopted.'

'Well . . .' He flushed.

'The rani is the most devout woman I have ever met, or expect to meet. She may not herself possess any royal blood, but she is the daughter of a Brahmin, which is the highest Hindu order of society, an inheritance that governs every aspect of her life and her behaviour. That she should have been married at the age of fourteen to a man she had never seen was to her entirely right and proper. That her husband died so soon was karma. But she still regards herself as bound by her marriage vows, and she considers promiscuity, any promiscuity, as the lowest form of human behaviour.'

'You'll forgive me for saying that is a damned shame.'

'I will not forgive you for *saying* it, Major, although I am prepared to do so for your thinking it. If you are interested, the child is my daughter.'

He stared at me, his mouth open even wider.

'Oh, come now, Major, surely you know that I have a daughter?'

'By . . .?

'By Abid Kala. Now you have seen enough. Come.'

Skene followed me back to the reception chamber, like a docile dog, clearly in a trance. 'Do you ever join the rani in her exercises?' he ventured.

Clearly his imagination was running wild. 'Sadly, Major,' I replied, 'I entirely lack the queen's horsemanship. I can shoot, though. She insists on that skill being achieved by all her women. We will take tea, Kujula.'

'Of course, Memsahib.' He summoned a servant and gave instructions.

I seated myself, gesturing Skene to do the same. 'I wanted you to see that because of the popular misconception held by the Raj that they are dealing with an inconsequential young girl, and their only knowledge of these are based on British young ladies such as their own daughters, who shriek with fear and climb on to chairs at the sight of a mouse, and faint if they inadvertently glimpse a nude man. Lakshmi Bai may be a girl, but she is a Brahmin, the highest Indian caste, and now she is also an Indian queen. Her life is governed not by prurience, but by an awareness of her ancestors, her surroundings, and by her duty, to those ancestors, to the memory of her dead husband, and even more to her son, and above all, to her people, as she was instructed to do by her husband on his deathbed. In pursuance of this duty she will fight, if need be. Can you convince the Company of this?'

'I assure you, Mrs Hammond, I shall do my best. I admire the rani greatly.' I assumed he was still mentally seeing the vision he had just been given. 'But . . . there are things she could do to help her cause.'

'Tell me. As long as they do not impinge on her sovereignty, I am sure she will be receptive.'

'One of the things that most concerns Calcutta is her continued correspondence with known Anglophobes like Nana, and the Begum of Oudh. If this were to cease . . .'

'They are both very old friends.'

'None the less, I am sure you have heard the saying that a man, or in this case, a woman, is known by the company she keeps. Tell me, have you ever met either of them?'

Met! I thought. How little you know. 'Yes. Nana visited us about three years ago.'

'For what purpose?'

'He had some business to discuss with Gangadhar Rao.'

'What sort of business?'

'Now, Major, six years ago I made it perfectly clear to Colonel Sleeman that I would not act as a Company spy as to what went on within this palace. That was a simple act of loyalty to the rajah, who employed me as governess to his young bride, the rani. In the years since he became my friend, as the rani is now my closest friend. So I am even more unlikely to betray any confidence concerning them. But as it happens, I have no idea what Nana and the rajah discussed; I was not present at their meetings.'

'I did not mean to cause offence. But will you at least give me your opinion of him? Nana, that is.'

Opinion! Nana had looked at me, liked what he saw, and demanded that Gangadhar Rao give me to him for his harem. For a moment my fate had hung in the balance, Gangadhar Rao, however much he might value my services and, indeed, my company, being terribly aware of Nana's superiority, in wealth, power, and above all, lineage, to himself. Manu had saved the day in the only way she had been able to think of, by informing Dhondu Pant that he could not take me to his harem because I was betrothed to be married, and when Nana, correctly suspecting subterfuge, had demanded the name of the man, she had selected the captain of her guard, Abid Kala, who was present and was as dumbfounded as myself. But Nana had also insisted upon staying for the wedding, and thus I had been forced to embark upon my second disastrous marriage.

From which, as I have related, this man had sought to release me by proclaiming the marriage to be invalid in British law, but he knew nothing of the background to the event – nor should he. So I said, 'It is not my position to air opinions upon a royal prince, Major.'

He decided against risking further offence, and waited while two girls served us tea, which was taken without milk or sugar. Then he said, 'As I have indicated, in Calcutta he is regarded as a most dangerous man. You would be doing the rani a considerable favour were you able to dissuade her from further correspondence with him, and certainly from entertaining him in Jhansi again.'

'I cannot possibly do that, Major. As I said, the rani and Nana are the oldest of friends. Although he is some years older than her, they played together when she was a child in Benares.'

He sighed. 'Well, then, the Begum of Oudh. You have also met her?'

'I have. She visited Jhansi a few years ago on her way to Bombay to board a ship for a ceremonial visit to England, where she was received by Queen Victoria.'

'That was an idea of Lord Hardinge. She is regarded in Calcutta as the most dangerous woman in India.'

'You mean, more dangerous than the rani?' I smiled at him, but he was a difficult man to tease.

'Do you know anything of her? Her background?'

'If you mean, do I know that she began life as a prostitute, whose beauty, charm and wit, undoubtedly assisted by her sexual skills, brought her to the attention of a court official, who passed her on to the nawab, who took her into his harem, and then made her his number two wife . . . yes, I know these things.'

'From which position she has virtually forced her husband into retirement and now rules the state as if she were born to it. Or perhaps you approve of her.'

I do approve of her, I thought, but for reasons you would be quite unable to understand. So I said, 'Well, at least her career, in addition to being an almost incredibly romantic story, proves that not only men can rule.'

'Oudh is a far larger and more powerful state than Jhansi,' he said severely. 'And she rules it absolutely. How, I do not understand. According to her title, she is a Muslim. Yet Oudh is a predominately Hindu state.'

'She rules because her people adore her. And because she is beyond the Company's reach: she has a husband, who is alive and well, even if he has abdicated all power to her. And she also has a healthy son.'

'She *thinks* she is beyond the Company's reach.' This remark I found somewhat sinister. 'Tell me, is she as beautiful and as sensual as they say?'

'Hazrat Mahal is the most beautiful and sensual woman I have ever encountered.' I spoke almost dreamily, remembering the night I had spent in her company. Like Nana, Hazrat had looked at me and liked what she saw, and like Nana, she had requested that I come to her bed – there was no condemnation of homosexuality amongst the Hindus and, although it was forbidden by Sharia law, Hazrat Mahal did as she pleased. Unlike Nana she had only required me for one night, and even more unlike Nana, apart from her beauty she possessed charm, charisma and sheer style that was beyond his reach, as well as that sensuality that apparently so fascinated Calcutta society.

I had, of course, been both horrified and terrified at her proposal, but on this occasion no help had been forthcoming from either Manu or the rajah, neither of whom was prepared to refuse the Begum of Oudh, ruler of the powerful and enormously wealthy Kingdom of Oudh, anything she wished. Thus I had spent the night with the begum, and undergone, to my initial consternation, an experience that had turned out to be the most sublimely rewarding of my life. My only previous experience of sexual desire had been in my six years of marriage to Mr Hammond – an ongoing purgatory with occasional descents into hell. That he had brought me to India as part of his missionary activities was the only good memory I had of him. Our marriage had entirely negated my interest in sexual matters, although I was well aware that those around me, following my rescue from the hands of the thugs, were often more than a little interested in my striking looks and full figure. If I had ever felt the slightest attraction for any man it had been the one who had actually carried out my rescue – James Dickinson.

It had not seemed relevant at the time, as our lives had been headed in such different directions, but he had managed to have himself appointed to the caravan bound for Cawnpore, which I had joined after accepting Lady Hardinge's offer of employment as governess to the teenage rani, which had brought me to Jhansi, and thus eventually to my present situation, when I was only one level away from being mistress of all around me.

'She also hates the Raj.'

'Not at that time. I think her dislike for the British arises from her treatment on her visit to England in 1850.'

'I am not aware that she was ill-treated.'

'Of course she was not *ill*-treated, Major. But she was treated as an unimportant provincial, forced to take her place behind the ladies of the court. Hazrat Mahal is the reigning queen of a country not greatly smaller than England itself. Whatever her background, she expected to be treated as visiting royalty, which she is. When she was not so treated, she took deep offence. And I can tell you, the begum is a woman of intense emotions.'

'You admire her.'

'Certainly, I do.'

'Despite the fact that she rules the most corrupt and dissolute court in India?'

'Major, the biggest problem you, and every white man or woman in India, has is that you are incapable of viewing life except through the eyes of a white, Anglo-Saxon Protestant. You may, thanks to your aggression and superior weaponry, have been able to conquer a huge empire, but it is still, like all empire, ephemeral in terms of history, and the British White, Anglo-Saxon, Protestant composes but a microcosm of the population of the world, most of whom has been around, in terms of civilization, centuries longer than you. They have different cultures, different codes of conduct, and of honour, different concepts of morality, and above all, of course, different views of religion. But they were here, practising their way of life, long before Britain became a nation, and they will still be here long after you have gone away again.'

'Did you learn all this . . . well . . .?'

'Claptrap?'

'I would not have said that. But did Mr Hammond have . . .'

'Believe me, I learned nothing of any value from Mr Hammond. I worked it out for myself.'

He considered. 'You do realize that in Calcutta, you are also regarded as a very dangerous woman?'

I smiled. 'As dangerous as the begum, or the rani? But I have no kingdom.'

'You are chief adviser to the rani.'

'I'm afraid you are flattering me, Major. I am the rani's friend, and her interpreter in matters relating to British laws and customs.'

'The estimate is that you are more than just a friend.'

I gave him my most steely stare. 'Just what do you mean by that?'

He flushed. 'Please do not take offence. It is simply that you have achieved a position of wealth and prestige in relation to an Indian ruler that is unprecedented.'

'I achieved my position in regard to Gangadhar Rao before his untimely death. The rani, you could say, inherited me. And . . .' I held up my finger. 'In case you are suffering any other misconceptions, I was never the rajah's mistress.'

Another flush. 'Believe me, I did not . . . well . . .'

'I think it is necessary for us to be absolutely straight with each other,' I suggested.

He finished his tea. 'You have been most cooperative, and informative. I only wish we could have had this conversation earlier in our acquaintance.'

'Thank you. I feel the same way. May I hope that I have persuaded you to regard the rani in a different light?'

'Oh, you have,' he assured me, fervently.

'And will so present your new opinion to Calcutta?'

'Indeed, I shall.'

'Well, then . . .' I made to rise.

'May I venture to impinge on your wish to have me understand the true situation here in one last direction?'

I looked at the window; the sun was very high. 'If we can be brief; I have certain other duties.' Mainly to acquaint the rani with the contents of our discussion.

'As I said just now, your position is unique. It would be of great interest to me to understand just how this was achieved, if not . . . well . . .'

'Lying on my back or kneeling before masculine desire?'

'Mrs Hammond!' I had, as usual, shocked him with my boldness.

'I am simply stating a fact that is known to every man, and every woman, in India. And I am sure in England as well, even if they are afraid to mention it. As for me, is there not a file on me in Calcutta?'

'It is very brief, and therefore incomplete. It merely states that you arrived in India in 1843 at the age of twenty, as wife to the Reverend Charles Hammond, that he was murdered in 1849, and that you then obtained employment, through the good offices of the wife of the then governor general, Sir Henry Hardinge, as governess to the Rani of Jhansi.'

'That is broadly correct. Although it is based on a mistake.'

He raised his eyebrows.

'I was born on the fourteenth of December, 1825. Thus I was eighteen when I arrived in India.'

'But . . .'

'I felt it to be necessary to add two years to my age when being interviewed by Lady Hardinge.'

'Forgive me, but isn't that very unusual, for a woman to *add* two years to her age?'

'I suppose it is. But you see, in my anxiety to obtain the employment she was offering, I told her I had spent two years as a schoolmistress. Well, as she knew that I had been married to Mr Hammond for six years, almost all of which were spent in India, had she known I was only just coming up to twenty-four when we met, I would have had to start my teaching career at fifteen, which she would hardly have believed.'

'You mean you lied to Lady Hardinge?'

'Yes, I did.' And not only in that direction, I thought.

'Well . . .'

'I was endeavouring to survive, Major. I do not suppose you have ever been in that position.'

He cleared his throat. 'But is it true that you married Mr Hammond at the age of eighteen?'

'Actually, it was seventeen. The voyage to India took some time.'

'He was much older than you?'

'He was considerably more than twice my age.'

'But you lived with him, happily, for six years, and yet, I have been told, revealed no trace of grief when he was so brutally murdered, before your eyes.'

'That was because, Major, he was not murdered before my eyes, and I did not live happily with him for one day, much less six years.'

'I'm sorry. I don't understand. You married him . . .'

I considered. My sentence for accidentally killing my employer's housekeeper had been for ten years exile, married to the man who had offered to take me and keep me out of England for that time. That Mr Hammond had been able to come to such an arrangement with Lord Stapleton, chairman of the local magistrate's bench, had been because a trial might have involved His Lordship himself in an unseemly scandal, he having been somewhat close to the lady I had inadvertently pushed to her death. His Lordship had, not unnaturally, assumed that Mr Hammond's offer had been an act of extreme charity by a man of the cloth; it had never crossed his mind that my husband, man of the cloth or not, had had only one ambition: to get his hands on my body just as soon and as often as possible, and the idea of being able to take that body with him to share the discomforts of his Indian mission had been irresistible.

Well, that six-year purgatory had been brought to a sudden end by the thugs he had carelessly invited to join our caravan. What mattered now was that my 'crime' had been committed eight years ago. Thus technically, I was still under sentence of death in England. But I felt quite sure that British law could not reach me in Jhansi, certainly while I was the rani's favourite. 'I married Mr Hammond because it was a choice between that and the hangman's noose.'

'*What* did you say?'

'You asked me.'

'Would you mind explaining?'

I shrugged. 'I do not think it matters, now. I am the daughter of the Reverend John Weston, Vicar of Lower Stapleton, in Hampshire. As we were very poor I was put out to work at the age of fourteen, obtaining a position as chambermaid at Stapleton Manor, the country seat of Lord Stapleton. I worked there for three years, until there came the day I had an altercation with another member of the staff, and endeavoured to push my way past her. But, tragically, I must have pushed too hard, for she lost her balance and, as she was standing at the head of a steep staircase, fell down it. I think she must have hit her head on every step, because she arrived at the bottom quite dead.'

'Oh, good heavens! What a catastrophe! But wasn't it obviously an accident?'

'Only to me. Unfortunately, she happened to be the housekeeper, and even more unfortunately, she was the mistress of Lord Stapleton, who was in residence. His wife seldom left the fleshpots of London to bury herself, as she saw it, in the country. My story was of course, necessarily incomplete. Daily growing more aware of the poverty of my family and the way my father was sinking into debt, and finding a mass of guineas scattered across Lord Stapleton's dressing table, clearly the previous evening's winnings at cards, I had succumbed to temptation and pocketed five of the coins. Unfortunately when I encountered Mrs Houston at the top of the stairs she heard a clink from my apron pocket and demanded to see what I had in there. I panicked and, my sole desire being to get out of the house,

I attempted to push my way past her, causing the accident that followed. Believe me, Major, I was forced to expiate my crime a thousand times beneath Mr Hammond's sweating weight.'

For the moment he was at least partly sympathetic. 'I can understand your misfortune, and your feelings on the matter. But you have just admitted that you lied to Lady Hardinge, on several counts, in order to obtain this position.'

'As I have told you, I was endeavouring to survive, Major. Had I been returned to England, as was the Company's intention, I would have been hanged. And I should point out that Lady Hardinge was equally desperate. She was stuck with this request from the Rajah of Jhansi, a long-time friend and supporter of the Raj, that she obtain a tutor for his child bride. His terms were strict. A five-year contract, which would require cutting oneself off from all but the most casual contact with European society, and for which, of course, she would have to be unmarried, a widow or a spinster, again with no prospect of altering her condition until her five years were complete. Lady Hardinge had found it quite impossible to discover anyone willing to accept such a situation, despite the considerable remuneration offered, as quite apart from being required, from the point of view of a Calcutta memsahib, to plunge alone into the wilds of darkest India, there was all the consequent risk of encountering savage behaviour, not to mention rape. I suspect that Lady Hardinge regarded me as a gift from the gods.'

Skene was looking embarrassed again. But he was becoming accustomed to my use of words unacceptable in a British drawing room. 'Oh, quite. Absolutely. And so you came to Jhansi, and prospered, thanks to . . .'

I held up my finger.

He flushed. 'I was going to say, your talents. Or was it good fortune?'

'A bit of both. The rajah found me both intelligent and attractive, and then I was able to help the rani survive an attack of smallpox.'

'Good heavens! But . . .'

'You have never observed the evidence? Actually, she was very fortunate. Because, as her sole nurse, I prevented her from scratching as much as I was able to, she was left with very few marks, and only one on her face, a pit above the right eye which is only noticeable on close inspection.'

'But weren't you at great risk yourself?'

'No. Because I had survived an attack myself as a girl, and was therefore immune.'

'And you . . .' He could not stop his gaze wandering, and as usual I could not resist the temptation to tease him.

'I have one or two pits on my body, yes. Would you like to see them? Or is this interview now concluded?'

He was flushing again, but again recovered. 'There is just one more matter.'

I sighed. 'Yes?'

'It is of a rather intrusive nature.'

'You mean more so than whether or not I am marked with smallpox? Very well, Major. Just so long as it does not take too long.'

He cleared his throat. 'There is a rumour prevalent in Calcutta, and indeed, here in Jhansi, that you have renounced Christianity in favour of Hinduism.'

'And my religious beliefs, or lack of them, are so important to anyone?'

'Well, in view of your position as adviser to the rani, and your background . . . I mean, as a parson's daughter and you were the wife of a missionary . . . you never attend the Christian church here in Jhansi.'

'What you mean is, from the day of my birth to the night Mr Hammond was murdered, I was submerged beneath a consistent torrent of religious dogma, which I increasingly found difficult to relate to the actual teachings of Jesus Christ as reported in the gospels.'

'You mean you did not believe the teaching of your own father?'

'I am grateful for most of the non-religious things he taught me, and which have proved most useful, especially his knowledge of, and interest in, history and politics. But when I needed him, and his religious beliefs, more than ever before, he chose to disown me.'

'Well, after your confession to me one can hardly blame him.'

I gave him another of my most steely stares. 'I have *confessed* nothing to you, Major Skene. You asked me for a résumé of my life, and I have given it to you. As a man of God, my father's business was not to condemn, but to forgive and pray for my redemption. As for attending church, I am well aware that I am an object of prurient curiosity to the English residents. I do not enjoy mixing with people who I know are vilifying me behind my back. Besides, would I not be a distraction to the parson, as he would know that his congregation was more interested in me than in his sermon?'

'Do you see all life through a screen of laughter?'

'That has to be preferable to seeing it through a veil of tears. In any event, I fail to see that my religious beliefs can be of the slightest interest to Calcutta.'

'They are of interest to everyone, Mrs Hammond, where you have the ear of an Indian queen.'

I sighed. 'As I have told you, you are mistaken. I do not have the ear, as you put it, of the rani. I am her friend, and I am proud to be so. I only advise her when she asks me to do so.'

'Then may I ask, how would you advise her if it ever came to an open conflict between the princes, and princesses, of the Bundelkhand and the Raj?'

I stood up. 'I earnestly hope that such a day will never come. And now, Major, I'm afraid I have things to do.'

Hastily he scrambled to his feet. 'I have taken up sufficient of your time, Mrs Hammond. Thank you for being so frank with me.'

'And will my frankness now be recorded in my file in Calcutta?'

'Not without your permission.'

'Which I shall not give. But tell me, Major, has my frankness enabled you to obtain any . . . insight into the rani's true character?'

'Indeed it has. And into yours.'

'And will *that* be reflected in your next report to Calcutta?'

'It will colour it, certainly.'

'In whose favour?'

'Why, the rani's. And yours, to be sure. Have confidence in the future.'

'Do you?'

'Yes. The Earl of Dalhousie retires as governor general in a few months' time. And I have been told that this new man, Canning, is an entirely different character. He may not have the aristocratic ancestry of Dalhousie, but his father was prime minister of England, thirty years ago, and I am told he has an altogether more pragmatic outlook, and will be prepared to listen to argument with an open mind.'

'Thank you, Major. Kujula will show you out.'

The Storm

I went to the rani's office, where I knew she was to be found at this late hour in the morning. Except if there was a crisis, Manu lived in a very orderly manner, rising before dawn, indulging in her exercises, then having her bath in the fast-flowing stream that cut through the rock on which the palace was built, then attending to her devotions which, as I had explained to Skene, she took very seriously, then breakfasting, then holding court, when she could be uncompromisingly severe – and there was no appeal from her judgement – before retiring to her office to deal with correspondence, accounts and reports, usually in company with her father, while several secretaries waited to carry her directives to the appropriate departmental heads. Following this she had her midday meal before retiring for a rest, then she spent an hour or two with me, often requesting me to read to her from some classic or history book; she had never fully mastered the nuances of English and preferred me to explain everything to her, although with her acute and inquiring intelligence, in many cases inspired by her intensely anti-British sentiments, there were few statements and opinions she was not eager to argue, and we had some enjoyable debates. In the evenings she usually entertained one or two of her ministers or family members before retiring early, as she was up so early every day.

As was usual around the palace, she wore a sari, today in pale blue, with her hair loose and still damp from her bath, with several rings of enormous value on her fingers, as well as gold anklets and bangles on her forearms, studded with rubies. The picture was utterly exquisite. But then Manu was exquisite in everything she did or wore, even the yellow jodhpurs and green tunic topped by a gold-coloured turban, with a tulwar, the Indian sabre, and two revolvers that she preferred when on official business or going about her people, determined to leave no one in any doubt that she was as much a ruler in her own right as any man.

She looked up from the document she was studying. 'That was a very long interview.' Her voice was low and soft, and she gestured me to take the chair on the other side of the desk, beside her.

I sat down. 'He had a lot to say. And to ask.'

'You mean he has forgiven you for refusing to accept his judgement last year?'

'He seems to be prepared to accept it, even if I doubt he is capable of understanding it.'

'Was any of his news truly important?'

'It was very important. The war in the Crimea is over.'

'And has ended, no doubt, in an English victory.' Her tone was contemptuous.

'The tsar has sued for peace, yes.'

'And Major Skene considers that this is of importance to us?'

'Well, it means that the soldiers taken away from the Indian army will be returning, so it will be back to full strength.'

'Yes,' she said, thoughtfully.

'And that therefore they will all be able to return to more normal duties.'

'Ah. You are saying that Colonel Dickinson may be returning to Jhansi?'

'Possibly.'

She gazed at me. 'Am I then to lose you, my Emma?'

'The only way you will ever lose me, Manu, is if you send me away. But . . . I would like to be allowed to see him.' After close on two years!

She rested her hand on mine and gave my fingers a gentle squeeze. 'And so you shall. But did Major Skene take an entire morning to tell you this?'

'No. There was something else.' I drew a deep breath. 'Dhondu Pant has lost his appeal.'

Manu's face seemed to stiffen.

'Then we are lost,' Maropant Tambe said. He was a little man, but there could be no doubt from whence Manu had obtained her beauty; her mother had died when she had been a child.

'The major does not think so.' I hurried on. 'He considers that there is no possible connection between Nana's appeal for the restoration of his pension, and ours for the recognition of your son as the legitimate heir to the throne of Jhansi.'

'What does he care?' Manu asked. 'He hates me.'

'Not any more. Now he wishes to assist you in every way possible.'

'Indeed? What changed his opinion?'

'I allowed him to watch you exercising.'

Manu had been staring at the sheet of paper on her desk as she took in the news of the rejection of Nana's appeal. Now her head turned, slowly towards me, while her father snorted in condemnation. 'I am sure you had a reason for doing that,' she said, quietly. 'Apart from gratifying the major's senses.'

'Yes. The Raj has always held you to be a pampered child, raised, if you will pardon me, Maropant Tambe, above your station by the lust of a lonely widower. I wanted him to see the real Manu, the spirited, athletic woman, capable of taking her place beside, or indeed at the head of an army, and loved and admired by her people.'

'You think, and plan, so deeply, Emma, that sometimes you frighten me, even as it makes me realize how much I need you. Do think you succeeded, in more than merely arousing his manhood?'

'Yes. He has promised his support in whatever may lie ahead.'

'And of course you believe him, because he is an English officer and a gentleman.'

'I regard that as important, yes.'

'And I must put my trust in your judgement.'

'There is, however,' I said, cautiously, 'a caveat.'

She raised her eyebrows.

'He quoted an English saying, that a man is known by the company he keeps.'

'Was he referring to you?'

'I am not the most popular person in Calcutta, yes. But he was thinking more of your friendship with Nana and the begum, both of whom are regarded as hostile to the Raj.'

Manu's eyes flashed. 'Am I then to have my friends chosen by Calcutta?'

'He made the point, Manu. He means well. I am sure of it.'

'And you agree with him.'

'No. You must know how warmly I regard the begum.'

Her eyes softened. 'Yes, I do. But you still would have me obey the dictates of some distant clerk?'

'I would beg you to be patient. It has been two years since Mr Lang launched your appeal. Nana's took just over two years to be brought to a decision. Yours cannot be delayed much longer. And now that the distraction of the war will no longer interrupt their Lordships' considerations . . . If they find in your favour, then you can snap your fingers at Calcutta.'

'And if they find against me?'

'We have another saying in England, that one should never cross a bridge until one gets to it. The major believes that we have every reason to be optimistic.'

'The major,' she mused. 'I would have you write to Lang, Emma, and ask for his assessment of our situation.'

I did as the rani wished, but of course it took more than a month for my letter to reach Calcutta, and I did not expect a reply for another six weeks after that. So it was necessary for me to practise the patience I had recommended to Manu, and in the meantime enjoy the peace and tranquillity of Jhansi. This was, in fact, an almost perfect summer, with the monsoon not due for another few months.

Indeed, almost the whole world seemed peaceful, as the Crimean War had finally come to an end – despite Major Skene's claims, it was difficult to determine whether anyone had actually gained a victory at the cost of an inordinate number of lives. True, Great Britain almost immediately became embroiled in another war, this time with Persia – which necessitated drawing on yet more British units from India – and there were ongoing troubles in China, but these, as Colonel Sleeman, the political agent when first I had come to Jhansi, had once pointed out to me, were the concomitants of empire.

As far as we were concerned, there was the imminent departure of Dalhousie to anticipate. We were told he was not in good health, that he had worn himself out in the administration of his duties. This may very well have been true, for he certainly had been tireless in his determination to bring the entire subcontinent into the nineteenth century as envisaged by the Raj, regardless of the feelings, or the desires, of the mass of the population. Railways had proliferated during his tenure of office, and as James had once laughingly said to me, there were few Indians who could resist riding on them. They were less happy with the spreading tentacles of the telegraph system, regarded as most valuable by the various far-flung military commanders, but with increasing distrust by the indigenous population.

For me, however, this period of apparent tranquillity, the last I, or any of us, was to know for some time, was distorted by the memory of my conversation with Skene. I knew my considerations, and Manu's, were being coloured by our anxiety about the future, whether or not Dalhousie's determination to force her abdication and have the Company take over Jhansi would be upheld by the British Government, but mine was further confounded by what he had told me of the estimation held of me by the English community. I had always treated their criticisms with contempt, and I was genuinely not interested in their opinions, as I knew that I could never re-enter the British world of nuances and double entendres, of never saying what was one's actual feelings but always disguising them beneath a veneer of hypocritical politeness.

But as I had entirely rejected such behaviour, I had to face the question of who was I? And in what did I believe? Was I a Christian? This might well become a matter of life and death should the unthinkable happen: looming above it all was the question of religion.

If my six years of marriage to a tub-thumping doom and gloom fanatic like Mr Hammond had left me almost numb with distaste for him and all he stood for, I had yet been brought up in a vicarage. I certainly believed in God. But whose God?

I have to confess that I found Hinduism most attractive. This was partly because of its tolerance of other beliefs, in such contrast to Mr Hammond's utter intolerance of any opinions that did not coincide or accept his version of the deity. Which is not to suggest that the Hindus did not take their own seriously. Indeed, they were far more devout in their daily lives than most Christians, certainly in India, just as they held their beliefs – their worship of, for instance, the cow, the preservation of which was so important to their daily lives. Sadly, and to their terrible cost, the British regarded this as an idle, and often irritating, superstition.

I cannot pretend, and I would not presume, to understand the true nature of Hinduism, of its deeper meanings and concepts; I can only say that in contrast to the Christianity I had been taught from birth, under which, in the person of Mr Hammond, I had suffered for so many years, I found it refreshing. But as to what I truly was . . . I could only remind myself that I was Manu's friend, her confidante and, I liked to think, provided a strength on which she could draw when necessary. I knew that I could never desert her, no matter what circumstances might arise, and certainly not until the business of her sovereignty had been resolved.

In response to my letter, Mr Lang made the journey to Jhansi himself to discuss the situation. 'There is no need to be despondent,' he told us, while I wondered if he had heard anything of my own marital crisis; if he had, he gave no sign of it. 'I said from the beginning that Nana's case had no substance. There is still every cause for confidence on our part.'

'I must write to him, conveying my condolences,' Manu said.

'No, please,' Lang begged. 'Under no circumstances should you do that. He is currently, so I am informed, making all manner of threats. For you to be associated with any of those would be a grave mistake.'

Manu accepted his advice, which supported that of Skene, with ill grace, but it was only a few months later that we were rocked by far more serious news. In almost his last act as governor general before leaving India, the Earl of Dalhousie announced that the Raj was taking over the government and administration of the State of Oudh.

Major Skene himself brought this news, which he delivered with a good deal of justified apprehension.

'That is preposterous,' Manu declared. 'How can he do that? The nawab still lives, and the begum is a mother.'

'This has nothing to do with the Doctrine of Lapse, Your Highness,' Skene explained. 'The governor general has acted because of the chronic and serious misrule that obtains in Oudh. It is hardly possible to believe the evidence of corruption and injustice that exists there.'

'What will happen to the royal family?' I asked.

'Oh, the nawab will be required to abdicate, and will be suitably pensioned off.'

'What does the begum say to this?' Manu inquired.

'I understand she is very unhappy about it,' Skene replied.

If my memory of Hazrat Mahal was at all accurate, I had to consider that was the understatement of the century.

Major Skene duly took his leave, and Manu and I gazed at each other.

'I must write to her,' Manu said.

'Did she write to you when you were deposed?' I asked.

'I have not yet been deposed,' Manu riposted. 'My case is still in abeyance.'

'Do you suppose she will appeal?'

'She may well wish to do so, as she is a friend of Queen Victoria's,' Manu said.

Remembering what Skene had told me, I gave a little cough at this, but Manu ignored it. 'But it will rest with her husband, and he is a useless excrescence. She has told me this herself.'

'I remember,' I said.

'But I will write to her,' Manu insisted. 'We are two queens in distress.'

'And if the British learn of it and hold it against you?'

'Am I to live my entire life at the behest of the British?' she demanded, angrily.

There was no further argument. And perhaps, I thought, the worst was over, as Dalhousie duly took his departure.

Skene was reassuring. 'As I mentioned, this new man, Canning, is entirely different,' he told us. 'His business is to restore the popularity of the Raj, and I know he will do this.'

We had no choice but to believe him. But before the end of the year the blow fell. Mr Lang appeared in Jhansi, looking thoroughly miserable.

'I am sorry to tell Your Highness that your suit has been thrown out by the House of Lords,' he said. 'They have delivered an almost unanimous decision that the Earl of Dalhousie not only acted within his rights as governor general in invoking the Doctrine of Lapse as regards Jhansi, but that he was entirely correct to do so, in view . . .' he cleared his throat, 'of the rani's known association with various dissident elements. I am quoting, you understand, Your Highness.'

'I am sure you are not finished, Mr Lang,' Manu said, speaking quietly but each word like a drop of ice. 'Did they not name these dissident elements?'

'Well, Your Highness . . .' He gave me an anxious glance.

'Name them,' Manu said.

Lang cleared his throat again. 'They list your lifelong friendship with Nana Sahib.'

'Go on.'

'And with the Begum of Oudh.'

'I understood that the begum no longer rules.'

'The nawab has been required to abdicate, and has been removed to Calcutta, where I understand he is living in luxury and complete contentment. The begum, unfortunately, has refused to accept the ruling and has removed herself, and her son, who she claims is now the nawab, from Lucknow into the interior.'

Hoorah for Hazrat, I thought. But I had never doubted that she was not the sort of woman tamely to surrender what she considered to be her rightful position.

'Where,' Lang continued, 'she is apparently stirring up the populace against the Raj. Oh, she will be brought to book, but Oudh is a very large country, and it may take time. But you will understand, Highness, that she is now an open enemy of the Raj.'

Manu's expression had not changed. 'Was there anything else?'

He sighed. 'The fact that your father spent most of his life working for the family of Baji Rao, the deposed peshwa.'

'If he had not, I would not have known Nana,' Manu pointed out. 'Continue.'

This time he licked his lips. 'They also list your employment of, again I quote, the widow Hammond, who is well known as an agitator and an enemy of the Raj.'

'How interesting,' Manu said, 'if somewhat out of date. Thank you, Mr Lang. I know you have done everything possible to assist me. Do you have any idea how much time I have before I am deposed?'

'It will take some time. Mr Canning has to settle in, pick up, as we say, the reins of government, and then he must prepare a new government for Jhansi.'

'So I may have a few months left to me. To prepare myself, and my people, for the headsman's axe.'

'It will not be as bad as that. I am sure Mr Canning will handle the matter with both tact and diplomacy.'

'You are a most reassuring man, Mr Lang. Again, I thank you.'

'As I thank you, Your Highness, for your unfailing courtesy towards me . . .' Yet another clearance of the throat. 'Ah . . . to whom shall I submit my account?'

'You may submit your account to that well-known enemy of the Raj, my father.'

'Thank you. You understand, Your Highness, that this business has not been cheap. The journey I had to make to England . . .'

'I understand that,' Manu said. 'Present your account, and it will be paid.'

'Although I do not know from where,' she confessed to me when we were alone. 'Thanks to my husband's overspending, I am still deeply in debt.'

'I have brought you nothing but ill-fortune,' I said.

'That is not true. Your company and support have been two of the few blessings I have enjoyed these past few years. As for my associations, was I not a friend of Dhondu Pant before I even knew you existed? Would I not have been accused of friendship with Hazrat whether you were here or not? Was not my father employed by the peshwa's brother? They would have done me down no matter who I employed. But, oh, to be riding beside Hazrat now.'

'Well . . .'

She glanced at me. 'I know. You would give up everything to lie in her arms again.'

'Manu,' I protested. 'I went to her bed because Gangadhar Rao commanded me to do so, because he dared not offend the Begum of Oudh.' But I knew I was blushing.

'And you loved every moment of it. I am not blaming you, Emma. Perhaps I, too, could find solace in those arms. But I cannot desert my people.'

'Then what will you do now?'

She walked up and down the room, went to the table and picked up her favourite tulwar, which had a jewel-encrusted hilt, and swished it to and fro, then laid it down again. 'What can I do, save wait, and hope? Great Britain seems so powerful. One cannot escape the feeling, as there are many more people in Hindustan than in England, that we should be even more powerful. But it is not so. I am in despair, Emma.'

'Nothing lasts forever,' I reminded her. 'The British will eventually go away again, or dwindle. Did not the Mughals eventually dwindle?'

'Over several hundred years. That will be too long for me.'

But only a few weeks later she was again exhilarated, as she received a letter, which she waved at me in her excitement. 'Dhondu Pant is coming to visit!' she cried.

I was aghast. Of course it was possible to say that now the rani's appeal had finally been turned down, who she associated with no longer mattered. But I was too aware of the apparent omnipotence of the Raj, the way its decrees had to be carried out, and the way that those decrees could be quite ruthless. I did not doubt that it was possible for Calcutta to determine that Manu no longer had the right to live in her palace, or worse, to cancel her pension, as they had done to Nana himself – unlike Nana, without Jhansi she had no independent source of income.

On the other hand, surely a prince was entitled to visit a queen, even if she no longer ruled, who also happened to have been a childhood friend?

I put this point to Major Skene when, having learned of the impending visit, he hurried up to the palace in some agitation.

'If it concerns you so,' I said, 'can you not forbid Nana to come here?'

'I have no legal right to do that.'

'Well, then, it is simply a visit of one old friend to another. Can you not see it like that?'

'If only it were that simple,' he said. 'Calcutta is sure that Nana is making plans for a revolt. We know that he has been corresponding with the Begum of Oudh. It would be very unfortunate if he were to attempt to involve Jhansi.'

'I very much doubt that the rani would be interested in a revolt,' I said, knowing that I was lying. I could not doubt that Manu would be *very* interested in a revolt, if she thought it could succeed.

'Nevertheless,' he said, 'we know that Nana is very popular here. I must warn you that if there were to be a demonstration when he comes, and this got out of hand, the garrison will respond vigorously.'

'I am sure they will,' I said. 'But I am also sure Nana is aware of this.'

'And then . . .' He looked embarrassed. 'I believe you are a confidante of the widow Gangadhar?'

'You know that I am proud to be a confidante of the widowed Rani of Jhansi, yes.'

'So . . . would you by any chance be present when the rani and Nana have their meetings?'

'Very probably, yes.'

'I don't suppose you would feel able to inform me of what is discussed?'

I realized that I was in a very difficult position. I could not doubt that were Nana to attempt to take on the Raj he would be defeated, and severely punished. Equally would any of his allies be so treated, and the thought of that happening to Manu was not acceptable. Therefore, would it not be better for everyone if any proposed revolt should be nipped in the bud?

But if there was a plot, and it was proposed to Manu that she should join it, would not any information involving her lead to her arrest as well as that of Nana? That was not something I could contemplate.

In any event, I was entirely on the side of these people.

So I temporized. 'That would depend upon what was being discussed, Major,' I told him.

This actually seemed to reassure him.

He was certainly proved right about Nana's reception in Jhansi. As always, the Prince travelled in extravagant style, a whole entourage of richly caparisoned elephants surrounded by equally richly dressed horsemen, mounts and riders. Nana himself rode in the first howdah; those behind carried members of his harem.

Slowly he made his way past the houses and the two forts and up the hill to the palace, cheered by, it seemed, the entire population. There was not a British soldier to be seen, nor a sepoy, as they had all been confined to barracks to make quite sure there was no trouble.

Manu and I stood on the porch, surrounded by our guards and her ladies, to watch his approach. 'Is he not a king?' Manu asked. 'Every inch of him?'

I could not argue that he *looked* like a king, his turban and his clothes as well as the hilt of his tulwar gleaming with precious stones, his moustache carefully waxed to turn up at the ends. His face was as I remembered it, large and harsh, his eyes as cruel as before.

And I remembered that the last time he had visited Jhansi, I had had to be hastily married to keep me out of his clutches, whereas now . . . but I was still a married woman, at least in Hindu eyes, even if estranged from my husband, and given Manu's strict moral principles I should be in no danger.

But she was certainly pleased to see her old friend, whatever *his* morals. She wore a cloth of gold sari and all her jewellery to receive him, and bowed low before him. He held her hands to raise her up. 'It has been too long,' he said.

'Too long,' she agreed.

'And you are as beautiful as ever.'

'You flatter me,' Manu said. 'I am a queen without power.'

'Who can tell the future?' Nana asked, and gazed at me.

I curtsied also. 'Your Highness.'

'And you too, Mrs Kala, have lost none of your beauty. I am told you are a mother.'

'That has been my fortune, Highness.'

He looked me up and down again. Whenever he did that he gave me goose-pimples. Then he looked at Abid, standing with the guard behind the rani. Then he turned back to Manu, waiting patiently.

'My house is yours,' she told him.

As Skene had suspected, Nana had come to discuss the current situation, and was taken aback when he discovered that I would be present.

'Can this woman be trusted?' he asked.

'Emma? Of course.'

'She is a *feringee*.'

'She is my friend. Would you ever dream of repeating anything you heard me say, or heard said to me, in private, Emma?'

So there it was; I had no further room for consideration. 'No, Highness,' I said.

'It would still be better were we alone,' Nana grumbled.

'But we are not alone,' Manu pointed out, looking at Tatya Tope, Nana's guard commander, who as always stood immediately behind his master, as fierce as ever.

'He is my right-hand man,' Nana said.

'As Emma is my right-hand woman,' Manu countered.

'Then let her swear.'

'There is no need,' Manu protested.

'I swear,' I said.

He continued to regard me for some seconds, then nodded. 'Very well.' He turned to Manu. 'I have heard that your appeal to the House of Lords has been rejected.'

'That is true.'

'Will you accept this?'

Manu shrugged. 'I have no choice, as things are at present.'

'The begum has not accepted her family's deposition, any more than I am prepared to accept the rejection of my appeal,' he said.

'What will you do?'

'I will strike a blow for freedom,' he declared.

'We will drive the British into the sea,' Tatya Tope announced.

Manu sighed. 'Many people have had dreams such as you.'

'Perhaps,' Nana agreed. 'But how many have acted? Two generations on, we are still suffering from the defeats inflicted upon our forefathers by the British. By the Duke of Wellington. But the Duke of Wellington is dead.'

'Are his successors inferior?' Manu asked. 'What of Sind? What of the Punjab?'

'Baluchis,' Tatya said, contemptuously.

'And Sikhs,' Nana said, equally contemptuously. 'And yet, the Sikhs nearly defeated the British. And what of Afghanistan?'

Manu stroked her chin.

'The British are not the men they once were,' Nana claimed. 'We only *think* they are. Listen to me, Manu. For the last three years my agent, Azimullah Khan, has been living in England, representing me in the courts.'

'Unsuccessfully,' Manu pointed out.

'That does not matter now. For those three years he has observed the British at close quarters. He was there throughout the war in the Crimea.'

'Another victory for the British.'

'The British declare it to be so, because the Russians wished to stop fighting when Tzar Nicholas died. The new tzar is a man of peace, not war. But what did the British take away from the Crimea? Nothing. Not a single thing. What did they leave behind? More than twenty thousand men. And of the rest more than half died of sickness or were frozen. Azimullah Khan says that the British people were fed up with the war long before it ended. It even caused the fall of a government. He says they will not support another such war for many years. But more, he says the incompetence of the British generals is all but unbelievable. He says that but for the presence of the French the British would have been thrown out of the Crimea in weeks. Is not now the time to test them with another war, on as grand a scale, and at a greater distance?'

'They already have an army in Hindustan,' Manu pointed out. 'They do not have to send one. And there are no winters here as there are in Russia.'

'Tell her Highness about the British army in Hindustan, Tatya Tope,' Nana invited.

'At the last count,' the general said, 'there were two hundred and sixty-nine thousand troops under British command in Hindustan.'

'That is a nation,' Manu observed. 'That is more people than I have here in Jhansi, men, women and children.'

'Go on, Tatya Tope,' Nana invited.

'This army,' Tatya said, 'is divided into the three Presidency commands: Bombay, Bengal and Madras.'

'Which can easily be united.'

'Not that easily, Highness. If the Marathas were to rise as in days of old, we would have only the Bengal army to deal with for some considerable period. But there is a more important factor yet. Of these two hundred and sixty-nine thousand men, only thirty-three thousand are British. The rest are sepoys.'

'Not even the British could cope with such an army,' Nana said.

'You expect the entire sepoy army to fight for you?' Manu asked scornfully. 'That really is a dream. For one thing, half of them are Muslims, and only half Hindu. You expect Muslim and Hindu to fight shoulder to shoulder? Under you, a Maratha? Did not the Muslims, before the British came, devote all their strength to fighting and conquering the Hindus?'

'That is history. Now we have a common foe. When the war begins, the begum is content to place her forces under my command.'

'The begum has a personal grudge against the British. The sepoys do not. What they do have is generations of discipline, of watching their British officers perform wonders in the field, of observing the British war machine at close quarters and understanding that it is invincible. To make them fight for you, together, you would have to find a cause, a cause so great that they would be prepared to unite, that they would be able to overcome their ingrained fear of the British. You would have to turn every man in Hindustan into a fanatic. I do not see how that can be done.'

Nana smiled. It was one of the most sinister sights I have ever seen. 'I have the cause, Manu.'

Manu snorted. 'Your pension?'

'Tell me, what is the worst fate that can befall a Hindu?'

'To lose their caste.'

'And how can that happen?'

'By defilement. But are not the sepoys composed entirely of men of high caste?'

'And can not any man lose his caste? And be defiled, forever?'

'How can an entire army lose its caste, at the same time?'

'Have you ever heard of the Enfield rifle?'

I caught my breath. Suddenly I knew his plan.

'Oh, yes,' Manu said, enthusiastically. 'I have seen it. I have fired one, lent to me by a British officer, oh, it must be two years ago now. It is a wonderful weapon. Such accuracy.'

'Did you know that the entire sepoy army has been re-equipped with this rifle over the past two years?'

She sighed. 'That is another cause of the British superiority, the possession of weapons like that.'

Nana waved his hand impatiently. 'Were you shown what gives this rifle its range and accuracy?'

'I was given to understand that it is the new cartridge, the Minie, which fits the barrel more closely than previous ones.'

Nana nodded. 'That is right. And it is greased, to force it down the barrel and make that tight fit.'

'Yes. I have done this.'

He stared at her. 'You have loaded this rifle yourself?'

'Of course.'

'But . . . did you not have to bite the head from the cartridge?'

'That is right.'

'You are saying that your lips touched the grease?'

'Well, of course they did.'

'Do you realize that you have been defiled?'

It was the rani's turn to stare, most imperiously. 'Just what do you mean by that?'

'The grease is made of a mixture of cow fat and pig fat,' Nana said.

Manu's jaw sagged in consternation, then came up again with a snap. 'This is the truth?'

'By all the gods, it is the truth.'

She looked at me. 'Did you know of this?'

'No,' I lied. 'I know that Captain Wilson was reluctant to let you bite the cartridge.' The captain had explained about the greased cartridges to me before showing Manu the gun, but she had been so determined to load it herself I had been reluctant to interfere.

'How noble of him.' Nana sneered.

'But . . . you are saying . . .' Manu was clearly in a state of some confusion.

'Every Hindu soldier in the sepoy army has been defiled, and is defiled, every time he fires his rifle.'

'Do they know this?'

'Not as yet. The Raj is keeping it a deadly secret. But I have found out, and my agents are even now travelling the country, telling the soldiers the truth. Do you suppose any Hindu will fight for the British after such a betrayal? Or the Muslims? It is not as strict a religious matter with them, but they still regard pork as unclean. When they find out they too will renounce their allegiance to the Raj. All they will then need is a leader. That will be me. I will rally all India, and I will unite Hindu and Muslim in the cause, not only because both religions will hate the Raj more than they hate each other, but because I will restore the Mughal to his throne in Delhi.' He grinned. 'Do not worry. When we have completed our triumph, I will see that he rules as we wish.'

'I have been defiled,' Manu muttered, the horror of her situation only just sinking in.

'That is nothing to worry about, as it was inadvertent,' Nana said.

'You must give me time to consider the matter. I have been defiled.'

Obviously this was more important to her than any incipient revolt, as Nana realized. His expression indicated his impatience. 'I should not consider for too long,' he said. 'When the time comes, there will be only two sides, against us, or for us. Those who are against us, against the greatness of Hindustan, will be considered to be our enemies. Remember this.'

Manu spent the next two days at her devotions, seeking purification for what had happened. At the same time, she did not wish anyone to know *what* had happened, lest she be the one to spark the conflagration.

I had never known her so upset. But she was also angrier than I had ever seen her, more even than on the day she had learned she had been deposed as Rani of Jhansi.

'That foul thing, that Wilson,' she said. 'He knew it when he gave me that cartridge to bite.'

'He wished to load the gun for you,' I reminded her.

She glared at me. 'They are your friends.'

'They were never my friends. Mrs Wilson was an acquaintance from my visit to Calcutta. I quickly realized that we never could be friends.'

'He should be impaled.'

My imagination boggled.

'Will you join with Nana?'

She walked up and down. 'What would you do?'

'I would not.'

She stopped, and gazed at me. 'Because, as he reminded me, you are a *feringee* yourself.'

'Because I do not believe the British can be beaten.'

'Not even if the whole sepoy army rises in our support?'

'I do not believe that will happen.'

'You think they will allow themselves to be defiled?'

'I do not know. I am sure the British will somehow explain it all away. And when Nana talks of the immense supremacy of numbers . . . the British have allies they can call on.'

'Such as who?'

'Well . . . what of the Sikhs?'

'The Sikhs,' she commented, as contemptuously as Nana.

'They are great fighting men. They proved that over the past few years, and before that. And they will be untouched by this cartridge business, because they do not believe in caste. Is that not the principal difference between them and you?'

'They are heretics.'

'And they hate you.'

She resumed her perambulation. 'To go to war, against the British,' she said. 'That has been my dream, since birth.'

'But to be defeated will bring catastrophe upon your people,' I pointed out, 'who are your ultimate responsibility.'

'Have I any people? They have been taken away from me.'

'That is another important point, Manu. Should there be a revolt, and you refuse to take part, but instead demonstrate your loyalty to the Raj, no matter how badly they have treated you, that will give you another weapon to use, in a fresh appeal against Dalhousie's ruling. They say this man Canning has an entirely different point of view, and is anxious to be on good terms with all the kings. And queens,' I added.

Once again she paused to gaze at me; I had touched a very important chord.

'Then what of Nana's threat to treat us as an enemy if you do not support him?' she asked.

'That can only be effective if he were to win,' I said. 'And I have said, I do not believe he can.'

My arguments persuaded her into the path of peace, however reluctantly. For while her every instinct was to fight, given the slightest opportunity, common sense and her natural caution convinced her

I was right. There was a week of entertainments for Nana, which put a considerable strain on our already diminished finances, and then she had to tell him what she intended.

'I have found what you have had to say of great interest,' she said.

'Then you will await the summons.'

She had considered her reply with great care. 'I doubt I have anything to offer you,' she said. 'I am restricted to a palace guard of a hundred men. That is hardly an army.'

'There are a thousand sepoys in the garrison.'

'They are not my people.'

'Do you not suppose they will follow you?'

'I have said: they are not my people. Do you make them follow you, when the time comes?'

'But you will declare for us.'

'It would be the height of folly for me to declare for you,' Manu said, 'until after the garrison has done so. Otherwise they will simply march in here and lock me up.'

They gazed at each other, then Nana looked at me. He clearly understood that Manu had discussed the situation with me.

'But once the garrison has declared for me, you will do so also.'

'I will declare for you, for Hindustan, the moment I can do so safely and to worthwhile effect.'

Once again, a long stare. Then he nodded. 'I will regard that as a promise. Now, listen to me. As I have said, my agents are already circulating amongst the various garrisons, explaining to them the composition of the cartridges they are required to bite every time they fire their rifles. But of course it would equally be the height of folly for anyone to act individually, or precipitately. The signal for a rising must be a general one, so that everywhere and at once the British may be overwhelmed. This will be accomplished by means of a message.'

'Which will immediately be betrayed to the British.'

'Not this message. Do you not eat *chupatties*?'

These being a type of biscuit commonly part of most Indian meals.

'Of course I eat *chupatties*.'

'Well, then, one day, one day soon, you will receive a box of *chupatties*, only these will be marked. The mark will be an impression of the lotus flower.'

A holy flower to the Hindu religion, I thought.

'When you receive these *chupatties*,' Nana said, 'you will calculate the distance from Jhansi to Delhi in English miles. Whatever figure this is, you will halve it, and on that number of days from the one on which you receive your gift, the rising will commence.'

'That sounds very complicated.'

'It is not in the least complicated. It is a matter of simple arithmetic.'

'But I will not be rising until the garrison has done so.'

'Certain members of the garrison, their secret leaders, will receive their *chupatties* at the same time.'

'Well,' Manu grumbled, perceiving that she was in danger of being outmanoeuvred and forced to act whether she wished to or not. 'I still say your plan is overelaborate.'

'It is secret,' Nana said. 'That is the essential thing. But there is one thing more. This will be a life or death struggle for our people. The *feringees* cannot merely be driven from Hindustan, or they will simply come back. They must be destroyed. Utterly. Men, women and children.'

'You cannot be serious!' I spoke without thinking.

'I am very serious, Mrs Kala. This must be a calamity the like of which has never before befallen the British. The Raj must be extirpated, root and branch, in such circumstances that they will never dare return. Their men must be shot or cut down, their women and children must be violated and cut into pieces. The dread news of what has happened here must spread around the world, a warning to all other would-be violaters of Hindustan.'

I looked at Manu. Her expression was difficult to decipher. And after all of these years of intimacy I still did not know her well enough. I knew that she worshipped the gentle Sita and identified herself with the loving Lakshmi. But I also knew that she revered Durga, the goddess of death and destruction, and dreamed of acting in her name. This was reasonable, given her background and her mistreatment by the Raj. What I did not know was whether or not, deep under those three eminently respectable goddesses, there also lurked a secret desire to emulate the hell-goddess Kali.

Nana was still speaking. 'Bearing this in mind, it follows that we must take every opportunity to carry out such destruction. Azimullah Khan has told me much about these people, and I have observed much myself. They, too, are utterly ruthless when they fight, which is why they have so often conquered. But because of their religion they believe that when the fighting is over, for whatever reason, they should, as they say, shake hands with their foe, whether victor or vanquished, and say bad luck, old fellow. For this reason, and for the protection of their camp followers, when they see that they cannot win, they will offer to surrender. You will remember they did this in Afghanistan. We must do as did the Afghans. We will agree to accept their surrender, wherever it is offered; indeed, we will invite them to surrender, providing they evacuate their position, so that they come out into the open, and then we will massacre them.'

'Every man, woman and child,' Tatya Tope said, gleefully.

'If you do that,' I said, with fervour, 'your name will be damned forever throughout history.'

'English history,' Nana sneered. 'What do I care about English history? The man who frees Hindustan from the British yoke will be revered forever in Hindu history.'

'The British invaded Afghanistan to avenge the massacre,' Manu said, more practically.

'That is because they had India to draw upon. When we have finished with them, they will have nowhere to draw upon. Now prepare yourself, Manu. When next you and I meet, it will be as the rulers of this great land.'

We watched the caravan winding out of sight, the elephants visible for a long time.

'Every time he visits me, I feel as if I have been out in a storm,' Manu remarked.

'Because he is a monster,' I suggested.

She glanced at me. 'Yes,' she agreed, to my surprise. 'He is a monster. There can be no doubt of that. But then, Emma, was not Genghis Khan a monster? And Timur the Lame? Aurungzeb was a monster, to my people. And before him, Nadir Shah. Yet these men are famed as much as they were feared in their lifetimes. Sometimes it is necessary, for a monster to appear, to change the course of history.'

'I cannot believe that you can compare Nana with Genghis Khan or Tamerlane,' I protested. 'If you ally yourself with him, you will lead your people to disaster.'

She smiled. 'My own people will still love me.' Then she was serious. 'If we win.'

'And after he has carried out his horrendous threat? How do you suppose history will judge you?'

'That will never happen. Dhondu Pant has always dreamed of being a reincarnation of such heroes from the past, who created empires by massacring all who stood in their way. But he has not the stomach ever to carry out such a threat.'

It may well be imagined that this conversation, taken together with Nana's visit, left me profoundly disturbed. For all Manu's dismissal of him as a dreamer, I could not doubt that Nana intended to provoke an uprising. Equally, I had no doubt that the British would quickly suppress it. What concerned me were Jhansi, and the rani, because she had virtually agreed to join in, if the Jhansi garrison did so. I knew nothing of this garrison, or even any of the officers, including the new commander, a Captain Gordon. But I did know there were several hundred sepoys and only half-a-dozen British officers. If they *did* decide to rise, to be crushed in due course as the British marched against them, they would leave Manu irretrievably compromised, certain to be rendered destitute by the conquerors, at worst perhaps even to be confronted by gaol.

Like a caged tigress, Manu would certainly die in captivity.

And there was nothing I could do. I contemplated even breaking my oath, and going to Skene with what I knew, but I was back to the old problem, quite apart from earning myself Manu's undying enmity – a thought I could not bear – she was already compromised.

I could only wait, and pray, that Nana's hopes would come to nothing, that the sepoys would simply not respond to his agents.

Thus the year continued in apparent peace. As although Manu had apparently been deposed, no overt move had yet been made to replace her as ruler of the state; she continued to collect the taxes, hold her courts of law, met her ministers to give them directives, and entertained her leading people to lavish dinners as if nothing had changed. She even held the occasional polo match, although much of her love for the game had disappeared with Gangadhar Rao's death, as that had been largely caused by a fall on the polo field.

Her dinner parties invariably included one or two of the more prominent members of the English community and their wives who, as usual, I observed were watching me with a great deal of speculative interest; at these functions, of course, I wore not only the sari but also my best jewellery, including my necklaces and bangles, all priceless in European eyes, especially the bangle given to me by Hazrat Mahal as a remembrance of our night together, and which was studded with diamonds and rubies.

None of them gave any indication of knowing anything about what might be going on behind the scenes. Neither did Skene, who was a regular guest. But both Manu and I were in a state of continual apprehension. What disturbed me most was that Manu started receiving certain more prominent local people for private conversations – from which I was excluded. As I could not believe she would ever suppose I would betray her, this rejection had to be because she knew my aversion to any talk of revolt, and did not wish me present when she was sounding out her people, obviously as to whether or not they would support her. Even more disturbingly, she invariably emerged from these meetings in high good humour.

The monsoon came and went – it seldom had much impact in Jhansi, removed as the state was from the proximity of any coastline or even large river, although it did restrict travel outside of the city by the damage it caused to the roads – and in December we were visited by a certain Ahmed Shah, who called himself the Moulvie of Fyzabad.

We were informed of his coming long before he reached Jhansi, for it appeared that he was a famous *fakir*, or holy man, who possessed great prestige. Manu was all agog, especially as she hoped he would finally be able to cleanse her of the defilement incurred in biting the greased cartridge. I was very unhappy about the whole thing, as I could not doubt that he was in the pay, or certainly the confidence, of Nana.

He was a little man, very humble, and very devout; he spent a good deal of his time either in silent prayer or contemplation. He was indeed able to reassure the rani as to her religious cleanliness, pointing out that her tasting of the defiled grease had been entirely inadvertent, and that the gods would understand that. I was happy for her, but I was concerned to see him go down to the cantonment and move amongst the sepoys; again I could not doubt that he was passing the word, both about the cartridges and the *chupatties*. I was very pleased to see the back of him, and I may say that he hardly deigned to notice my existence.

'He gave me the shivers,' I confided to Manu.

'He is a holy man,' she said, severely. 'And is entitled to respect.'

It was at the end of January that Major Skene requested an interview.

'Have you heard any news from Calcutta?' he asked.

'I have no correspondent in Calcutta,' I reminded him.

'Ah, yes. Well, I feel you should know that there has been some trouble there.'

'Trouble?' I suddenly felt short of breath. But there had been no delivery of any special *chupatties*.

'At a place called Barrackpore. That is a few miles north of the city. A sepoy regiment mutinied, and burned down a telegraph station. A British officer was murdered.'

'Good heavens,' I commented.

'Oh, it has been suppressed. The murderer was hanged. And I suppose it was bound to happen. We have known for some time that many of the locals are distrustful of the telegraph, which is really beyond their ability to understand.'

As usual, I found his chauvinistic arrogance irritating even if what he had to say was reassuring in that Nana had never mentioned anything about the telegraph playing any part in his plans.

Then he spoiled my morning by continuing, 'There is also some talk concerning discontent amongst the sepoys about the cartridges they are being required to use, because they are coated in animal fat which may contain beef or pork. The government has been trying to keep this business quiet, until everyone got used to the idea, and accepted it. But someone must have spoken out of turn, with the result that a bearer, who was without caste, asked a sepoy, who was actually a Brahmin, for a drink from his canteen, and when the Brahmin told him to get away as he did not intend to defile himself by allowing a casteless person to drink from his bottle, the bearer laughed at him and told him he had already lost caste because he had bitten a defiled cartridge. There was an explosion of violence. As with the event in Barrackpore, it was pretty rapidly put down, but the governor general has considered the incident sufficiently serious to recall the eighty-fourth from Rangoon. The eighty-fourth is, as you may know, an entirely British regiment.'

'What are the feelings of the sepoys here?' I asked, with some anxiety.

'Oh, there will be no trouble here. The troops are utterly loyal.'

I thought of the Moulvie, and decided against mentioning him. Although . . . 'But are they not using the same cartridges?'

'Certainly. But as I say, they are utterly loyal, and will remain so, unless they are in any way suborned. That is why I am here. I know that in the past you have refused to cooperate with us, but I know you are as interested as ourselves in preserving the peace, and in this instance we are talking about a possible loss of lives. It really is essential that you do everything in your power to reassure these people that it is most certainly not our desire to defile anyone, and it is important that we know the rani's attitude to this situation.'

'So far as I know, Major, our guard here in the palace has not been permitted the use of the new rifle, or the new cartridges. As for the rani, she is not even aware that there is a "situation", as you call it.'

'But she is bound to learn of it, sooner rather than later.'

'No doubt.'

'And then . . .'

'She may well have an opinion on it. However, as you well know, whatever the rani may feel about it, or about anything else, for that matter, can be of no possible interest to you, simply because she no longer has any authority over her people. This was your decision.'

'Not mine, I do assure you,' he said, hurriedly. 'I only carry out the orders of my superiors. Do I understand that once again, Mrs Hammond, you refuse to cooperate?'

'Like you, Major, I only carry out the orders of my superiors.'

He glared at me, and then left.

I thought it best to tell Manu what had happened in Calcutta. She was as confused as I. 'But there has been no signal,' she said.

'Thus either Nana has got his plans mixed up,' I said, hopefully, 'which was always likely to happen, or this incident was spontaneous.'

'Hm,' she commented.

'Either way, Manu,' I said, 'this is going to turn out very badly. You see how the British have reacted, calling in their own people. They will be prepared to do this on a much bigger scale. I beg of you not to become involved. No matter what happens, even here.'

'I gave Nana my word.'

'You promised to be sympathetic, but only to take part if you could be of use. How can you help, with but a palace guard of a hundred men?'

'I agree that my guard could have no influence upon events, but I told Nana that my decision would depend on the attitude of the garrison.'

I could understand the questions that were ranging through her mind; her anxiety to do the best for her people mingled with her desperate desire somehow to regain control of her kingdom and overlaid by an even stronger wish to fight for her rights, especially as part of a general movement to drive the British from India. I thus also understood that I was in for a difficult period, and could only hope, but my hopes were dashed when on 27 February a large box of *chupatties* was delivered to the palace.

The Mutiny

Manu stared at the box as if it contained a nest of cobras. I reacted more quickly, and ran behind Kujula, who had brought it to us.

'Where is the messenger?'

'I do not know, Memsahib. He rode a horse, delivered the box, and left again immediately.'

I returned to Manu, who was releasing the string. I knelt beside her as we looked at the biscuits. She took one out, and sure enough it bore the imprint of the lotus.

'At last,' she whispered. 'Have you worked out how far it is from Jhansi to Delhi?'

'Yes. As the crow flies, two hundred and thirty-five miles.'

'And half of that is?'

'One hundred and seventeen and a half. We had better forget the half.'

'One hundred and seventeen days from today by the English calendar. When is that?'

I kept a calendar in my apartment. Vima fetched it for us. 'June twenty-third.'

'The date of Plassey. What is more, this is 1857, and the Battle of Plassey was fought on the twenty-third of June, 1757. That is exactly one hundred years since the victory that gave Clive the kingdom of Bengal, from which the Raj has derived its power. There has long been a Hindu tradition that the Raj would last a hundred years and then disappear.'

'That is incredibly simplistic,' I said. 'The whole world knows of it.'

'Perhaps there is method in his madness,' Manu said. 'If the whole world knows of that date, then no doubt the whole world will suppose no leader would be mad enough to call a revolt for that date. There is also sound military strategy behind the date. June twenty-third. In not more than six weeks after the rising, the monsoon should be with us. That will make it very difficult for the British to move troops from one area to the other until December, while Nana can use those six months to recruit as well as consolidate his hold on the places he will have seized.'

I scratched my head; her reasoning revealed a very sound understanding of military strategy . . . but I could not convince myself that Nana was capable of that. 'What are you going to do?' I asked.

'What I said I would do. Nothing, until I see what happens here in Jhansi.'

This was a relief, but I was curious to discover who else in the state had received a gift of the biscuits. I had Vima make some surreptitious inquiries, but as I couldn't tell her why I was interested I didn't get very far. As usual we had little news from outside, and heard nothing from Nana. But for the arrival of the *chupatties* it might have been possible to consider the whole thing a bad dream.

And then, in mid-March, there was a letter from the begum.

Her Royal Highness, Hazrat Mahal, the Begum of Oudh, sends cordial greetings to her beloved sister, Lakshmi Bai, Rani of Jhansi, and looks forward to associating with her in the great venture now underway.

'What shall I reply?' Manu wondered.

Much as I knew that an answer might well enable me to see Hazrat again, and perhaps renew our intimacy, even if only for one night, I could have no doubt as to the course we should take. 'You should not reply at all,' I told her. 'It is too dangerous.'

Manu chewed her lip.

Naturally, since our separation, I had endeavoured to see as little as possible of my husband, Abid. This was difficult, as he remained an officer of the palace guard, but whenever we encountered each other we exchanged a brief bow, while when he came to visit Alice, which was not very often, I always made sure Vima was present. She stood by the cot, or the pram as my daughter reached the age of three, while I remained on the far side of the room. But here again Abid seldom touched the child, preferring to stand and stare at her, although occasionally he brought her a present.

I was the more surprised, therefore, when one day early in April, he stopped beside me as I left the schoolroom. He bowed to Damodar, who was with me, and then addressed me. 'You know of the biscuits.'

It was not a question.

'Does not everyone?' I countered.

'My brother wishes to know if we are to fight.'

'That decision will be the rani's.'

'When will she make this decision?'

'When the time comes.'

'The time is come.'

'The time will be twenty-third June.'

'It has come now,' he insisted. 'A British officer has been murdered.'

I felt as if I had been kicked in the stomach. 'Here?'

'No, not here,' he said impatiently. 'In Barrackpore.'

I gave a sigh of relief; he was several weeks out of date; but I decided it was best to pretend ignorance of the matter. 'And what has happened?'

'The man who killed him was seized and hanged.'

'Well, I think that is something you all need to reflect upon. Anyway, it must have been an isolated incident.'

'It is the beginning. It is the talk of the barrack rooms. You will tell the rani.'

'Yes,' I agreed. 'I will tell her, because I am sure she will be interested. But I repeat, this is an isolated incident.'

'It is the beginning,' he insisted. 'Tell the rani. And tell her, too, that those who do not lead must follow.'

'The insolent dog,' Manu grumbled.

More than ever I felt we were sitting on a powder keg, especially when I recalled the words of Risaldar Khan, Abid's elder brother, and the commander of the Jhansi army, after the death of Gangadhar Rao, when he had pledged his allegiance, and those of his people, to the rani, provided she *ruled*. He had accepted that, following the invocation of the Doctrine of Lapse by Dalhousie, we should wait on the result of our appeal to the House of Lords before taking action, and we had told no one of the calamitous result, but this was an entirely new situation. I could only reflect that we still had two months to wait for the day. But as it turned out, and I would say this was inevitable given the over-elaborateness of Nana's plans, there were those who wished to jump the gun, as it were.

It was in the middle of May that the explosion took place. The news came to us via Major Skene, as usual. He hurried up to the palace to find me.

'Mrs Hammond!' he gasped. 'The most terrible thing has happened.'

'Tell me.'

'A week ago there was a mutiny at Meerut.'

This was a garrison town only a few miles north-east of Delhi, and therefore some two hundred and fifty miles away from Jhansi.

'It was to do with these confounded cartridges,' the major went on. 'The thirty-fourth Native Regiment refused to use them, so the commanding officer placed the entire regiment under arrest and then ordered them to be disbanded. It does not seem to have occurred to him that they might resent this. So on Sunday all the British officers and NCOs trotted off to church with their wives and children, and while they were worshipping, the regiment rose. There was the most frightful massacre. Men, women and children, torn to pieces, raped and then mutilated . . . do forgive me.'

I had clasped both hands to my neck, but not in outraged modesty. This was what Nana had called upon his people to do.

'And then . . .' Skene looked ready to burst into tears. 'Having completed their dastardly deed, the mutineers marched on Delhi itself.'

'But . . .' I frowned. 'There is a British garrison in Delhi, several thousand men.'

'There *was* a British garrison in Delhi. Four thousand strong. But only a quarter of those were actually British. The rest rose with the mutineers, as did the people of the city. There was another most ghastly massacre, and what was left of the British troops had to evacuate as best they could. At least the rebels did not get the main magazine. That was blown up, at the cost of the lives of several gallant fellows. But the city is in the hands of the insurgents. They have placed old Bahadur Shah back on the throne, and proclaimed him once again Mughal Emperor.'

'But . . .' My brain was spinning. 'What of the European community?' As I recalled, this had numbered several hundred.

'Massacred,' he moaned. 'Women and children. Massacred. Raped and . . .'

I held up my hand. He had been through this already, and I had no desire to hear it all over again.

'What will happen now?' I asked.

'God alone knows. It is spreading. There is a rumour of trouble in Lucknow, encouraged of course by that dreadful woman the begum.'

'What about here in Jhansi?'

He gave a little sigh. 'We seem to be all right, at least for the moment. I had a word with Captain Gordon as soon as I heard the news and he has spoken with his officers.'

'The garrison consists of the Twelfth Bengal Native Infantry, I understand,' I said.

'And the Fourteenth Irregular Cavalry,' he added.

'Those are all sepoys, except for their officers.'

'Yes, yes. But I have just said – they have renewed their oaths of allegiance to the Raj.'

'And you believe them.'

'Certainly, I do. I have telegraphed Calcutta that they may rely upon the people of Jhansi.'

'I see. Well, let us hope that you are right. However, Major, will you take a word of advice from a woman?'

'What advice?'

'That you hold the two forts in strength, with men you are certain you can trust. That you provision them with arms and ammunition and food to stand a siege, if need be, and that you further alert all the Europeans in the city . . . how many are there, anyway?'

'Oh, perhaps seventy, including the children.'

'Well, as I said, I think you should warn them to be prepared to leave their homes at a moment's notice, and retire to one of the forts. I would recommend the City Fort, as it is the larger, and besides, does not the Star Fort house the magazine, and the state treasury?'

'Yes, it does.' He was frowning.

'Then it is the more likely to be attacked, should there be trouble.'

'I think you are overreacting, Mrs Hammond. Or attempting to get me to overreact.'

'I can't see that there is any suggestion of overreacting in preparing to handle a possible situation, however unlikely it may be to occur.'

'And you don't think such measures might inflame the situation?'

'Not if it is done with a minimum of fuss. And when your movements are discovered, as they will be, you are entitled to say that while you have every confidence in the people of Jhansi, and the garrison, there is always the possibility that a body of mutineers from outside the state may move this way, and you are taking proper precautions.'

'Hm,' he commented. 'Hm. I will discuss the situation with Gordon.'

'Then do so. I would recommend, immediately.'

He took his leave, a sorely troubled man. But then, I was a sorely troubled woman.

Manu was in a state of high agitation. 'There are all manner of rumours,' she said.

'All of which are true.'

'You mean there has really been a massacre at Meerut? And Delhi has fallen?'

'Yes.'

She clapped her hands. 'Then it is the end of the Raj!'

'I wouldn't be too sure about that. Skene says the garrison here in Jhansi is absolutely loyal.'

'Ha! And what of Nana?'

'There is no word of Nana. I would suppose he has been as surprised by this as are we, and everyone else. This has probably upset all his plans.'

'And the begum?'

'Nothing is known of her either, at the moment. She is supposed to be stirring up trouble in Oudh, but it is only a rumour.'

'But when Nana takes control . . .'

'If he takes control,' I said. 'I imagine he will wait to see what is going to happen.'

She pinched her lips.

The next fortnight was very tense, as rumour and counter-rumour spread through the entire subcontinent, of risings here and suppressed risings there, of troop movements . . . and nearer to hand, of the situation in Delhi where, amazingly, the small British contingent had only retired as far as the hills surrounding the city, and had there entrenched themselves to await reinforcements. That they were being allowed to stay there, when the Indian troops in the city outnumbered them many times over, suggested to me that the rebellion was still in a most chaotic state – it certainly was a serious strategic blunder. Although the British problems seemed to be multiplying, as the officer intended to take over the force and no doubt lead it into action, General Anson, died of cholera before he could reach his post.

But in Jhansi all remained quiet, until the morning of 4 June, when we were awakened by gunfire. I sprang out of bed and hurried in to the rani, Vima at my heels.

Manu was also getting out of bed, assisted by her maids, Mandar and Kashi. 'It has started,' she declared. It was difficult to tell whether she was alarmed or exhilarated.

We dressed ourselves and went on to the porch. Risaldar Kala was there, as well as Abid and most of the guard. The city appeared quiet, but the firing was coming from the Star Fort.

'It is under attack,' I said. 'The sepoys have risen.'

'I must go down there,' Manu said.

'No,' I protested. 'You must not. You will be seized and used as a figurehead.'

'I gave my word to Nana.'

'Wait, I beg you,' I said. 'Even Nana is waiting.'

We retired to our apartments and endeavoured to begin our normal day's activities, but in the middle of the morning we were told that Captain Gordon urgently requested an audience with the rani.

We looked at each other. 'You will attend me, Emma.'

We went to the reception chamber where Captain Gordon was walking up and down, wearing a blue uniform and a white peaked cap. He was certainly very agitated, but then, he always had an agitated air about him. I had only ever seen him at a distance on the polo field. He had somewhat indeterminate features and sported a small moustache.

Now he bowed. 'Your Highness. You have heard the news?'

'I have heard gunfire,' Manu said. 'But no news.'

'Well, madam, I have to inform you that a part of the garrison has risen in revolt.'

'A part?' I asked.

He gave me what could be described as an old-fashioned look. 'That is correct, Mrs Hammond. The mutineers are some of the men of the Native Infantry, led by one of their sergeants, a scoundrel named Gurbash Singh. These men, several hundred in number, have broken into the Star Fort. Obviously they were resisted, but the men on duty there were surprised and expelled, and my officers were killed. Murdered, you could say. Only one, Lieutenant Taylor, managed to escape, and he is badly wounded.'

'You mean the fort is in the hands of mutineers? With the state treasury and the main munitions store? What measures have you taken to restore order?' I asked.

'There is the problem,' Gordon said, miserably. 'At present it is a matter of containment. Major Skene has ordered all European non-combatants into the City Fort, and I have garrisoned it with men I can trust. But they are really in an intolerable situation, with very little room, just sufficient food and water for survival, and of course the civilians are terrified after what happened at Meerut and in Delhi.'

'How many are there?' Manu asked.

'About sixty, including the children.'

'Major Skene told me there were some seventy Europeans in the city.'

'Well, some have refused to leave their homes, or have been coerced.'

'Can you not find them, or force them to leave?'

'I dare not send my men into those narrow streets. If they were not suborned they would stand a chance of being cut up.'

'You mean the rebels are in command of the city?'

'No, they are not. They are holding the Star Fort and firing at anyone who comes too close.'

'In other words, they are terrified at what they have done,' I said. 'If you were to launch a counter-attack now, this thing could be settled by tonight.'

'What am I to attack with?' he demanded.

'You have at least half the garrison left.'

'But I cannot count on their loyalty, especially if they are required to march against their comrades. And I doubt there is sufficient powder and ball for a sustained attack.'

It occurred to me that he was so shocked by what had happened he was totally incapable of arriving at a decision. 'Then what *do* you propose to do?'

'Well . . . I have sent for help, but I doubt this will be forth-coming, at least in the immediate future, the country is in such a state. If I could be sure of the loyalty and support of the mass of the population . . .' He suddenly went very red in the face.

'What is it you wish from us?' Manu asked.

I wondered if, like me, she was anticipating the incredible.

Correctly. 'Well, Your Highness,' Captain Gordon said. 'It occurs to me that if you would resume your position as Rani . . .' He licked his lips, while we stared at him. 'You see,' he went on, 'there can be no doubt that your people love you, madam. They adore you. They will follow your lead in everything.'

'The men in the fort are not my people,' Manu pointed out, no doubt giving herself time to think.

'But even they, if confronted by the entire population of Jhansi, would have to realize that their position is untenable. You would be doing us a great service. I suspect that you might even be saving our lives. You may be sure that the Raj would be eternally grateful.'

Manu regarded him for some seconds. 'You are asking me to resume my rule?'

'Yes. Yes, I am.'

'You have the authority to do this?'

'I am the Raj's military representative on the ground. I may say that the civil authority, as represented by Major Skene, is in entire agreement with me.'

'What powers will I have?'

'Well . . . everything. All the powers you would have were you the ruler of Jhansi.'

'You have just said that I *will* be the ruler of Jhansi.'

'Yes. Yes, that is what I said.'

'I will have the power to enforce the laws?'

'Yes.'

'To collect the taxes?'

'Certainly. I am sure Mr Thornton will be of every assistance.'

Manu tossed her head. She did not like Mr Thornton, who was the Company's Collector of Taxes. 'I will require you to put these things in writing.'

'Ah . . . I'm afraid I do not think my Marathi is sufficiently good.'

'Then write them down in English, Captain. Mrs Kala will make a translation, and you will sign it.'

Gordon gulped. 'I will do this.'

'I will also require your request to be endorsed and confirmed in Calcutta.'

'I will obtain that endorsement as soon as it is possible.'

'It is possible now, Captain. The insurgent forces are nearly all north of Jhansi. Calcutta is to the south.'

'Yes,' he said. 'Yes. I will draw up the document now, and send a copy to Calcutta.'

'Thank you, Captain Gordon.' Manu stood up with a penetrating slither of muslin. 'Then I will resume my reign.'

'And you will put an end to this madness?'

'If that is possible, yes.'

She was far more elated than she would permit Gordon to see. When we were alone, she embraced me for several minutes.

'Can it be true?'

'It certainly seems so.'

'To think that the Raj, who so contemptuously cast me aside, should now appeal to me to restore order . . . it almost makes me want to laugh. And to weep. Did not those fools know that had I been left in control this situation could never have arisen?'

'You must make them understand that now,' I said. 'You must write letters, to everyone who matters, utterly condemning the revolt, whether here or at Meerut or Delhi.'

'I do not utterly condemn the revolt.'

'Nevertheless, it would be prudent to make the British think that you do.'

'You would have me tell a lie?'

'Is not all diplomacy a series of lies?'

'I must go about my people,' she said.

I have to confess that I was a little doubtful about this, if the populace was indeed in a state of some excitement. But I worried needlessly. Excited though the people of Jhansi certainly were, the excitement was over the presence of their queen amongst them after so long. They clamoured about our horses – we were accompanied by a somewhat bemused Maropant Tambe – and had to be driven back by Abid and Risaldar and their men.

'Do not harm them, I command you,' Manu said. 'They are my people.'

I thought I made out the face of Mrs Mutlow in the crowd, but dismissed it as a fantasy; she was surely in the City Fort with the other 'white' women and children. Or would she suppose herself inviolate? She was a woman that I most detested. A Eurasian, which is to say that she was of an English father and Indian mother, she had married an English merchant and insisted upon taking her place in the British community. Soon after my arrival in Jhansi she had invited me to dine with her and her friends, in the most condescending manner, referring to me as the 'unfortunate widow Hammond', as if I were an object to be pitied. I had declined, simply because Gangadhar Rao had intimated that he did not wish me to leave the palace complex, and he had been my employer. But she had chosen to take my refusal as a snub, and begun spreading the most scurrilous rumours both about my background and the orgiastic rites to which I undoubtedly subscribed in the secrecy of the palace. That she would have arrogantly refused to take shelter in the fort was quite in keeping with her character.

We received less of a welcome when we rode out to look at the Star Fort, and were greeted with some shots from the men defending it. I knew that this was not the first time that Manu had been under fire, but it was uplifting to see how undisturbed she was, which could not be said for me.

What disturbed me even more was that at least as many people in the crowd who had accompanied us were cheering for the mutineers as were cheering for the queen, although this may have been because we were joined by Captain Gordon.

'Will you order an assault?' he asked.

'I do not think that would be wise, at this time,' she said. 'I must sound out our people first. Those men are making a lot of noise, but they are not causing any trouble.'

'They are mutineers . . .'

'Who, if they surrender, are liable to be hanged? Do you not think they know this?'

'Then what do you propose to do?'

'I will talk with my people, and we will see.'

He didn't look too happy with this.

From the Star Fort we visited the City Fort, where the welcome was somewhat suspicious. But as the rani was accompanied on this part of her tour by both Captain Gordon and Major Skene they had at least to be civil. What they principally wanted to know was when they would be allowed to return to their homes. On my advice, Manu prohibited this, as the situation was still unsettled, but they were allowed to visit their houses in groups and under guard to collect some additional clothing, food and any valuables that had been left behind.

When we returned to the palace, tired but, at least in Manu's case, utterly happy, Captain Gordon's assignation of full powers was waiting for us. I immediately made the translation, and returned it to him for signature. Then we bathed together and lay together on her bed. 'There is so much to be done,' she said. 'First and foremost, I must write those letters.'

'And then,' I said, 'you must find some way of ending the rebel position in the Star Fort. You must recruit an army from amongst your people.'

'Do you suppose Captain Gordon will allow me to do that?'

'I think at this minute Captain Gordon will allow you to do anything you please, if you can end the crisis in Jhansi.'

'Hm,' she commented. 'We must speak with him tomorrow.'

Things having settled down somewhat, Captain Gordon was actually less receptive than I had expected, or hoped. He handed over the precious document, signed by both himself and Major Skene, and told us that he had despatched a copy to Calcutta for confirmation.

'As for the situation here, I have considered the matter, and am inclined to agree with you, Your Highness, that premature action might be unwise. Thus I am negotiating with the mutineers,' he told us. 'I think this is the best way to handle the situation. If we were to attempt an assault, and it turned out badly, there might be all manner of repercussions.'

'You are afraid of these rebels,' Manu suggested.

He refused to take offence, although he flushed. 'My business is the preservation of law and order, Your Highness.'

'Two of your officers have been murdered. Is that law and order?'

'The murderers will be arrested in due course, and placed before the courts. But these are military matters, Your Highness, and while I look to your continued support, and especially as regards keeping the rest of the population quiet and loyal, I must ask that you allow them to be handled by the military authorities.'

'Meaning you?'

'I am the military commander, yes.'

'You told me I must rule. As rani I am superior to the military.'

'Theoretically, yes. But in practice, it is your duty to bow to our opinions. Believe me, the same situation exists in England. Queen Victoria is theoretically the head of our armed forces, but she does not interfere in our conduct of affairs.'

'I doubt Queen Victoria has ever had to deal with a situation like this,' I suggested.

'Indeed she has, Mrs Hammond. Just under ten years ago England was very close to revolution. It was called the Chartist Movement. An army of several thousand men was marching on London. The queen left matters entirely in the hands of the Duke of Wellington, and the business was settled, without bloodshed.'

It was difficult to argue with that, especially lacking, as we did, all knowledge of what was happening beyond the boundaries of the state.

But four days later Abid came to see me. 'We have had news from Nana.'

'*You* have had news?'

'There was a messenger with a letter, for the rani. My brother intercepted him.'

'Both you and your brother go too far,' I told him.

He grinned. 'It was nothing personal. It was merely to inform her Highness that he has taken the field, at the head of a huge army, has captured Cawnpore, and is besieging the garrison.'

'Give me the letter.'

He did so, and I scanned it. What he had said was true, the news I had feared.

'The time has come,' he said, 'for the rani to place herself at our head and lead us to glory.'

'That decision must be the rani's and hers alone,' I said.

'And you will advise her against it.'

'I will advise her as to the best course to follow,' I said.

'Beware,' he warned. 'Those who do not lead are forced to follow.'

'You've said that before,' I reminded him.

I took the letter to Manu.

'At last,' she said. 'He was not waiting, he was recruiting. Now . . .'

'Please hear me,' I begged.

'Well?'

'Nana says he has captured Cawnpore, with a vast army. We do not know how true this is.'

'You are accusing Nana of lying?'

Actually, I was; I had no doubt of it. But I considered it best not to say so. 'What is or what is not a large army is a matter of opinion,' I said. 'I would have supposed, if he really commands sufficient men, he would have done better to march to Delhi and secure the city. And anyway, how can he claim to have captured Cawnpore if the garrison is still holding out?'

'Delhi *is* secure.' She studied the letter again. 'And it makes sense for him to settle with the garrison first; Cawnpore is only six miles from his home in Bithur. He says this will be accomplished within a few days. He will no doubt march on Delhi when it is. He says Lucknow is also being besieged. He says the begum has escaped the city and is with him with most of her army. It is all happening. Now we must act.'

'And do what?'

'Well . . .' She hesitated.

'Do you suppose you can suborn the rest of the Jhansi garrison without Gordon learning of it? He would place you under arrest.'

'He would not dare. The people would not stand for it.'

'You must be logical, Manu. If you now take the side of the rebels, the people are going to rise against the Raj anyway, and Gordon will know this. To have you under arrest and in his power will give him a bargaining counter. You will be a hostage.'

She chewed her lip. 'He would never get in here. My guards would see to that.'

'It would still be a mistake. Manu, Highness, can you not see that you are about to regain everything you wish? You have already regained most of it. You are the ruler of Jhansi . . .'

'Under the Raj.'

'As was your husband and his forebears. If you stay loyal to them, they cannot help but confirm you in your position once the rebellion is put down.'

'You are assuming that it will be put down.'

'I am certain of it.'

'With all of Hindustan in arms against the British?'

'We do not know that *all* of Hindustan is in arms, Manu. What we do know is that those who are in arms appear to be totally disorganized, lacking a decisive and capable leader . . .'

'Nana will give them that.'

'Then why is he not at the decisive place, Delhi, instead of Cawnpore?'

'I have explained this. He wishes to regain his patrimonial lands, and he cannot leave a British garrison behind him.'

'And that is the point I am making. If every prince wishes only to be certain of his own patrimony, the British will be able to defeat them, piecemeal, one by one. For this rebellion to succeed, all the elements must act together. Until and unless they do, it will fail, and the British will take a fearful vengeance for the deaths of their loved ones.'

All of those memsahibs, raped and murdered!

'So you would have me do nothing?'

'I still think it would be wise for you to wait and see how things develop, for just a while longer.'

'Ha!' she commented. But I knew she would take my advice.

Was I wrong? I do not believe so. My whole idea was to avoid the tragedy, or indeed, the tragedies, which were soon to crowd upon us. Where I was definitely wrong was in not repeating Abid's warning to her, so that she might have been able to take a pre-emptive position towards the brothers. But would she have been able? The guards, however much they might respect and even adore their queen, were very much Risaldar's people; when Manu's original army had been disbanded, he had chosen those who would remain – they were entirely loyal to him.

I saw no reason to inform Captain Gordon or Major Skene of what was happening at Cawnpore. I had no doubt they would soon enough find out, and I could not see how it might affect us here; for surely, even if Nana's boast was accurate, and the garrison surren-dered within a week, he would then have sufficient military acumen to march to Delhi rather than a place as militarily unimportant as Jhansi.

Thus I retired that night, uneasily to be sure, but still feeling time was on our side. I slept alongside Manu in her bedchamber, for we both needed all the comfort we could get, and we both awoke in the same instant, and the same horrified alarm, to find the queen's bedchamber filled with armed men.

Manu sat up in outrage.

It was just on dawn, and the light was already good, thus we recognized our invaders as members of the palace guard, with Abid and Risaldar at their head, and if they had both had the opportunity in the past to survey my naked body, they had never been so privileged as regards the rani save during her morning exercise, and especially in such circumstances, for she seemed to glow with indignation. I may say that over the years Manu had filled out considerably from the slender little girl I had first encountered. The vigorous life she insisted on living had prevented her from ever becoming fat, but she was certainly voluptuous, and had them gaping, so much so that they largely ignored me, to my relief.

But Manu, as always, was little concerned with modesty, and now swung her legs from the bed. 'What is the meaning of this?' she demanded.

Risaldar Khan licked his lips and stepped forward. 'We have waited long enough, Highness. Now you must lead us in the destruction of the *feringees.*'

'You seek to give me orders?'

'We would have you give *us* orders, Highness.'

Manu flung out her right arm, finger pointing. 'Then leave my apartment. Return to your quarters, and pray that I do not punish you for this outrage.'

The men hesitated, and one or two shuffled towards the doorway. Almost I thought that the rani had carried the day, but Risaldar knew that he could not stop now. He stepped right up against the bed, and seized Manu's extended arm.

'The orders we seek are to lead us into battle against the *feringees,*' he said in a low voice. 'We will accept no other. Now, join us and lead us, or die.' And he drew his tulwar.

Manu gasped, I do not believe in terror, for I had never known her to be afraid, of anything, but in utter consternation that such a thing should be happening to her.

'And we will begin with this one,' my husband said, seizing my arms in turn and dragging me so that I fell to the floor. Now he rolled me on to my back, stood astride me, and also drew his tulwar.

'Manu!' I cried, and I will confess that I certainly was terrified.

Manu continued to pant, but as always she was determined to survive, and rely on an upturn in her fortunes. Indeed, I believe her mind was already ranging to her next project, supposing she could reach it. Besides, what Risaldar wanted was what she wanted as well, however unadvised it might be.

'Very well,' she said, her voice also low. 'I will lead you.'

The tulwar blade was only an inch from her heaving breast, and Risaldar had seized the opportunity, which might never arise again, to throw his arm round her and actually clutch the pulsating flesh.

'Where is my father?' she demanded.

'Maropant Tambe is under arrest.'

'You . . .'

'But he will not be harmed, unless you force us to harm you.'

'I wish him released.'

'He will be released. After you have promised to lead us.'

'I have just promised that.'

'Swear,' he said.

'I swear,' she said. 'By the goddess Durga, lady of death and destruction. Now release me.'

Slowly, reluctantly, Risaldar released her arm, took his fingers from her breast and stepped back; this was the closest he had ever been to a woman he clearly worshipped, at least physically.

'And you,' she told Abid. 'Get away from my woman.'

Equally reluctantly Abid moved to stand beside his brother. I do not suppose he still worshipped me, physically or otherwise, but he certainly had a great yearning to cut bits off me.

'Now leave us,' Manu said. 'We would get dressed. I will join you within the hour, and give you your orders.'

They hesitated. Then Risaldar said, 'One hour, Highness,' and led his men from the room.

We gazed at each other.

'Thus, you see,' Manu said, 'I have been overtaken by events.'

'Are you not angry?'

'Yes,' she said. 'I am angry.' And from her tone I had no doubt that she was. 'That such a lout should touch my person . . . we must have this matter settled.'

'But how? Will you inform Captain Gordon and have him lead his people against the palace?'

'His people would sooner follow Risaldar than any British officer. Besides, it is not my intention to employ *feringees* to war upon my own. This is an Indian matter, and will be settled by Indians. Summon Vima.'

She was in the next room, with several other women, trembling. A handsome woman, roughly my own age, like Kujula she had been given to me as my servant by Gangadhar Rao on my arrival in Jhansi, and for eight years had served me faithfully and well, as Manu knew. Vima it was who had taught me how to wear the sari, how to prepare and mix the spices to make what the Europeans called curry and, no less important, how to eat with one's fingers. Her loyalty could not be questioned.

'I wish you to leave the palace, clandestinely,' the queen told her, 'go to the cantonment, and tell Captain Gordon that I have been coerced by my own palace guard, and under threat to my life have been obliged to agree to lead them in rebellion. Tell him that by this time tomorrow all Jhansi will be in arms against him, and that he should immediately retire to the City Fort with all the people he can trust, and prepare to stand a siege. Tell him I will do what I can to make matters better for him, but that the business is, for the moment, out of my hands. Do you understand that?'

Vima nodded. 'Yes, Highness.'

'When you have done that, return here as quickly as possible, but still clandestinely.'

'Yes, Highness.' She hurried off.

'Will she succeed?' Manu asked.

'I have no doubt of it. But even so the Europeans must be in a most dangerous situation. You will not be able to prevent an attack on the fort, if Risaldar is determined on it.'

'I can delay it, for a while. Until we can get help.'

'From where can we do that?'

'From Nana.'

'What did you say?'

'Nana adores me. He also adores you, Emma. Or at least the idea of you. And he is a man renowned for his love of women. He will come to our aid.'

'But do you suppose he even knows of your situation?'

'Probably not. You must go to Cawnpore and inform him.'

'Me?!!'

'As I have said, once he sees you, he will wish to help us.'

My head was spinning. To give myself time to think, I took refuge in technicalities. 'But . . . he is already in arms against the *feringees*. He means to destroy the Cawnpore garrison. He will not abandon that to come here.'

'I am not asking him to do that. I am asking him to send a sufficient force to enable me to regain control of the situation here. A couple of thousand men and a capable commnder will do it. Tatya Tope. Tell him to send Tatya Tope.'

'But . . .' It seemed to me that my dearest friend was again losing mental control of the situation. 'Risaldar is in arms against the British. Nana is in arms against the British. Why should he send some of his people to prevent your people from doing what he wants?'

'He will do it, firstly, because he is my oldest living friend. He will do it, secondly, because I am the Rani of Jhansi, and supporting me is more important than defeating the British. He will do it, thirdly, because these vulgar men have laid their hands upon me and must be punished. He will do it, fourthly, because we will only succeed against the British by people such as me, and himself, to be sure, leading our armies, not itinerant captains of the guard. He will do it, fifthly, because he will hope to share my bed if he helps me. And he will do it, sixthly, because you will persuade him.'

'Persuade him?' I shouted.

'You will leave Jhansi tonight. You may take Vima with you, and Kujula. You will travel to Cawnpore as rapidly as possible to tell Nana what has happened here. You will make yourself as agreeable as you can to him, and persuade him to send people to our help.'

'But . . .' More technicalities to stop myself from screaming. 'You are telling me to ride across a country which is in open revolt . . .'

'It is only a hundred and twenty-five miles to Cawnpore. You could be there in three days, five at the outside.'

'I will be waylaid and murdered within a day of leaving here.'

'No, you will not. You will have Kujula to protect you, and I will give you letters saying that you are my accredited agent and are not to be hindered or molested in any way.'

I could not help but wonder if waving a letter, even when written by a local potentate, would have saved Mr Hammond from being murdered by the thugs? But by now my mind was already racing ahead.

'What of Alice?'

'She will remain here with me, under my care, as if she were my very own. Besides, Abid would never harm his own child, or permit anyone else, even his brother, to do so.'

In view of the love Manu had always shown for my little girl, I could not disbelieve her, but her safety would yet depend on that of Manu herself, and I had just seen an example of how fragile that might be . . . unless I returned with help. On the other hand, she had to be safer here than riding through the mutiny-ridden countryside.

There was, however, another less palatable reason for Manu wishing to take care of the babe: it would ensure that I did not give way to any temptation to betray her and run off to the British. As if I would ever have considered that, despite what she was asking me to do.

'You said I must be agreeable to Nana. How agreeable did you have in mind?'

'Whatever he wishes. Whatever he *desires*.'

I was appalled. 'No. I could not. He is utterly repulsive to me.'

'You will be doing it for me, and for Jhansi,' she said. 'And Alice,' she added.

I gulped. But I couldn't possibly refuse to undertake the mission, however dangerous and however distasteful. There was more than just Manu and Jhansi at stake; there were also a great many lives. Perhaps I still had some idea of averting the looming tragedies I saw on every side.

But there was one last argument. 'Nana desires you more than he desires me. Should you not go yourself?'

'That would be madness. If I abandon Jhansi to the Kalas and their supporters, I will never get it back. Nor could I do anything to preserve the peace here, until rescue comes, if I am not here. And what of Damodar? If I leave him he would become a puppet of Risaldar, while if we *were* to be waylaid on the road, even if I survived, were he not to, or be made captive, the dynasty would cease to exist.'

From her point of view, with which for eight years I had willingly associated myself, these were irrefutable arguments. And now she rested her hand on my arm. 'Complete this mission successfully,' she said, 'and I will honour you above all other women.'

I thought she already did.

Cawnpore

Vima, having completed the first part of her mission successfully, was somewhat dashed to discover she was setting out on a much longer journey. Kujula also had to be told, and briefed. He was happy to accompany me, having been as taken aback as anyone by the way in which the guard had invaded the rani's private apartments, and feeling decidedly guilty, as having not been given any orders as to what to do in such unlikely circumstances, he had done nothing. I was only happy that he had not attempted to prevent their entry, or he surely would have been killed.

Manu wanted to offer us the use of one of her remaining elephants – the guardsmen had made off with the others – but I decided against that. Our departure, and our journey, was to be as clandestine as possible, and there is no way an elephant can be overlooked. Kujula saw to the saddling of three horses, and the loading of two others as pack animals, and that night we stole out of the palace, using unguarded passageways and staircases. Manu gave me a last loving embrace, and bestowed on me a bag of rupees to pay our way. 'Come back safely,' she said.

I could not help but feel she was being optimistic, and yet I must be honest here, and admit that deep in my heart I was not as afraid of the immediate future as I had appeared, even of another encounter with Nana, with all that might entail, in view of Manu's instructions. When I had first met Dhondu Pant, and he had demanded me for his harem, I had been very close to at least a mental virgin. My six years as wife to Mr Hammond had been, as far as I was concerned, two thousand, one hundred and ninety-one days of continual rape, into which the art of love had never once been allowed to enter. Now, eight years later, I had not only studied, at Gangdhar Rao's insistence, both the *Kama Sutra* and *The Perfumed Garden*, and experienced the delicious lust of Hazrat Mahal, but I had known the equally delicious lust of both Abid Ali, who whatever his murderous outrage at my betrayal of his bed, had been a consummate and gentle lover, but also James Dickinson. I was no longer afraid of what might lie in a man's bed, and if this makes me sound like a wanton, it should be remembered that for all my determined optimism, I could not shake off the suspicion, almost the certainty, that we were all standing on the edge of a precipice that was steadily crumbling beneath us. So, eat, drink and experience whatever was left to me, because I would soon be dead? This was perhaps an essential point of view, and one I have never regretted, certainly in view of what actually *did* happen.

I kissed the sleeping Alice goodbye then joined my two servants. We led our horses across the polo field and away from the city without a challenge, mounted when we felt safe, and rode to the north east.

This was the first time I had left Jhansi in more than seven years. They had been a fairly hectic seven years, with sufficient highs to offset the several lows, and I knew I would not have refused if required to live them all over again, but I could not doubt that here I was embarking upon the most important, and potentially the most dangerous part of my entire life. Yet I was exhilarated at the prospect of perhaps taking my place upon the stage of history.

I was also concerned about the situation of Deirdre Wilson and her two children, who would have been caught up in the sudden explosion. She was the only Englishwoman in India I had even remotely considered a friend, when her husband had been commander of the Jhansi garrison. Our friendship had been brief, as I had been furious when I had learned that Captain Wilson, in demonstrating the new Enfield rifled musket to the rani, had permitted her to load the weapon and thus to bite the end off the fatal cartridge without first telling her of what the grease was composed. Deirdre had felt obliged to defend her husband's action, which I could understand, although I had not been prepared to forgive her, mainly because it had demonstrated the arrogant British dismissal of all religious beliefs not recognized by Christianity as absurd superstitions. Wilson had dismissed condemnation of his action as the ravings of a hysterical woman. But I knew that he had been transferred to Cawnpore, and presumably she, and all the other women and children in the city, were sheltering with and being protected by the garrison, but should they be overrun . . . When I remembered the tales I had been told of what had happened to the European women and children at Meerut and in Delhi my blood ran cold, and even if we were no longer friends I was determined to get her and her family to safety if it was humanly possible.

By dawn we were out of sight of the city. I had the advantage of both Vima and Kujula in having made this journey before, if in the opposite direction. But that had been in October, in a year when the monsoon had been weak. This was June, with the rain clouds still building, and once the sun got up it became very hot. The last time I had been on the road in an Indian summer had been that final disastrous journey with Mr Hammond, and I was close to being overwhelmed. My distress was apparently visible, so that although haste was an imperative, Kujula considered it necessary for us to call a halt at eleven and rest until the middle of the afternoon. I, indeed, would have made this our main stop of the twenty-four hours, and continued through the night, but neither Vima nor Kujula would contemplate travelling in the dark. So we kept going until sunset, and rose again with the first light, so that we made good progress, at least twenty-five miles that day.

Although Vima had packed several saris for me to wear when we reached our destination, I had adopted Manu's principle of dressing as a man for the journey, in jodhpurs and a tunic, boots and a turban in which to conceal my hair, and rode astride. I had worn this garb often enough when riding around Jhansi with the rani, but this was the first time I had travelled so dressed, and I could not help being curious, as well as slightly apprehensive, as to the reactions of anyone we might encounter, in view of my essentially pale skin and blue eyes. Vima preferred to stick to a sari, however unsuited such a garment was to lengthy riding. Kujula, as always, bristled with weapons. I had the revolver given me by Manu, but I kept this discreetly out of sight.

For this first day we were still inside Jhansi State, and although we encountered several groups of people, and passed through several villages, we were welcomed as servants of the rani. Once we crossed the border it was a different matter; we attracted a good deal of attention whenever we were in company. As long as these were peasants and farmers there was no problem; as I have mentioned, Kujula had a tulwar thrust through his sash, a musket slung on his shoulder, and a long knife hanging at his side, and looked very fierce with his upturned moustaches. With my revolver, I considered myself as being even better armed, but I continued to keep the weapon concealed. Inevitably, however, on our third day, we encountered a body of mounted men, who rode behind us for a while, and then closed up on either side. As they wore no uniforms, I determined that they were not mutinous sowars, sepoy belonging to the cavalry.

'Do nothing rash,' I warned Kujula, who was starting to look more aggressive than usual.

By now the horsemen were close enough both to identify me as not being Indian, and for me to hear what they were saying.

'A *feringee!*' commented one.

'A memsahib,' said another, perhaps more to the point, revealing that my attempt to look masculine had failed.

'Halt there,' called their commander.

I reined my horse and waited, while he wheeled his and came right up to me.

'You are my prisoner,' he announced without preamble, his eyes drifting down my body; even totally concealed, the fact that I was well-endowed was obvious.

'Do you, then, declare war upon the State of Jhansi?' I asked. 'Or upon Nana Sahib, Rajah of Bithur?'

He frowned at me, no doubt surprised by my fluent Marathi. 'You are a *feringee.*'

'I am in the employ of Lakshmi Bai, Rani of Jhansi,' I said. 'I have documents to prove it.'

'The rani was deposed,' he pointed out, 'by the British.'

'The rani has regained all of her powers,' I told him. 'And she has sent me with a message of great importance to her friend and ally, Nana Sahib. You interfere with the delivery of this message at your peril.'

The utter confidence I projected – at such variance with the pounding of my heart and the seething of my stomach – carried the day. He did insist upon looking at my documentation, and as he had apparently seen the rani's seal before, instantly his sole idea was to entertain me. We jointly pitched our camps for the night, and when he discovered that we had no tents and were bivouacing, he insisted I have one of his. I expected that he might intend to share it with me, but he was in too much awe of the rani's envoy for that, and Vima and I had a relatively peaceful night for all the roistering going on about us.

Our host's name was Prince Dignaga, and he was a Maratha Brahmin, a distant scion of the House of Scindia. He was not very old, considerably younger than I, certainly, and was thus of an age to dream of deeds of derring-do; he was also very handsome. He had been thoroughly put out by the refusal of his cousin, the Maharajah of Gwalior, to give even verbal support to the mutiny.

'He says he gave his sacred word to the Raj,' he complained, 'and will not break it. Has not the Raj broken its sacred word to us, time and again, whenever it has been expedient to do so? Did the British not treat your own rani with contempt? This is our great opportunity, as your rani has clearly recognized. Like you, I and my people are on our way to join the forces of Nana Sahib at Cawnpore.'

I could not of course tell him that my intention was to be in and out of Nana's camp just as quickly as I could obtain the necessary support.

'Will not your cousin be angry with you?' I asked.

Dignaga snorted. 'He will need to look to himself when I return with an army to destroy his British garrison.'

'I have heard it said that Gwalior is the strongest fortress in Hindustan, and is utterly impervious to assault.'

'It would be very difficult to assault, I agree,' he said. 'Perched as it is on its high rock it is even safe from cannon. But there are secret ways into the fortress, which I know.'

'Surely these ways are always guarded?'

'Indeed, but there are many men in Gwalior who think as I do, and are only restrained from action by their loyalty to the name of Scindia. Were they to be convinced that such loyalty was misguided, in that it is actually *disloyalty* to Hindustan, all things might be possible.'

From my point of view, this conversation, and Dignaga's obvious ambitions, were purely academic at that time. I had no concept how valuable his information would be in only a year's time.

Provided with such an escort as Dignaga's troop of horses, we made the remainder of the journey in the most perfect safety, and on the fourth day we could hear the rumble of guns. The next morning we stood on a slight rise and looked down on the city, situated, as I remembered, on the west bank of the Ganges, here very wide, although because the monsoon had not yet arrived, very low, revealing innumerable mud banks fronting the shore, but approaching as we were from the west, they were no obstacle.

The city itself looked perfectly peaceful, save for the large bodies of armed men to be seen in every direction, but it was a different matter at the cantonments outside of the city, where there was some smoke and where the firing was coming from. Obviously that was where the garrison had entrenched themselves.

We rode down the hillside, but before we could gain the streets we were stopped by a body of horsemen, who went through the usual manoeuvres, physical and verbal, as they discerned that I was a white woman. However, I was in the care of Dignaga, who rapidly obtained their obedience, and we were forthwith escorted – through streets in which many of the houses bore every evidence of having been looted – to the palace occupied by Nana, he having made himself most comfortable in one of the principal buildings of the city, high enough to provide a glimpse of the cantonments from its roof, but yet far enough removed from the scene of fighting to be out of range of any cannon ball.

Here there was a large courtyard, thronged with officers wearing the most splendid uniforms, as well as a horde of chattering women, growling dogs and noisy children, all of whom stopped their activities to stare at us as we dismounted.

'Let your people wait in the shelter of that porch,' Dignaga said.

I instructed Vima and Kujula, and then followed him as he strode, tulwar swinging at his side, up the main steps of the palace.

'Halt there!' came a shout, and we were confronted by armed men.

But now I was amongst . . . I will not say friends. But certainly acquaintances.

'Have you forgotten me, Tatya Tope?' I asked.

The general peered at me, and perhaps I was difficult to remember, for the soignee creature he had met in the rani's palace at the time of Nana's visit was here covered in dust and distinctly travel weary.

'Mrs Kala!' he said. 'There has been some catastrophe.'

'Not at all,' I told him. 'The rani is once again in full control of Jhansi.'

'But that is splendid news. Nana will be pleased. But why are you here?'

'I have a most urgent message from the rani, which must be delivered to Nana personally.'

'Then you must come with me.'

At this point Dignaga, who was not used to being sidelined, cleared his throat loudly. Hastily I introduced him, and Tatya Tope invited him to accompany us. We followed him through a succession of large hallways, sumptuously furnished and decorated although not so well as at Jhansi, and up several flights of stairs, to emerge on to the flat roof of the building where there were several divans and sun umbrellas, as well as a large number of men. Amongst these, studying the cantonment and the shells bursting there through a telescope resting on the shoulder of a servant in front of him, was Nana.

He turned when I was announced, and stared at me in total surprise. 'Mrs Kala? What brings you here?'

'Great news, and an important message, Sahib,' Tatya Tope said.

'For your ears only, Sahib,' I said. 'But first, let me introduce you to Prince Dignaga, from Gwalior.'

'Come to fight under your banner, Great Sahib,' Dignaga said.

'That is very gratifying,' Nana replied, but he remained gazing at me for several seconds before recalling his manners. 'I would have you meet my brother, Balla Sahib.'

He was a somewhat smaller version of Nana.

'And my commanding general, Jowalla Pershad.'

The general was as resplendently dressed as most of his officers, and had fierce eyes.

'How goes the siege, Sahib?' Dignaga appeared to be solely interested in military matters.

At last Nana turned to him. 'It goes well. We have driven them out of the outbuildings, and now they are concentrated over there.' He pointed at a group of buildings, one quite large, from which issued the occasional spurt of smoke as a musket or cannon was fired.

'They do not appear to be fighting with great energy,' Dignaga suggested.

'That is because they need to preserve their powder and shot,' Nana pointed out. 'They foolishly allowed us to capture their magazine by a *coup de main*, permitting my people to enter under the impression that they were reinforcements, and we seized it before they knew what we were about. Now they have sealed themselves in that old building, it was once a barracks, and are attempting to hold out, presumably in the hopes that they will be relieved. But their position is hopeless. There is only one well, and that is exposed to our fire. Every time they draw water we bring one of them down.'

'But will they not *be* relieved?' Dignaga asked. 'I have heard that there is a large British force marching in this direction.'

Nana frowned at him. 'I have heard nothing of this.' He turned to Jowalla Pershad. 'Have you heard of this?'

'No, I have not, Sahib.'

'Well, find out. Send out scouting parties. Find out. Quickly.'

The general bowed, and hurried down the stairs.

'I am grateful for your information,' Nana told Dignaga.

'We will meet them in the field, and fight a great battle, and destroy them,' the young man said enthusiastically.

'No doubt,' Nana agreed. 'Now you must excuse me, Prince Dignaga. I must learn what message the Rani of Jhansi has sent me. Mrs Kala.'

I followed him down the stairs, my mind spinning; I could see that he was not at all pleased at the prospect of confronting a British army in the open field.

He led me into a small antechamber and waved his guards away, then turned to me. 'You are as beautiful as ever,' he remarked.

I managed to keep my nerves under control. 'You flatter me, Sahib.'

'That is hardly possible.' He threw himself on to a divan. 'What has my cousin to say to me that is so important she has sent her favourite woman to me?'

'Her Highness wishes you to know, firstly, Sahib, that she has been reinstated as Rani of Jhansi.'

He frowned at me. 'How can that be? Her petition was rejected.'

'There has been a mutiny in Jhansi, Sahib. Half of the garrison rose in revolt, and while it was contained, the British feared for their lives, and offered the rani back her prerogatives if she would protect them.'

Nana clapped his hands. 'But that is splendid. Truly an admirable reversal of fortune. So now she is ready to join with me?'

'The rani conceives that her duty is to the people of Jhansi, Sahib.'

'Ha! She has a greater duty to the people of Hindustan. Very well. Tell me the exact situation there. The British have all been killed?'

'Certainly not, Sahib. The rani promised that she would protect them, and this she is endeavouring to do.'

'I thought she understood that a promise made to a *feringee* is of no account? And she has sent you here to tell me *this*?'

'She asks for your help, Sahib.'

'My help? To do what?'

'As I have said, the mutiny was by only half the garrison in the first instance. The remainder appeared to be faithful. But then her own palace guard mutinied, demanding to be led against the British. They invaded her private apartment in the dead of night, and laid hands upon her naked body.'

His eyes glowed. 'They raped the rani?'

'No, Sahib. She brought them back to their senses by promising to do as they wished.'

'There is a relief. But surely she now has sufficient people serving her to overcome any British resistance? There cannot be more than a few dozen *feringees* in Jhansi.'

'She needs your help to put down the mutiny, Sahib.'

He frowned. 'I do not understand you, woman.'

'The rani sent me to appeal to you, in the name of your lifelong friendship, of your love for her, and of your respect for the principal of princely rule. She cannot continue to rule Jhansi by virtue of a mutinous mob. These people threatened her life as well as her chastity. She begs for your help in restoring order, and confirming her as the ruler of Jhansi.'

Nana was looking genuinely bewildered. 'Her people wish to destroy the Raj, and she wishes me to stop them?'

'She wishes you to help her overcome this challenge to her princely power,' I said again, beginning to feel desperate.

'She has lost her senses.'

'Do you not love her, Sahib, and honour her as the Rani of Jhansi?'

'Well, of course I love her. And I wish to see her continue to be Rani of Jhansi. But she will do this best by joining in our fight for freedom, and leading her people in that direction.'

I drew a deep breath, but there seemed nothing for it. 'The rani empowered me to tell you that there is nothing she, or hers, will not do for you if you agree to help her.'

He regarded me for several seconds. 'She, or hers?'

I drew an even longer breath. 'That is why I am here, Sahib.'

He stretched out his hand to stroke his finger down the line of my jaw. Then his hand slipped down my neck to my shoulder. I made myself keep still with an enormous effort. 'I am not clean, Sahib.'

'Yes,' he agreed. 'You need a bath. And then I will come to you. I have dreamed of this for a long time.'

Then I must prove worthy of your dream, I thought. But surely we were still at the negotiating stage.

'And you will send a detachment to aid the rani? She asks for no more than two thousand men.'

His fingers had closed on my shoulder, both squeezing and caressing; no doubt this was how he would make love.

'I shall have to consider the matter. There is this battle to be won, first.'

'In your letter you said it would be over shortly.'

'It will. I have said, their cause is hopeless. But they are stubborn. It is this stupid man they have in command, General Wheeler. He is seventy years old, and a complete nincompoop. I have met him several times. We have taken tea together. His manners are impeccable, but his brains . . . he believed everything I told him.'

Then he *is* a nincompoop, I thought.

'I treated him fairly,' Nana went on. 'When my army was ready, I wrote him a letter, informing him that I was going to attack him. Can anything be more fair than that?'

'What did he do?'

'He determined to defend the cantonments. But instead of holding the magazine, which is a very strong building, as I told you, he allowed himself to be tricked, and is reduced to holding that place to the rear. It is an old and long disused barracks, and as I said, has no adequate water supply. It is quite indefensible.'

'But he is defending it.'

'Because he has not the brains to surrender. But he will. And until then . . .'

He resumed his stroking.

'I cannot come to your bed until you have given me a firm promise that you will send help to the rani.'

He scowled. 'You think you can bargain with me?'

'That is why I am here, Sahib.'

'You? A *feringee*?'

I was determined not to be browbeaten. 'I am the rani's envoy.'

'You are entirely in my power. I can do anything I choose to you. I can have you flayed alive, or impaled. I . . .' He turned, violently, as the door opened. 'I gave orders . . .'

'Mrs Kala! Emma!' cried the Begum of Oudh.

For all my memory of the night we had spent together, seven years before, I had never supposed I would ever see Hazrat Mahal again nor, in view of the guilt involved in our relationship, was I sure that I wanted to, but at that moment she was the most glorious sight in the world, and in every possible sense, for quite apart from her statuesque beauty, she wore a crimson sari and dripped jewellery.

I shrugged myself free of Nana and bowed from the waist, hands pressed together.

'I could not believe my ears when I was told you were in Cawnpore,' the begum said. 'We must talk.'

'Oh, yes, Highness,' I said.

Whatever had to be involved, lying with Hazrat had to be a million times preferable to lying with Nana.

'You may have her when I have finished with her,' Nana said.

'Finished doing what?' the begum demanded. 'I know your little ways. When you are finished with her she will not be worth having. Lie with one of your other women. Anyway, what claim do you have on her?'

'That she is here, and in my power.'

'I am here as an envoy from the rani,' I said.

'And I shall be interested to hear what my dear sister has to say,' the begum announced. 'Come with me.' She glanced at Nana. 'You may have her when *I* am finished with her.'

Which was not very reassuring, quite apart from the fact that I resented being referred to as a toy – which I suppose was what I was to these people.

'You think . . .' Nana began.

'I *know*,' the begum pointed out. 'Is not half your army composed of my people?'

Nana opened his mouth and then shut it again, and we were again interrupted, this time by Tatya Tope.

'Sahib, Highness, news has just arrived. What Prince Dignaga has said is true. A British army approaches to relieve Cawnpore.'

Nana threw up his hands in apparent despair.

The begum was more practical. 'How many?'

'He does not report more than a few hundred. But they have cavalry and artillery.'

'And where is this force now?'

'Oh, it is still well over a hundred miles distant, Highness. The messenger says it is moving very slowly because of the great heat. He says men are dying like flies.'

'And you are afraid of a few hundred men, drooping with heat, at a distance of more than a hundred miles?' Hazrat inquired, contemptuously. 'Go out and meet them, and defeat them.'

Tatya Tope looked at his master.

'Yes,' Nana said. 'Jowalla Pershad, take as many men as you require, and defeat the *feringees*. Kill every man. Take no prisoners.'

Jowalla Pershad bowed. 'Will you not lead us, great Sahib?'

'Lead you? My business is here. I am sending you, Jowalla Pershad.'

Jowalla Pershad bowed again, and hurried from the room.

'Of course,' the begum said. 'Your life is too precious to be risked. We will leave you to conduct your siege.'

★   ★   ★

She escorted me through various corridors into her world of women, where her all-female personal bodyguard stood to attention at every doorway, clad in their splendid red jackets and white trousers, every one young, and tall, and handsome. I could not help but wonder if she had slept with all of them.

'My servants are with me,' I informed her.

'Of course. Vima, was it?'

'And my manservant, Kujula.'

The begum snorted, and clapped her hands. One of her women hurried forward. 'Fetch the woman Vima,' she said. 'And bring her here. Send the man Kujula to the men's quarters until he is needed.'

The woman bowed and hurried off.

'You,' Hazrat commanded. 'Fetch a bath for Mrs Kala.'

They scurried to and fro.

'Undress,' Hazrat told me. 'I wish to refresh my memory.'

I obeyed. My sole ambition at that moment was to remain in this woman's care until I could escape Nana.

She undressed as well, to reveal all the voluptuous splendour I remembered, and which remained unchanged through seven years of considerable incident and vicissitudes and, the bath being brought, sat me in it and soaped me herself, the most softly sensuous sensation I had ever known. Then we lay on her bed, nibbling a plate of sweetmeats while she stroked me, caressing my breasts and thighs, my groin and what lay between. I could do nothing less than reciprocate, with again a deliciously guilty awareness that I could contentedly spend the rest of my life in this situation . . . were there not huge events surrounding me, and Manu and Alice waiting to be rescued.

'Are your son and your husband here in Cawnpore with you?' I asked, politely.

'My husband is in Calcutta, accepting the British pension,' she growled. 'He has chosen to stay there. He is a cowardly cur. I have divorced him. My son is here with me; I have pronounced him Nawab, and he will be crowned as soon as the British have been defeated and I can recapture Lucknow. It will not be long now; we have the fortress surrounded and its surrender is imminent.'

Words I had heard very recently. 'But you are here.'

'I came here to reinforce Nana and correlate our plans. And have found you! Is that not a good omen? Now tell me,' she said, 'what the rani wants.'

I did so, with growing hope. To be dashed. 'If you could lend me some men, Highness . . .'

'That I cannot do,' she said.

'Oh, but . . .'

'My people will fight against the British. They will not fight against the people of Jhansi.'

'No one is asking them to fight against the people of Jhansi. Only to help the rani regain her power.'

'Lakshmi Bai has that power. All she has to do is point her sword against the British, with us, and her people will follow her. This she has not done.'

I was in a very compromised position. I dared not offend this woman, who stood between myself and Nana. Yet I still had no doubt that for Manu to join the rebellion would mean the end, forever, of her hopes of reigning over her people in peace.

'But when this business is over, perhaps Nana will do something about Jhansi.'

'It was supposed to be over by now,' I reminded her. 'And now that a relief force is on its way . . .'

'Bah!' she said. 'A few hundred men? What can they do against Jowalla Pershad? He is a great soldier.'

'How many battles has he won?'

She laughed. 'I do not think he has ever fought one, yet. This is his first campaign. But Nana says he is a great soldier. We must believe this.'

I slightly changed the subject. 'Do you know what conditions are like inside the barracks?'

'They cannot be very good. We know they are short of water, and there are quite a few children in there.'

'And how many fighting men?'

'Nana estimates about three hundred.'

'And he commands several thousand. But he will not attack.'

'Oh, he has attacked, several times. But each time he has suffered many casualties. The fact is that he has no real control over his men. Like that business of the people from Fatehpur.'

'What people from Fatehpur?'

'When the rebellion started, the British commander in Fatehpur, that is just upriver from here, you know, decided that with his small garrison he could not hold the place, so he determined to evacuate, and came downriver by boat, with his women. They came ashore here. Nana wanted to make them all prisoners, but his men attacked them and killed all the men.'

'And the women?' I waited for some horrific tale.

'They were made prisoner.'

'Where are they now?'

'They were brought into the city.'

'Were they . . .' I bit my lip.

'Well,' she said. 'They are prisoners of war. And you know what men are like. Slavering beasts.'

'My God! And then what happened to them?'

'Oh, they were locked up.'

'You mean they are here now?'

'In the dungeons of this very palace.'

'Here?' I looked at the floor. 'Being mistreated?'

'No, no. Not in any way they would understand. They are merely made to grind the corn every day. You know that is a Hindu's way of proving to the world that he has conquered his enemy's womenfolk.'

'Yes,' I said thoughtfully. 'What is to become of them?'

'I have no idea. I imagine they will be included in the general surrender of the garrison.'

'If that happens.'

'Of course it will happen.'

When Hazrat was sated, at least temporarily, I said, 'I have some friends in the Cawnpore garrison.'

'Do you?' she asked, lying on her back with her eyes closed and breathing very deeply. 'You are a busy little bee.'

'Women friends.'

'Ah.'

'Not in the way you mean, Highness. One in particular I have known for a long time. Is there any possibility of finding out how she is? She has two children.'

Hazrat opened her eyes. 'The only way of finding out how she is would be to go into the enemy entrenchments.'

'Oh.'

'But that might be possible. It might be a good idea. I am sure Nana would agree.'

'He might if you ask him.'

'He will because it may be to his advantage. You will go into the enemy barracks, and see for yourself what conditions are like, how close they are to surrender, and then come back and tell him.'

'You are asking me to play the spy?'

'It is a chance to save their lives − if they will surrender. If not
. . . once this relief force has been dispersed they will have no hope,
and Nana may well order an all out assault. It will be for the good
of everyone.'

We dressed ourselves and went to see Nana. I wore a green sari
with all the jewellery I had brought with me, including the ruby
and diamond bangle given me by Hazrat seven years before, which
seemed to please her. But I was prey to very mixed emotions. Both
Sleeman and Skene had asked me to play the spy for the Raj, and
I had refused. Now I was being asked to play the spy for a man I
loathed and feared . . . and I had virtually agreed. Because I might
be able to save lives? There was that chance. But more important
to me was the possibility that if this siege, which clearly could only
have one outcome in view of the situation of the garrison and the
disparity in numbers, could be brought to an end, Nana might be
persuaded to release some of his men to go to Jhansi.

Even if that meant I would have to sleep with him? But I would
be prepared to do even that to succour Manu, and Alice, although
I was relying heavily on Hazrat's possessiveness to save me from that
ultimate fate.

Nana was not in the best of humours; he was clearly very anxious
about the coming battle with the British, even if he was keeping
himself far removed from the conflict. But he perked up when he
heard what the begum had to say.

'Yes,' he said. 'Yes. They would receive you, would they not, Mrs
Kala.'

'I think they might.'

'Yes,' he said again. 'Then you shall go. I will give you a personal
message for General Wheeler. We are friends, you know. Good
friends. We have taken tea together.'

He seemed to regard this as very important. As to whether, the
odd tea party or not, the British general would still regard Nana as
a friend was an entirely different matter. But I decided against saying
this.

'May I ask what the message will be?' I asked.

'Why, it will be an invitation for him to surrender. You will tell
him that if he agrees to this, I will provide the boats necessary to
take him, and all his people, down river to Allahabad, which I

understand is still held by the *feringees*. You will tell him that this is
his last chance, that I have great difficulty in holding my men in
check, and that if his position is stormed there will be a massacre.'

'And do you think I will be able to persuade him that you can
be trusted to carry out your promise?'

'I am Nana Sahib,' he shouted. 'You dare to doubt my word?'

'That was unseemly,' the begum told me.

'Forgive me, Highness,' I said. 'I was but remembering a conversation his Highness once had with the rani, in my presence.'

Nana snorted. 'Plans, ideals, in fact, often have to give way to
actualities.'

'Then I can assure the general that you have given your word.'

'Yes. He and his people will be sent to safety.'

I had to accept this, whatever my secret misgivings, because now
even the begum was slightly estranged.

'You will not, I hope, yield to any temptation, to desert us and
remain with the garrison, Emma,' she said. 'I would take that very
badly. And when the garrison surrenders, as it must do if it does
not accept the Nana's terms for evacuation, I will have you impaled.
I will drive the stake myself.'

I swallowed, but managed a smile. 'How could I ever contemplate
deserting you, Highness?' But I could not resist adding, 'Or my true
mistress, the rani?'

She snorted. 'I have been considering the matter,' she said. 'I do
not think it will be safe for you to go into the *feringee* ranks alone.
I will have the Nana send one of his people with you. You will be
joint envoys.'

I understood that my careless words had entirely forfeited her
confidence in me.

The arrangements were made, and at dawn the next morning, while
it was still cool, I was escorted to the magazine, accompanied by
Nana's representative, Azimullah Khan, who had been the leader
of the delegation to England to appeal to the House of Lords, and
whose comments as to the unwillingness of the English people to
go to war again so soon after the conclusion of the Crimean affair
had done much to spark this revolution. He was a nervous little
man with a long beard, who obviously considered that he might
be going to his execution; his principal asset was that he spoke
English.

Dignaga himself, having heard of the plan, came with us as far as the outer position.

'You are a brave woman, Mrs Kala,' he said. 'I shall wait here for your return.'

I glanced at the riflemen lining the parapet in front of the magazine. For the moment the cannon were silent.

Dignaga smiled. 'Do not fear. Not a shot will be fired until you are safely home again.'

I hoped he was right. Then I drew a deep breath, nodded to Azimullah, who raised the short pole to which was attached a square of white cloth, and stepped out from the shelter of the building.

We had to cross a distance of several hundred yards to gain the barracks, and this felt about the longest walk I had ever made in my life. It was not merely that I knew I was exposed to the gaze, and the guns, of several hundred men, both European and Indian, or that there was a fresh morning breeze which was whipping the hem of my sari to and fro. Worse than either of these was the fact that there were still dead bodies scattered about the yard, some of them already reduced to skeletons, others grinning horribly at me as I stepped over them; the stench of death was heavy in the air. Worst of all were the clouds of insects I disturbed with every footstep, who rose around me in angry swarms at having had their meal interrupted. I was irresistibly reminded of that terrible day after the thug massacre of our caravan when I had returned from hiding into the encampment. Azimullah seemed unaffected by his immediate surroundings; he seemed more concerned with what lay immediately ahead of us.

Well, so was I, as slowly we approached the walls of the barracks. They were pitted with both musket shot and cannon fire, and in places crumbling. We reached the well, around which lay more dead bodies, and I was holding my breath now, for some of these were recent enough to make the air very heavy indeed. I looked at the iron-bound doorway, which was still intact. Now I was close enough to be able to see the muzzles of the muskets protruding from the loopholes in the walls, and a voice called out, 'Stop there, woman! Who are you, and what is your business?'

Clearly they mistook Azimullah for my servant.

I shrugged the sari from my head. 'I am an envoy from Nana Sahib.'

There was a brief pause, while no doubt they took in my auburn hair and pale skin, and discussed whether to accept me or not. I was terribly conscious that I was within a few feet of their guns, and it required only one trigger-happy soldier to lose his head for me to be blown into eternity.

Then the door swung in, and an officer stepped out. 'You may come in.' He peered at me as I came closer. 'My God,' he said. 'You're an Englishwoman.'

'To these people I am a *feringee*, sir,' I said.

'And this fellow?' He peered at Azimullah in turn.

'He is also an envoy from Nana.'

He stepped aside, and we passed him and entered the building.

My first impression was one of revulsion, even greater than that I had felt when crossing the yard. The smell outside had at least been tempered by the breeze; in here there was no movement of air and the odour, of unwashed bodies and human waste, surrounded me like a miasma, so that I could hardly breathe. The people were equally distressing. On this ground floor, and behind the door, where it had to be presumed the main assault would come, there were only men. Most were soldiers, but there were quite a few civilians, all armed and looking desperate. A considerable number of the defenders were wounded, their bleeding limbs or heads roughly bound up in not very clean looking cloths.

'This way,' the officer said. He gave Azimullah another glance. 'Both of you.'

We were escorted to an office, which was sufficiently exposed to have clearly been struck by at least one shell; the window was shattered and there was debris on the floor. Waiting for me were several officers, but none of them appeared to be a general.

'This woman claims to be an envoy from Nana,' our escort said.

Like him earlier, the officers peered at me. 'Are you one of the women from Fatehpur?' one asked.

'I am employed by the Rani of Jhansi,' I said.

That took them aback.

'Then what are you doing here?' asked another officer.

'I came here on a mission from the rani to Nana. And Nana has in turn employed me to offer you terms for your surrender. This gentleman will confirm what I have to say.'

Now they bristled. But the first man spoke quietly. 'For our surrender, eh? Can you prove who you are?'

'Do you have a Captain Wilson in your force here?'

'Why, yes, we do. But he is a major now.'

'I met Captain Wilson when he was stationed in Jhansi, some years ago. He will confirm who I am.'

'Send for the major,' the officer said.

'Now take me to General Wheeler,' I requested.

'The general will not speak with any envoys from Nana,' he said. 'He has empowered me to deal with you. My name is Colonel Moore.'

The continuing arrogance of these people amazed me. They were in the most dire circumstances, from which they would be very fortunate to escape with their lives, and yet they still sought to lay down the rules of engagement, as it were.

'Now, let me understand this,' Colonel Moore went on. 'You, an Englishwoman, are in the employ of these mutineers? Are you aware of their crimes?'

'I was in the employ of the Rajah of Jhansi, and then his wife, long before this mutiny broke out.'

'And have remained in that employment, regardless of events.'

'I have remained in that employment, sir, because Jhansi is my home. My husband – stretching a point – and my child are there, and the rani is my friend. In any event, I have no other employment to go to.'

'And now you run errands for these rascals,' he remarked.

'Now I am endeavouring to save your lives, Colonel. And those of your women and children.'

'Ah,' he said. 'Major Wilson. Do you know this lady?'

Mr Wilson came into the room, saluted, then looked at me. There was no doubt that he recognized me, but I had some difficulty in recognizing him, for in the several years since last I had seen him – the day he had allowed the rani to bite the defiled cartridge – he had aged considerably, and there was grey in his hair. His uniform was as decrepit as everyone else's.

'Yes, sir,' he said. 'She is an English lady, the widow of a missionary, who now goes under the name of Emma Kala.'

Moore looked at me. 'You said your husband was in Jhansi.'

'I was speaking of my second husband, Colonel. An officer in the Jhansi royal guard.'

'Good God! You mean you are married to a Hindu? *Married?*'

'That is my present good fortune, yes.' Stretching another point. But I did not see that my domestic affairs were any concern of his.

He looked at Wilson. 'And you *knew* her? Socially?' He was clearly wondering whether the major was to be trusted.

'She attempted to befriend my wife.' Talk about stretching points! I had met Deirdre Wilson in Calcutta before I had gone near Jhansi; when she and her husband had been posted there some years later, it was she who had sought to renew the acquaintance. 'She provided a useful contact with the Jhansi court. When last I saw her she was in the employ of the Rani of Jhansi.'

'Well,' Moore said, 'that establishes that at least part of what you say is true, madam.'

I ignored him. Nor did I take offence at the way I was being treated. These people might be enduring their last minutes on earth. 'Will you tell me how Deirdre is?' I asked. 'And the children?'

'They are as well as can be expected,' he replied, stiffly.

'I should like to see her, if I may.'

'Well . . .' He looked at his superior.

'That can be arranged,' Moore said. 'I believe you have brought us a message from Nana.'

'Nana offers you your lives if you will evacuate your position and leave Cawnpore.'

'Evacuate Cawnpore? To go where?'

'He will himself provide the boats necessary to carry you down-river to Allahabad.'

Moore stroked his chin. 'We anticipate that our relief will soon be here.'

'There will be no relief, Colonel,' I told him. 'We have learned that a small force is attempting to move this way, but Nana has sent out a strong contingent, under his most able general, to defeat this column and disperse it. The fact, knowing your plight, that the Raj has only managed to accumulate less than a thousand men to attempt your relief shows that, when this attempt fails, they will not have sufficient reserves to try again.'

'I think we should wait on the outcome of the impending battle, if there is one,' someone said.

'Nana said to inform you gentlemen that this will be his only offer. If it is rejected, then as soon as his people return from having destroyed the relief column, he will launch an all-out assault on your position, at which time no quarter will be given to men, women, or children.'

There were several sharp intakes of breath.

'Is the man a monster?' someone asked.

'I'm afraid he is,' I agreed.

'Yet you serve him.'

'I serve the Rani of Jhansi. I have told you, I came here with a message from my mistress to Nana. He has decided to utilize my presence to make you this offer, and I accepted the mission because I believe it is your only hope of survival.'

'And do you believe this scoundrel, who so treacherously attacked us in the first place, while swearing his eternal loyalty to the Raj, can be trusted?'

'He has given his word, Colonel.' A hollow assurance? Which could leave me utterly damned. But what was the alternative?

'I asked if *you* believed him, Mrs Kala.'

'I believe that for you to believe him is your only chance.'

'This woman is a renegade,' someone said. 'I don't believe we can trust anything she says. In my opinion she should be hanged. And this rascal.' He looked at the trembling Azimullah.

'Then you would be as criminally guilty as any Indian,' I told him. 'We came here under a flag of truce.'

The officer harrumphed and went very red in the face.

'In any event,' Colonel Moore said, 'it is not our practice to make war upon women. Major Wilson, you know this lady. Do you believe what she has to say?'

'I believe she is acting in good faith, sir. I cannot speak for Nana.'

'Yes. We will excuse you now, Mrs Kala, while we report this matter to the general. You said you were acquainted with Mrs Wilson. You may take Mrs Kala to visit your wife, Major.'

'Sir!' Wilson stood to attention.

'And your answer?' I inquired.

'I have said – Nana's offer must be discussed with our commanding officer. You will have our answer within the hour.'

The Massacre

Azimullah and I followed Wilson down the stairs. 'Will they accept the offer?' I asked.

'I imagine they will,' the major said. 'Reluctantly. You understand how much it goes against the grain to surrender, when . . . is there really a relief force on its way?'

'So I understand.'

'And is it really not strong enough to do the job?'

'So I have been told.'

'And if those devils were to break in here . . .'

We had reached the ground floor, and were surrounded by haggard soldiers, who regarded me even more hungrily than before. Wilson led me across this floor towards the back of the building, and I was afflicted by an even worse smell than earlier.

'The well,' he explained.

'You mean there is another well inside? I was told the only water available was out front.'

'That is true. This well is dry. So we are using it as a cemetery.'

'As a . . .' I swallowed.

'Well, there is no way we can bury our dead in the floor. This way they are at least out of sight. You get used to it.'

Get used to that?

He showed me to a door leading to the cellars. This stood open, and there was a considerable noise coming up the stairs, principally children wailing, although the noise was nothing compared to the stench.

I stood at the top of the stairs, looking down. Perhaps fortunately, the large room beneath me was in semi-darkness, illuminated only by a couple of oil lamps hanging from the ceiling. The entire area was packed with people, not less than two hundred, I estimated, and perhaps more. Of this number about a third were children, of whom one or two were playing, while the rest, like their mothers, lay on the floor and moaned. What was most striking, and most distressing, was that they were mostly only half-dressed, and their clothes, whether gowns or shifts, were filthy; there were no stockings or hats to be seen, many were barefoot, and not one of them had had her hair dressed in some time.

Were these truly the fearsome memsahibs?

'God, to be able to get them out of here,' Wilson said.

I recognized Deirdre immediately, principally from her yellow hair. She saw her husband, stood up and came to the foot of the steps. Her children – now handsome teenagers – accompanied her. All three were terribly thin. 'Emma?' she asked, incredulously.

'I am a bad penny,' I suggested.

'But . . . here?'

'Mrs Kala has come to help us, if it is possible,' her husband said.

His voice was loud enough to be heard by most of the women, and several more now came to the steps.

'*Can* you help us?' Deirdre asked.

'Are we going to die, Mrs Kala?' asked Mary Wilson.

'No,' I said. 'No, you are not going to die. If your general agrees, you will be taken down the river to Allahabad.'

'Oh, thank God,' Deirdre said, and several of the women clapped.

'My father will never surrender,' someone said.

She was a most handsome young woman, dark-haired and strong-featured, buxom and strongly built.

'This is Miss Wheeler,' Deirdre explained.

'The general is my father,' Miss Wheeler declared. 'I know he will never surrender.'

But at that moment an orderly appeared behind me. 'Colonel Moore requests your presence, madam.'

'That was quick.' I looked down at them. 'I will not see you again,' I said. 'I will wish you a safe journey.'

I turned to go with the orderly, and someone shouted, 'Mrs Hammond!'

I looked over my shoulder and saw an extraordinarily pretty young woman, with long, loose yellow hair, coming up the steps. Her handsome features were emaciated with grief and suffering. 'Please,' she said.

'What is it?' I asked.

'Don't you remember me, Mrs Hammond? Lucy Orr.'

I frowned at her; the name was ringing a faint bell.

'We travelled together, from Indore to here, oh . . . eight years ago. You were on your way to Jhansi.'

'I remember,' I said. 'You were with your family.'

'Yes,' she said.

'Are they here with you?'

'They're all dead.' Her eyes were filled with tears. 'They couldn't get out of the city in time.' She came right up to me. 'Please, Mrs Hammond, I don't want to die.'

'You won't,' I assured her. 'I said that you are going to be taken to Allahabad. All of you.'

She didn't look convinced, so I squeezed her hand and hurried behind the orderly, joining Azimullah, who had remained on the upper floor. Together we returned to the office.

'General Wheeler has considered Nana's offer,' Moore said.

A very brief consideration, I thought.

'And he is prepared to accept. Nana will, I am assuming, allow us to march out with our weapons and all the honours of war.'

'I am sure he can have no objection to that,' I said.

'Well, then, will you return to him and give him our reply? Or will you stay here with us and accompany us when we leave? This fellow can take our reply.'

'Why should I wish to come with you?' I asked. 'My home is in Jhansi, and my sole ambition is to get back there as quickly as possible.'

'I was offering you the opportunity to escape these people. You do understand, Mrs Kala, that when the general reaches Allahabad, he will be required to make a full report on events here. He will have to name you as Nana's emissary, and should you choose to remain with him, I am afraid you will have to be described as a renegade.'

'I am sure there are some people who will say that, Colonel. Just as I know that Calcutta already regards me as a renegade, for my criticisms of the way they are ruling India. I can only remind you that when I went to Jhansi it was as the employee of the rajah and then his widow who, in the difficulties that surrounded her accession, asked me to remain at her side as her advisor until these difficulties have been resolved. I gave her my word that I would do so, and I have no intention of breaking that promise. I may also claim, and I know this will be endorsed by Major Skene, that it is my presence at the rani's side that has kept Jhansi out of the present conflict.'

'You are an Englishwoman, madam. A white . . . woman.' Obviously he had decided against using the word lady. 'Your primary allegiance is to your race.'

'Again, I must disagree with your point of view, Colonel. If you intend to turn this into a racial conflict, then I am sure posterity will judge you very harshly. Now, if your people will allow my companion and I out of this building, we will return to Nana and inform him that you have accepted his terms.'

The colonel abandoned his attempt to suborn me, and Azimullah and I left that charnel house; even the air of the compound smelt sweet as I returned to the magazine.

Of course my heart went out to those unhappy women and their children, forced to exist in such unhuman conditions for so long. But I had to believe that their suffering was nearly over.

Dignaga was waiting for me, and he escorted me up to Nana, who was delighted.

Tatya Tope was not. 'You cannot accept this business of them marching out with the honours of war,' he said. 'They are surrendering. They must hand over their weapons and their colours. They must be seen by our people to have been defeated.'

'And if they will not accept that condition?'

He shrugged. 'Then they have to die.'

Nana tugged at his moustache. As I was coming to realize, for all his bloodthirsty rhetoric, he was opposed to extreme violence, at least in his vicinity. He came to a decision. 'They may keep their personal weapons.'

Tatya Tope snorted. 'So that they may resume killing our people the moment they are free?'

'But not more than five rounds a man. And they must leave their cannon behind. Undamaged. Nor must they destroy any of their reserves of powder and shot.'

So once again Azimullah and I had to return to the noisome fortress and confront the British officers; the general again refused to see us.

'That is outrageous,' someone said. 'Let us at least die like men, with our weapons in our hands.'

'And our women?' someone else asked.

'And our children?' Wilson inquired.

'You are still sure Nana intends to keep his word?' Moore asked me.

'I am *sure* of nothing in this life, Colonel. I can only say that there is no reason for him *not* to keep his word. He wishes to demonstrate his victory to his people. This is necessary for his prestige. But once that is done, he will surely have achieved everything he requires. And I can also only say that, however humiliating this surrender may be to you, it is your only hope of survival.' I looked at Wilson. 'And for your women and children.'

The colonel sighed. 'So be it.'

Looking back, my naivety may seem astounding. But actually, I was not naive at all. Deep down, I did not trust Nana. I remembered too well his words to Manu and me before the rebellion had started. Manu had dismissed his wild talk as rhetoric. I was not sure of that. I knew that for all his boast of taking tea with General Wheeler and his wife he hated the British and sought only their destruction.

There was also the certain fact that for all the prestige he had already gained amongst his people, because of their basic indiscipline when not under the command of British officers, once he committed them to action he had little control over their behaviour, certainly if he intended to remain within the luxurious and safe confines of this palace.

But I also believed what I had told the colonel: firstly that, having secured the surrender and evacuation of the garrison, with all the immense additional prestige that was going to accrue to his name for such an achievement, there was no *reason* for him not to keep his word; and secondly that, as he was very conscious of his name and his fame, he surely would not wish to sully it by an act of treachery; and thirdly, and most importantly, that there did not seem any alternative for the garrison other than to accept his offer. To attempt to hold out in such conditions and without hope of relief was to die. Evacuation at least gave hope. It was like being on a sinking ship in the middle of a storm. The ship was certainly going to sink, and everyone on board when it did so would drown. Taking to the boats, even in such weather at least held out the hope that some of the company might make the shore.

Thus I hoped, and prayed, with the entire garrison, I have no doubt.

For the moment all went well. The preparations began. Boats were gathered, and moored in the river just below the barracks. This was a relief to me, as if the garrison was to be simply marched down the slope to the river bank it would be saved a great deal of humiliation, such as would have followed had the defeated soldiers been forced to march through the streets of Cawnpore itself. Unfortunately, as I have mentioned, the river was low, and there were extensive stretches of mud next to the banks that would have to be negotiated before their boats could be reached.

The city was *en fête* as news of the agreed surrender spread, and decorations were already being put up, for Nana had announced his intention of being officially installed as rajah once the British forces had been removed.

He was himself in a high good humour, so much so that I approached him again regarding the rani's problems. It was now nearly three weeks since I had left Jhansi, and as no word had come from there I had no idea what might be happening, or had already happened; Manu might have been murdered in her bed, and with her, Alice.

'I will go to the rescue of my dear sister,' Nana promised, 'the very moment I have completed the business here, and Jowalla Pershad sends me news of his victory.'

'Then I would beg your permission to return to Jhansi now,' I said. 'So that I may acquaint the rani with the news that you are coming.'

'You have not yet completed your part of the bargain,' he pointed out.

'Well,' I said, 'I do not wish to upset the begum.'

He gave one of his evil smiles. 'The begum is planning to leave,' he said. 'As soon as I have been installed as rajah.'

This was very bad news. Without her protection I was utterly helpless. But perhaps . . .

'I am told you are leaving Cawnpore, Highness,' I remarked when next the begum and I were alone.

'As soon as the rajah is crowned, yes. I can do nothing more here, and I have business elsewhere.'

'May I ask where?'

'I am going to Gwalior, to visit the Scindia. The silly little boy has refused to take up arms with us, and he has a powerful army. I am going to have a word with him. It is my business to regain Lucknow, where the stupid garrison is still holding out.' She sighed. 'I had hoped that by bringing my people to assist Nana here, he would then send his people to assist me in turn. But he says that he must get on to Delhi. Men!'

She was going from Cawnpore to Gwalior. That meant travelling very close to Jhansi.

'I would like to come with you,' I said.

She glanced at me.

'Would you not like me to, Highness?' I asked, as seductively as possible.

'I think we have run our course, you and I,' she said.

I bit my lip. 'I had thought we loved.'

'We *shared* love, Emma. We have never loved. You, certainly.' She squeezed my hand. 'Oh, we have had precious moments together, and I shall always remember them, and cherish the memory. But you are too conscious of being a *feringee*. You do not really trust us, or even, perhaps, like us.'

She was remembering my incautious words to Nana.

'So you must make your own way,' she said, and gave a wicked smile. 'See what you can do with Nana.'

This was a savage blow. As with Hazrat, I dared not offend Nana, or he would not go to Manu's aid. My only hope had been that the begum would overrule him, as she had already done more than once before. But if she had entirely withdrawn her support I could do nothing more than pray that politics would take precedence over lust, and once Cawnpore was his, Nana would send a force, and me, to Jhansi.

I stood with her on the roof of the palace to look at the barracks on the day the British were to evacuate. It was 27 June 1857.

The evacuation began at first light, as it promised to be a very hot day. There was a huge crowd gathered below us to watch the surrender, and a great deal of noise, drums beating and tambourines clashing, bugles and fifes blowing; a large part of the crowd was made up of sepoys, incongruously most still wearing the red tunics given them by the Raj, who filled the front ranks. They were all armed, but this was natural. I was too far away to be able to hear anything that was said, but I could imagine some of the remarks that were being made, on either side.

Led by General Wheeler and his staff, clearly identifiable even at a distance because of their plumed hats, the soldiers climbed down the bank to where the mass of boats were waiting. Some waded through the mud and boarded immediately, others remained on shore to pull the craft closer in; still others waited higher up the bank to escort the women and children, who now began to file out of the barracks. They at least had to be happy to have at last escaped the noisome interior of their prison, and they had been provided with carts to transport their sick. Hazrat had a telescope, and she willingly lent it to me to study the faces. I picked out Deirdre Wilson, holding her children's hands and staring straight ahead, chin up. Lucy Orr was close behind her, obviously weeping. Miss Wheeler and her mother walked alone.

'It is always sad, to look upon a defeated army,' the begum remarked.

At that moment a shot rang out. There was no means of knowing the cause of it, whether it was an overt action by a British soldier, perhaps at seeing or hearing one of the women insulted, or whether one of the sepoys had lost his head, or indeed, whether someone had been ordered to start firing once the last soldier had left the fort. In any event, that first shot was followed by a fusillade, as it seemed every sepoy in Nana's army now commenced firing.

The scene was horrific. Red-coated soldiers fell left and right as the bullets slashed into them. Some attempted to form ranks and return fire. Others, already in the boats jumped into the water and tried to make the far bank, which was impossible because of the width of the river and the swift flow of the current. There seemed to be a complete absence of command on the part of the British officers, while Nana's men kept up as rapid a fire as possible, aiming at anything that moved, in or out of the water. The men on the bank were simply shot to pieces, and when sufficient of them were dead the sepoys dashed amongst them with swinging tulwars to complete the work of destruction, while the women and children huddled together on the bank, unable to move forward or return to the dubious safety of the barracks, now occupied by sepoys, and in any event paralysed with shock and terror.

As was I, for several minutes, by the end of which time, indeed, the massacre had been all but completed. Then I so far forgot myself as to seize the begum's arm. 'You must stop it!' I shrieked. 'Stop it!'

She was watching in as much stupefaction as I, but there was no condemnation in her expression. 'I never thought he would have the courage to do it,' she remarked.

I gazed at her in consternation, then released her and pushed my way through the other watchers to gain Nana, who was studying the scene through his telescope.

'Your Highness!' I shouted. 'You gave your word!'

His hands were trembling as he lowered the glass. 'I did not command it,' he muttered. 'I did not.'

'Then you must stop it.'

'How am I supposed to do that, woman? Do you suppose they will obey me, now, even if I could command them from here?'

Because you are so far removed from the scene. In complete safety. As usual. 'But the women and children,' I implored. 'You can save them.'

'The women and children! Yes. Send a messenger commanding that they be returned to the barracks.'

But still he would not risk going himself. He was too afraid of even risking a stray bullet.

'Bah!' said one of his aides. 'They are *feringees.*' He grinned. 'They *were feringees.*'

For the slaughter had all but ceased; the riverbank was littered with motionless redcoats, and more floated in the water, carried downstream by the current.

'But . . . the women and children,' I gasped. They were still gathered in a horrified mass.

'Have not been touched. They are being taken to safety.' He gave me the glass, and I watched the women and children being shep-herded back up the slope.

At least someone at the scene had acted, I thought.

'Do you suppose,' the begum asked, 'they will ever forget, seeing their husbands shot down in cold blood?'

I bit my lip as I realized what she had said, even if I did not believe she had considered the possible implications of her words.

'They can remember whatever they wish, once Hindustan is ours,' Nana said.

The begum took back her telescope, and I could no longer clearly see what was happening. But the dead bodies were being thrown into the river, and the women and children had been returned to captivity . . . and now it really was captivity. But for how long?

I retired to the begum's apartment and lay on a bed, my face buried in the cushions. I felt like a murderess. No matter that I had acted in good faith, I was the one who had persuaded General Wheeler and his staff to accept Nana's terms. I had convinced them it was the only way to save their lives, and in doing that I had sent them to their deaths.

And their women to a fate that did not bear contemplation.

Had it been planned? I wasn't sure that I ever wanted to find that out, as if so that would only compound my guilt.

'What are you weeping about?' Hazrat asked.

'Should I not weep?'

She sat beside me. 'It is a soldier's duty to die.'

'In battle. Not to be shot down in cold blood. Nana has committed a great crime.'

'Crimes,' she pointed out, 'are a matter of perception. Did not Napoleon Bonaparte massacre all of his Syrian prisoners, and there were several thousand of *them*, because he had not the men to guard them? But as that was in 1798, and he had his entire glittering career

in front of him, this is not held against him except by a few purists.
Nana's act in destroying this garrison will only be condemned by
the British, should they ever learn of it. In any event, *his* crime, if
you choose so to consider it, was simply an inability to control his
people.'

'That is in itself a crime, in a commanding general. And of course
they will learn of it. And condemn him for it.'

'By the time they do, it will not matter.'

'And you will not condemn him.'

'I will condemn nothing that works for the good, for the freedom,
of Hindustan.'

'And perhaps you knew it was going to happen,' I said, no longer
caring whether I made her angry or not.

'I think you should look to yourself,' she remarked. 'Ask yourself
if your great friend the rani would not have approved of what
happened here, no matter who was responsible.'

'Never,' I declared. 'Lakshmi Bai would never condone such a thing.'

She snorted, and left me alone. In fact, she never came near me
again, for which I was profoundly grateful, even if it meant an end
to the protection I had hitherto enjoyed.

And I remained in a most invidious situation. I desperately wanted
to go to the women, to tell them how sorry I was about what had
happened, but I dared not – they would tear me to pieces. Besides,
what could I now offer them? I now knew just how worthless Nana's
word was, in that he had absolutely no control over his people, and
for all his protestations, I could not shake off the suspicion that he
had meant every word he had said to Manu on that day in Jhansi,
that his sole intention was the destruction of every Britisher he could
lay hands on. I could only pray that his enmity was directed only
at British *men*. But then I remembered that he had said that both
the humiliation *and* the destruction of their womenfolk had to be
part of the plan to drive the Raj from the subcontinent entirely and
forever. And now, if I included the women from Fatehpur, he had
some three hundred of them, with their children, at his mercy.

And there was nothing I could do about it, nothing I could do
to oppose him. He remained Manu's only hope of regaining control
of Jhansi, and even if I no longer had any faith in his promise to
go to her aid, I still had to work to make it happen.

★   ★   ★

With the massacre behind them, everyone in Cawnpore was concentrating on only one thing: the rajah's coronation. Those who felt there might be greater issues at stake kept their thoughts to themselves. Save for Dignaga. I had not seen him on the day of the massacre, and I had not seen him since. But a couple of days later, walking with Vima in the palace yard, Kujula as always a few feet behind us, I encountered the young prince, who bowed to me most courteously.

'You have been hiding yourself,' he remarked.

'Should I not? I gave those people my word.'

'I can see this would trouble you.'

'But you do not condemn Nana.'

'It is not what I would have done,' he said. 'But Nana is our commander. He no doubt knows things I do not.'

'What things can possibly justify the murder of several hundred men?'

He shrugged. 'News, perhaps, from his army in the field.'

'What news?'

'I cannot say. I am not in his counsels. But do you not think it strange that there has been *no* news from Jowalla Pershad? He must have encountered the British by now.'

'You don't suppose he has been defeated?'

'I do not see how he can have been defeated, if he truly outnumbers the British by two or three to one. But I do know that had he gained a victory a messenger would have been sent to tell us of it.'

There was a provocative thought. If I still felt that, as the people who had conquered and looted this land the British had a great deal to answer for in their behaviour in Hindustan – principally of course, in my eyes, their brutal and unjustified deposition of the rani in order to annex Jhansi – they had never been guilty, to my knowledge, of any crime equal to that of the massacre. My every instinct was to wish Nana, as ultimately responsible, to be punished, even if I did not see how that would happen. But if a British relief force was to fight its way into Cawnpore, and hear what the women had to tell them . . . my own position would be highly dangerous. I would have to get out before that happened.

'Could it happen?' I asked Dignaga.

'It has happened before,' he said. 'Men like Clive defeated vastly superior armies. But that was a hundred years ago, when the British had the advantage of modern weapons. Now that we have them also . . . I do not think it could happen now.'

Certainly Nana was allowing nothing to interfere with his coronation, which took place 15 July 1857; I had now been away from Jhansi for five weeks, with no idea as to what might have been happening. The coronation was a tremendous occasion. Drums, tambourines, flutes and zithers kept up a constant racket, elephants trumpeted, horses whinnied. The streets were packed with celebrants, everyone in their finest clothes, spoiled only by the absence of Manu, although I had to believe that her absence meant she was still a prisoner to the mutineers.

However, Nana himself was smothered in jewels worn over rich fabrics, as was the begum. All the ladies of the court, as we might be called, were also dressed in our best; I wore a silver sari as I took my place with the others, behind the throne, which had been placed on the porch of Nana's palace, so that everyone could see him, while cannon roared blank shot to overcome even the other noises.

It was impossible to imagine what the captive women thought of it all. The celebrations continued all night, and became wilder and wilder, with muskets and pistols being fired at random, and a good deal of alcohol consumed. I retired as soon as I could. Sleep was for a while impossible, but eventually I nodded off, and awoke to daylight and a profound silence. I scrambled out of bed and ran to the balcony outside my room, to gaze on a scene of utter devastation. Cawnpore might well have fallen to another assault. But the bodies lying about the place were merely drunk, and they slowly returned to life, although it took several days for the city as a whole to function normally. I had to act on my own initiative, go down to the magazine, shake the captain in command there awake, and insist he send in food and water to the captives. This he did very reluctantly, and his men obeyed him even more reluctantly; had the smallest British force been able to reach the city on this day they would have gained the easiest of victories.

I also endeavoured to visit Nana, but he was unable to do any business for some three days, and then there was a good deal of business to be done. I was therefore left to myself for upwards of a week, feeling increasingly desperate. It would have been the simplest thing in the world, given the prevailing conditions in Cawnpore, to have Kujula saddle up our horses and ride out and back to Jhansi, but I could not do that without the certainty that Nana would follow with support.

As soon as she had recovered from her excesses, the begum departed for Gwalior, taking with her her Amazon bodyguard and the main part of her troops. They paraded away from the city with a great deal of pomp and ceremony. She did not say farewell to me, and while I toyed with the idea of asking her to detach one of her people with a message for the rani, as she would be passing so close to Jhansi, just to let Manu know that I was still working on her behalf, I decided against it, as I had no certainty that she would not say something derogatory about me.

It was a couple of days after the begum's departure that Nana sent for me; I assumed that until that moment he had presumed I was still under her protection.

'Kneel,' he commanded. 'Kneel, to the Rajah of Bithur and Cawnpore.'

I obeyed. I had to believe that we were about to get down to the nitty-gritty, as it were.

'I had assumed that you would be leaving with the begum,' he remarked.

'It is my business to stay here, Highness,' I said, 'until I can return to Jhansi, with an armed force for the support of the rani.'

'The rani no longer needs my support,' he said. 'She is in full control of Jhansi, as she is now wholeheartedly on our side.'

I frowned. 'You have heard from Jhansi?'

'A messenger arrived yesterday. She has taken my example, and destroyed all the *feringees.*'

I could not believe my ears. 'Destroyed them?'

'I sent her a message, after I had dealt with the garrison here, enjoining her to do the same in Jhansi. It seems that the *feringees* there were confined to a single fort, as here.'

'Yes,' I said, my head swinging. 'The City Fort.'

'That is it. Well, almost as soon as she heard the news from here, the rani ordered her forces to attack the fort. The attack did not succeed in forcing an entry, but the *feringees* suffered many casualties, amongst them their commanding officer, a Captain Gordon. Did you know this man?'

'Yes,' I muttered. 'I knew him.'

What on earth could have possessed Manu to do something like this?

'So she then offered them terms of evacuation, that they should leave the fort, with their women and children, and make their way out of Jhansi. They accepted these terms.'

I clasped both hands to my neck; he was smiling his evil smile.

'What happened to them?' I whispered.

'Once outside the fort, they were attacked by the rani's people and massacred, every one.'

'No!' I cried. 'I will not believe that of Manu. I cannot.'

'It happened,' he said. 'She is to be congratulated for acting with such decisive ruthlessness.'

'I must get back there. Please, Highness, grant me an escort, I beg of you.'

He regarded me for several seconds, while I held my breath. But I was determined to go, with or without support, and find out the truth of the matter. I simply could not accept what he had told me.

'Well,' he said, and looked up as there was a commotion at the door.

'Highness!' It was Jowalla Pershad.

'Haha!' Nana shouted. 'You have defeated the British.'

But he frowned as he spoke. This figure was a long way removed from the resplendent warrior who had ridden off to war a month before. His clothes were dust- and mud-stained and even torn in places, he had clearly not bathed in several days, and fatigue lines were etched on his face.

'The British are coming,' he said.

'What? What are you saying? You have not beaten them?'

'We fought them,' Jowalla Pershad said. 'We fought them at the river, and they came on like devils. They would not stop. So we withdrew.'

'You let them across the river?' Nana was aghast.

'We had no choice. Our men would not face the bayonets. We withdrew, and regrouped, but still they advanced, so we fought them again. And again we were forced to withdraw.'

'Three thousand men?' Nana shouted. 'How many *feringees* were there?'

'Several hundred. They were the Scotsmen, who fight in skirts. They would not stop. So we fought them a third time, and a third time were forced to withdraw.'

'You are cowards!' Nana shrieked. 'I should have your heads.'

'You were not there, Great Sahib. You do not know what it is

like to fight these people. They form up in two ranks, and advance,
step by step, while a drum beats. There is no other sound. It is a
terrifying prospect. Then, when they're about five hundred yards
away, there is a command, and they halt. Another command, and
the front rank falls to one knee. The rear rank then levels their
muskets and fires a volley. It is a perfect hail of bullets. The moment
they have fired, they advance, through the kneeling men, who then
stand and fire in turn. Meanwhile the front rank is reloading, with
such speed as you could not believe, and the manoeuvre is repeated,
again and again, while they move inexorably forward, firing volley
after volley, so that more and more of our men fell as they came
closer.'

'Were you not firing back?'

'We did, Great Sahib, but our shooting was wild, and it took us
too long to reload. Some of the redcoats fell, but that did not stop
their advance. Then, when they were a hundred yards away, they
halted again, but this time the front rank did not kneel. Instead,
there was a command, and they drew their bayonets. You have never
seen such a sight, Sahib. The sun glinting from all that steel, as the
entire force seemed to move as one man, and the click as they locked
the bayonets to the gun barrel was the most frightening thing of all.
Then they advanced again, still step by step, still without a sound
save for the drum beat. Then, when they were perhaps thirty yards
away they halted, for a moment, and then they gave a great cheer
and charged. Some of our men were already fleeing; they could not
face that wall of steel. Those who stood and fought died, stuck like
pigs. It was a terrible experience. Perhaps, had you been there to
lead us, Great Sahib . . .'

Nana continued to glare at him for several seconds, but the general
had made a telling point. He regained control of himself. 'Where
are they now?'

'They have halted, perhaps fifty miles away, Great Sahib. They are
awaiting reinforcements. They have lost many men through the heat.'

'Well, then . . .'

'But the reinforcements are coming, Great Sahib. A thousand men
at the least, with cavalry and guns. They are coming. Their
commander is the man Havelock, one of their greatest soldiers.'

'What am I to do?' Nana wailed. 'What am I to do? Can we not
stop them, here?'

'I do not think so, Great Sahib. They are devils who are destroying everything and everyone in their path. They are burning villages, and what they do to those taken, even the women, I cannot repeat. They have artillery, and will bombard the city. The people here will not be able to withstand that. You must withdraw, and regroup, and place yourself at the head of your armies, and confront them again, with every man who will follow you.'

'Withdraw,' Nana muttered. 'Yes, that is what we must do.' He looked brighter at the thought that he would not have to face the dreaded Highlanders in person. 'You will give the orders. But . . .' his face fell again, 'those men we killed . . .'

'Dead men tell no tales, Great Sahib.'

'But the women and children . . .'

The two men gazed at each other, and I realized what they were thinking. 'No,' I said. 'No,' I shouted. 'No!' I shrieked. 'You cannot do it.'

'Remove this woman,' Nana said. 'She is hysterical. Go back to Jhansi, Emma, and tell the rani to prepare to defend herself. Against the British. Tell her I will send her what help I can.'

I would have protested further, but my arms were seized by his guards, and I was hurried through the corridors to my own apartment.

'Memsahib?' Vima was anxious.

'You are to leave this place,' my escort told her. 'You will return to Jhansi. These are the orders of Nana Sahib.'

Vima looked at me, as the men left again.

'You had better tell Kujula,' I said.

'Yes, Memsahib. But . . . will we have an escort?'

'It does not appear so. Just let us get out of here.' I was running. For my life? No doubt that came into it. As Colonel Moore had pointed out, the British had no reason to consider me other than a renegade, and as guilty as Nana himself. But I was also running from that guilt, of what had happened, of what was about to happen. All of those women, Deirdre, her children, Lucy Orr . . . one half of me still could not believe that it would happen, that he could possibly allow it to happen, much less command it. He was a ruling prince, even if not recognized by the Raj. Had he fought, honourably, and lost, honourably, he could have hoped for perpetual exile or some such thing. After 27 June he could expect nothing more than execution. But if in addition he had the deaths of three hundred women and children to be laid against him . . .

And what was I running to? According to Nana, the rani was every bit as guilty of cold-blooded murder. That was something else I could never accept as true, until I heard it from Manu's own lips. But there was nowhere else I could go. My daughter was in Jhansi!

Vima stood in the doorway. 'Prince Dignaga is here, Memsahib.'

'Oh!' I stood up and straightened my clothes.

The prince was as handsome and debonair as ever, even if his face was grim. 'I am told you are leaving, Mrs Kala.'

'Yes,' I said. 'My mission has failed. I must return to Jhansi.'

'I and my people will escort you.'

'You?' My heart leapt. 'But . . . are you not with Nana's army?'

'What army?' he asked contemptuously. 'This is a cowardly rabble, planning to run as far and as fast as they can. I and my men will return to Gwalior. But on the way I will see you safely to Jhansi.'

'And I shall be forever grateful,' I said. My mind was already racing ahead. If he came to Jhansi, might he not be persuaded to help the rani? He commanded two hundred men. 'I am ready now.'

He shook his head. 'My people cannot be ready before tomorrow morning. We must equip ourselves with food as well as ammunition. We will leave at dawn.'

'Oh,' I said. Another twelve hours in this place! But again, perhaps . . . 'Those women,' I said.

'Which women?'

'The *feringees.*'

'If it is true that Havelock is on his way, they will be rescued.'

'Nana will not permit that. If even one of them was to give evidence against him . . . He means to kill them all.'

'Well,' he said, 'when you have committed one big crime, another is not so difficult.'

'Can you not stop him?'

'I?'

'You are a prince of the House of Scindia. Is that not the oldest and most powerful in all Hindustan?'

'It was once,' he said. 'Those days are history.'

'Surely the name still counts for something.'

'Not sufficiently – certainly since my cousin refuses to support the movement. In any event, what can my two hundred men do against Nana's army?'

'A cowardly rabble, you said.'

He smiled. 'I believe they are. But still the odds are too great. And I do not think my men would follow me to war upon their fellows in defence of *feringees*.'

'So those poor women must die.'

'They are *feringees*,' he repeated. 'Perhaps they are fortunate to have lived this long. Do you not know that, had they been Hindus, they would have taken their own lives once their husbands were dead?'

Becoming angry with him would have been a waste of time. I believe he was in every way a noble and honourable man, but his religion was composed of different values to mine . . . and I could not forget the comparison with some past Christian deeds as outlined by the begum. This was a war of religion far more than a fight for independence.

As for what would happen afterwards . . . but first it was necessary to have it happen. I had hoped to be away from Cawnpore before the slaughter commenced, but it was not to be. Vima was with me, packing up our few belongings, that afternoon, when we heard firing. Then, even from the palace, a distance of a mile or more from the barracks, we heard screams and shrieks, of agony and terror. I could not stop myself from going up to the roof, where Nana and his staff were gathered. I learned later that the sepoys had at first absolutely refused to kill the women and had had to be bullied by Tatya Tope into opening fire, through the windows. Once they had begun the bloodlust took control and they fired again and again, until the building was wreathed in smoke. Then the firing ceased, and the men laid down their muskets and drew their tulwars.

The doors were thrown wide, and the men rushed in. It seemed impossible that anyone inside the building could have survived such concentrated firing at close range, but now there were more shrieks and cries for mercy, clearly audible in the still air – not one of the considerable crowd of onlookers was making a sound, all overwhelmed by the awfulness of the deed they were witnessing.

This second wave of the massacre lasted longer than the first, before the last of the shrieks ended. A few minutes later one of the sepoys came out, and marched towards us. In his right hand he held his tulwar, stained to the hilt with blood, as was his arm, stained to the elbow. In his left hand he held a human head, by the hair, long and yellow; beneath the hair was the tortured face of Lucy Orr. Blood still dripped from her neck.

I wished to be sick and I wished to faint. I could do neither.

'It is done, Great Sahib,' the sepoy shouted. 'What is to be done with the bodies?'

'Did not the *feringees* put their dead down a well?' Nana said. 'Let them be joined by their women.'

I fled down the stairs. At the foot I encountered another blood-stained sepoy. 'Is there no one left alive?' I asked.

'None, Memsahib,' he answered. 'Every last one is dead.'

The Ruler

Vima and Kujula and I could only complete our packing and await Dignaga. We did not discuss what had happened: our points of view were too different. I knew they were unhappy that I should be so grieved, but I also knew that they did not condemn Nana. To them, he had done what had to be done. It was unthinkable that any group of Hindu women would have allowed themselves to be placed in a position where they could be torn to pieces by their enemies. Memory went back to the famous incident at Chitor in 1567, when the Maratha stronghold had been surrounded by the Mughals. There had been no hope of succour from any direction. So all the men had marched out and died in battle, and all the women, several hundred strong, had set fire to the fortress and perished in the flames. There was no point in attempting to remind my faithful servants that General Wheeler and his people had been promised a safe conduct by Nana. To them, his betrayal of his word had been a legitimate act in time of war, just as suicide, so opposed to Christian teaching and belief, was a legitimate and indeed honourable act for any women about to be made captive. Equally, believing as they did that their superiors had to know best, Nana's decision to abandon the city rather than face the vengeful redcoats was high strategy rather than cowardice.

All of these points had to be considered in forming my own judgement of what had happened, or was likely to happen. My condemnation of Nana's action, or lack of it to stop the massacre, was complete and irrevocable, compounded by the part I had unwittingly played in the tragedy, over and over again: apart from conveying Nana's terms to the general – and I had at least refused to guarantee them – I *had* guaranteed the lives of the women and children, to their faces, because I had been unable to believe their lives, for all Nana's threats, could possibly be in danger. Nana had surely rubbed shoulders with European customs and beliefs for long enough to know that they simply did not make war upon women. Although, if the reports arriving of the behaviour of the British troops during their advance were to be proved true, I would have to revise that cherished belief . . .

In any event, as for all my instincts I had opted to support the Indian cause, at least where Manu was involved. I was well aware that when the facts became known I would be put in the same class, and more, in the same dock if the British ever got hold of us. But what could I do save continue on the path that had been chosen for me by both fate and the rani?

The rani! It was only to her that I could now flee, not only because she was the only person in India who would protect me, but because she was in possession of my daughter. But according to Nana, she had committed no less a crime, save in actual numbers. I still could not believe this, but I dreaded to find out. And yet I had to.

My brown study had not lightened when the prince came to dine with me that evening, because by then it had started to rain, a steady drizzle as if the skies themselves were weeping for the tragedy of Cawnpore. But we knew this was just an indication of the arrival of the monsoon, although Dignaga suggested that I might wish to postpone my departure until the weather improved. 'We have nothing to fear for the time being,' he said. 'The rain will slow, if not halt, the British advance. The difficulties of moving large bodies of troops with their supply wagons will be enormous.'

'I do not think they will allow the weather to halt their advance,' I argued. 'When they are so close and they have Nana's army on the run. They will certainly wish to occupy Cawnpore before waiting for the next campaign season, and if opposed, they will rely on the bayonet. Anyway, I could not consider spending any more time in this charnel house.'

He rested his hand on mine. 'You grieve for those people.'

'Should I not? One of them was my friend.'

'War is a sad and bloody business. And yet it is man's natural environment.'

'Do you believe that?'

'Of course. War, the possibility of death, the *risk* of death, is man's most exalted state.'

'And you consider that massacring women and children is exalted.'

'I know that it is difficult for a woman to understand. Let me put it this way. War is a coin and, like all coins, it has two faces. The first is what appeals to us, battalions of men, clad in bright uniform and with their weapon gleaming and their flags flying, their bands playing, marching proudly to the beat of the drum, determined to do or die. But then the coin turns over, and the doing and dying commences. Then your warrior is consumed with fear of death, or of having to live with a shattered body, with revulsion at seeing his comrades scattered about the field, dead or dying in agony, with guilt that he should still be alive, and perhaps unharmed, in the midst of so much carnage. But most of all, he is consumed with anger, with hatred of his enemy. This hatred is necessary, and it is installed by his officers, or he would not fight at all. It burns like a fire that sustains him throughout the battle. But when the shooting stops, it is still raging. It cannot be extinguished by throwing water on the flames. It must burn itself out. And until it does, woe betide any of the enemy's people, be they old men, or women, or children, who are encountered. All will suffer as if they had weapons in their hands.'

I found myself squeezing his fingers. I had recognized this man's worth, as a man, from the moment of our first meeting, but had not realized that behind the charm and the obvious courage, there might lie a thoughtful and sensitive personality. 'You must forgive me,' I said, 'but as a woman, one of those who must suffer that masculine fire if captured by a victorious enemy, I cannot accept your point of view, even if I believe it to be true. And in any event, those women were not the victims of blood lust, at least in the beginning. Their deaths were the result of a cold-blooded decision.'

He nodded. 'There is always additional hatred when the fighting is against the infidel.'

'In your eyes, I am an infidel,' I pointed out.

'You are unique.'

'I could easily have been one of those helpless women, to be shot, or cut to death.'

'But you were not. That is the hand of fate. It was not your karma, your destiny.'

I knew those were meant to be reassuring words. If only I had some idea of what my destiny actually was. Or even if it truly existed.

Dignaga's admiration for me was evident, and growing, and I understood that it might become a problem. In other circumstances, had I not been engaged to another, I might even have responded. He was young, strong, virile and, I felt, intrinsically noble. That he would not condemn Nana for what he had allowed to happen, while prepared to condemn his stupidity and lack of leadership was, like Vima and Kujula, an aspect of the ethos into which he had been born and educated. He was also a prince, with all that rank suggests in terms of wealth and upbringing.

Fortunately, he seemed to hold me in some awe, and for this I was intensely grateful. I would have hated to fall out with him by rejecting an advance, the thought of forming a relationship, whether emotional or sexual, with anyone was utterly repugnant to me at that moment. I could not be sure which I hated more, myself or all mankind. I dreamed only of regaining Jhansi, and my daughter, and the reassuring comfort of Manu's company . . . supposing, if what Nana had told me was true, that was still available.

To my consternation, that night, after Dignaga had left me, and just as I was preparing for bed, there was a peremptory knock on my door. Vima and I looked at each other. Then I said, 'You had better open it. Otherwise it may be knocked down.'

She gulped, but went to the door, opened it, and stepped back as Tatya Tope entered the room. My heart seemed to slow. If Nana intended to carry me off with him . . . there was nothing I could do.

The general bowed, most courteously. 'Mrs Kala. Forgive this intrusion.'

I'm afraid I goggled at him: I had never known this man to be other than violently aggressive, towards all *feringees*, and towards me in particular.

'I have come to inquire into your intentions.'

'Nana has sent you.'

'Nana does not know I am here. Will you wait for the British?'

'I will return to Jhansi, and my mistress.'

'You are a loyal servant. So tell me, will Lakshmi Bai, understanding that the British will certainly now turn on her, defend Jhansi? Or surrender?'

'She will fight.'

'How can you be certain?'

'For two reasons. One is that on Gangadhar Rao's deathbed she swore an oath to defend Jhansi as long as it is humanly possible to do so. The other is that she wants to fight, more than anything else in the world.'

'Whatever the outcome?'

'Whatever the outcome.'

Tatya Tope sighed. 'How I wish Nana could have been cast from the same metal. I know our strengths, and I know our weaknesses. I accept that on an open field, the British, with their discipline and their fire power, are nearly impossible to defeat. But if we are behind fortifications, that would be different. I believe that if we were to stay and defend Cawnpore, we might gain a victory that would rouse all Hindustan in our support. But Nana is reluctant to commit his forces, and as I am his principal officer I must obey his will, and hope that we may yet be able to fight a battle on ground of our own choosing. But listen to me – I have a personal following of two thousand men. As we retreat, I will leave spies to keep me informed of the British movements and intentions. And the moment I learn that they have turned against Jhansi, I will bring my people to the rani's support.'

I gazed at him, my heart pounding. I did not like this man. I had no proof that he had not been involved, if indeed he had not actually ordered the massacre – he had advocated it often enough. But I would have sold my soul to the devil to preserve Manu. And if it seemed that she no longer needed any help to regain control of her city and people, I had no doubt at all that she would need professional help to oppose the Raj. 'You will swear this?'

'You have my word. If you will give me your word, on behalf of the rani, that she will stand.'

I drew a deep breath. 'I give you my word.'

He gave another bow. 'Then may the gods go with you.'

He left me staring at the door as it closed. Could it be possible that I had found salvation, whatever the source?

★   ★   ★

Dignaga presented the three of us with hooded cloaks, which, if not entirely waterproof, kept out the worst of the wet, and of course I changed into my male attire for the journey.

We stole out of Cawnpore in the dawn. Not that we were alone, as Nana's army was also evacuating the city as fast as it could, but the sepoys were making north-west while we headed south-west. I did not confide Tatya Tope's promise to the prince. I had no doubt that he would support me, and the rani, to the limit . . . but that was as long as his support did not clash with his overwhelming sense of duty, to his race, his religion, and his superiors. Nana, as the heir to the peshwa, was superior in rank to any other Indian ruler. I could not be sure how he would react to learning that his principal general was prepared to abandon him and fight for another, even another so charismatic and courageous as Manu.

Our progress was not as fast as I would have liked. Apart from the persistent rain, which turned narrow streams into broad and turbulent currents, the country between Cawnpore and Jhansi was seething, bands of men marching to the support of Nana, as they assumed he would be fighting for the city, other bands moving away from the city as they had heard of the inexorable advance of the British troops, all seeking or offering information, very little of which bore any resemblance to the truth as we knew it.

Thus it took a week for Jhansi to come into view. It looked utterly peaceful save in the cantonments outside the walls, where there were large numbers of men being drilled, regardless of the weather. I wasn't sure whether to be alarmed or relieved at this, or at the sight, as we grew closer, of the rani herself, seated on a white mare, and surrounded by officers, overseeing the proceedings. But certainly she appeared to be in complete command of the situation, and I had no doubt that beneath her cloak she was armed.

'Is that her?' Dignaga asked.

'That is her.'

'You will introduce me.'

'Certainly.'

We moved closer, now attracting some attention ourselves, while I looked at the forts. I was naturally more interested in the City Fort, and it certainly showed considerable evidence of conflict, some of the wall blackened and all pock-marked with bullet holes. But the only people to be seen were definitely Indian. Then I realized that the whole place had changed in the month I had been away.

Jhansi had always been walled, although the palace had stood outside the enclosure. But now the walls were being extended from the city to surround the palace itself. In every way, Manu was preparing for the worst.

We skirted the city and reached the cantonment.

'She is as beautiful as they say,' Dignaga observed, reverently.

I glanced at him; his eyes glowed, and I had to wonder whether he might have aspirations in *that* direction. But now our approach had been observed by one of the rani's escort, and she turned her head, and then her horse, to canter towards us.

'Emma!' she cried. 'I have feared for your life.'

She looked exactly as I remembered her, as her cloak flopped open to reveal that she wore her male uniform with her hair coiled beneath her turban, and was indeed armed with her sword and her revolver, and as always exuded energy.

Dignaga stared at her in rapture; she was clearly fulfilling all of his dreams.

'I am not that easy to kill, Highness,' I said, wishing to match her mood, at least in public.

'For which I must thank the gods. There is so much you have to tell me. We have spent these last few weeks existing on rumour.'

'So have I,' I said.

She made a moue. 'Then we have lots to tell each other,' she said, quietly. 'Are these Nana's people?'

She did not seem unduly concerned that there were only two hundred of them.

'These men are from Gwalior,' I said.

She raised her eyebrows.

'And are commanded by Prince Dignaga, of the House of Scindia.'

'Prince Dignaga!' She extended her hand, and he took it and pressed it to his lips. 'Welcome to Jhansi. You will take tea with me. This afternoon.' She turned her horse again. 'General, see to the billeting of Prince Dignaga and his people.'

Risaldar Khan bowed in the saddle, and then looked at me. 'Welcome home, sister,' he remarked.

'Come with me, Emma,' Manu said, and set off for the palace.

I urged my horse up to be beside her. 'Highness . . .'

'Later,' she said. 'Are you not anxious to see your daughter?'

'Very anxious.'

'She is waiting for you.' Manu rode into the courtyard and

dismounted, grooms hurrying forward to take her bridle as they did for mine. I followed her up the stairs, and at the top encountered Abid, resplendently uniformed, standing to attention. 'Highness! Emma!'

He had obviously seen me coming. And the last time I had seen him he had been standing over my naked body with a drawn tulwar in his hand. I gave him a brief bow, and followed Manu into her apartments. We took off our sodden cloaks, and a moment later I was holding Alice in my arms. She appeared delighted to see me, and was certainly in the pink of condition; I had a suspicion that she was not really aware that I had been away at all.

Manu allowed us several minutes of kissing and cooing and then called for the nurse to take the child away. Once we were alone, she embraced me most tenderly, and then led me down the stairs to the rushing stream that flowed beneath the palace and provided the communal bathing chamber for the ladies of the court. Several of these were present, but when they realized that the rani was accompanied by her favourite, they withdrew to be out of hearing.

Manu herself undressed me, before removing her own clothing and stepped into the water with me to soap me, her hands as softly sensuous as ever. 'Tell me of Cawnpore,' she commanded.

'I have to say it was an act of the foulest treachery,' I said, and told her what had happened.

She listened in silence, her face expressionless. 'And you say Nana has now abandoned the city?' she asked when I had finished.

'He was advised to do so by his generals. But I think he would have gone anyway.'

'The British will call him an outlaw.'

'He *is* an outlaw. At the very least.'

'His problem is an inability properly to control his people,' she said. 'It is the problem of every ruler.'

'Highness . . .'

'Yes,' she said. 'You have heard what happened here.'

'Rumours, which I have refused to believe.'

'Sadly, the rumours are true.'

'You commanded a massacre?'

'No,' she snapped. 'I neither commanded it nor wished it. I was helpless. You know how it was when you left here? I sent you for help.'

I hung my head. 'And I failed you.'

'You tried your utmost, I have no doubt. It is Nana who has failed me, as he seems to have failed his own people. But in your absence, I could do no more than temporize. Indeed, when your flight, as they interpreted it, became known to Risaldar and his brother, I thought I was again in danger of my life. And remember,' she added for good measure, 'that my murder might have been followed by that of your daughter; Abid was just as angry at your departure as his brother. I had to lie. I told them that I had sent you to Nana for assistance in overcoming the *feringee* resistance here in Jhansi. They believed me, but were contemptuous of Nana – it would seem with justification. "We need no help to take the City Fort," Risaldar said. He had by now released the occupants of the Star Fort, and had control of all our reserves of powder and shot, not to mention,' she added darkly, 'all of my treasury. They took thirty-five thousand rupees from my personal strongbox. There was no way I could stop them, so I pretended to lead them, from a distance. Well, the assault failed. The British defended themselves most ably. Unfortunately, during the battle your friend Captain Gordon was killed, and equally important, the defenders used up most of their ammunition and powder. Thus it was that Major Skene raised a flag of truce and sought an interview with me. I may say that he was disturbed to find that you were no longer here, but to him also I said that you had gone for help, which but made his position the more hopeless. He then asked if I would allow him to evacuate the fort and take his people out of Jhansi. I told him that I would. Naturally, he then wished guarantees for their safety. Emma, I could not give him a guarantee. I was at that time still virtually a prisoner of my own guards. I told him that I would do everything in my power to ensure his safety, and that of his people. He seemed satisfied with that, and returned to the fort. The next day they began the evacuation. No reference had been made to weapons, and many of them were armed. But of course once they were out of the fort they were defenceless. I had told Risaldar that they should be allowed to leave the city, and the country, unmolested. I told him this would be best for us. He seemed to agree with this. But when the last of the *feringees* had left the fort, his men, who were assembled to either side, opened fire. He has told me that he did not order this, but that he could not stop it once it had started.'

'And you believed him?'

'I had no proof either way. In any event, as he could not, or would not, stop the firing, there was nothing I could do. I stood on the porch and watched them shot down, every one.'

'Every one?' I asked. 'Annie?'

Manu nodded. 'She was amongst the dead.'

I was aghast. Annie Marjoribanks had been my maid, appointed by Lady Hardinge to accompany me to Jhansi eight years ago. I had let her go when I had married Abid Kala, assuming that she would return to Calcutta. But she had preferred to remain in Jhansi, and had obtained employment in a European household. 'Major Skene?'

'Him, too.'

'Mr Thornton?'

'No. He had never gone to the fort, but had hidden in the city. There were some others. These were rounded up later.'

'And also murdered?'

'No. I had things under control by then. I was able to have them escorted to the frontier. I do not know what happened to them after that.'

'I am quite confused,' I said. 'You say that you had no power to stop Risaldar Khan's men from carrying out a massacre, yet a few days later you were in control?'

'Fate takes many strange twists, does it not? On the morning of the seventh of July I was helpless. By that night I was undisputed ruler of Jhansi. The people have got it into their heads, you see, that I had ordered the massacre, that I was entirely on the side of Nana and the begum and indeed everyone who would fight for the independence of Hindustan from the Raj. They surrounded the palace and cheered me and vowed to follow me to the ends of the earth if I so wished. In that moment, Risaldar Khan was reduced to what he was, no more than the commander of my guard.'

'I heard you address him as general.'

'Well, that is his rank. I appointed him commander of my army. He is the most capable soldier I have.'

'And you are now raising an army?'

'I think that is very necessary. So many of my people are volunteering that I have not sufficient arms for them all. Even the women wish to fight.' She smiled. 'I am forming them into a regiment.'

'Your intention is to go and fight with Nana?'

'When he would not send me help? Certainly not.'

I breathed a sigh of relief. 'Then you intend to defend Jhansi against the British.'

'Against anyone who tries to invade me. These are troubled times.'

It seemed to me that that was a considerable understatement.

'I think the British will certainly come,' I said.

'I do not believe they will. I have done what you might have recommended, Emma. As soon as I was in control here, I wrote to the Commissioner at Sagar, Major Erskine, to explain what had happened.'

I was intrigued. 'What did you say?'

What *could* she say? I wondered.

'I condemned my own people, Emma. I regretted the faithlessness, cruelty and violence my troops had used towards the *feringees*, and I pointed out that this could never have happened had I remained in control. I also told him how I had been assaulted in my own bedchamber by the mutineers, who had threatened my life.'

'Did he ever reply?'

'Yes. I heard from him a week ago. He told me he had forwarded my letter to Calcutta, and that what I said agreed with what he had heard from other sources. So you see, there is nothing for us to worry about.'

I hoped she was right. I could not help but remember how Major Ellis had been entirely supportive after Gangadhar Rao's death, only to be overruled from Calcutta. 'You say you heard from this man Erskine a week ago?'

'That is correct.'

'He would probably not then have known what happened at Cawnpore.'

'Am I responsible for what happened at Cawnpore?'

'I think the British will regard every Indian as being responsible for what happened at Cawnpore.'

'I cannot believe that,' she asserted. 'They have a great deal to do to contend with the situation as it is now, without adding to their enemies. And I have been confirmed in my position.'

'Yet you are preparing a defence.'

'It is my duty, as Rani of Jhansi, to defend my people. But here again, as with the size of my army, these new walls will discourage *anyone* from attacking us.'

My brain had gone off on another tack. 'Did Erskine mention the people who survived the massacre? Who you allowed to leave?'

'No, he did not.'

'Because they had not reached him yet. Do you not suppose they will certainly tell what happened?'

'What can they say that I have not said? They know nothing of what happened, anyway. They were not present when I saw Major Skene. Nor were they present at the massacre. If they had been, they would be dead. They can only know that I protected them.'

'I doubt that is how they will see it.'

'I have Erskine's letter accepting my version of what happened.'

I held her hands. 'That is one man, and he seems a reasonable man. But I do not think the British as a whole are in a reasonable mood. When they start to think about it, and listen to what the survivors have to say, they will only understand that more than fifty people were murdered here in Jhansi. They will never forgive you for that, if only because instead of punishing Risaldar you have promoted him.'

'They have to have proof of my involvement,' she insisted. 'And they do not have any. Nor can they obtain any. They are always carrying on about how the law must be obeyed. Well, the law requires that they have proof before they can condemn me. The massacre here in Jhansi was an unfortunate concomitant of the war in Hindustan. I did not give those people a safe-conduct. It was their wish to leave the fort and Jhansi, and I said I would do what I could to ensure their safety. As it turned out, I was unable to do anything. I regret this, but it is a fact of life. That is what I explained to Erskine, and that is what he has accepted. As to promoting Risaldar instead of punishing him, as I have said, in these troubled times it is my duty as Rani of Jhansi to protect my people. Risaldar is my best soldier. It would be a dereliction of my duty to dismiss him from command.'

'But still . . .'

'There can be no case against me. I resumed my rule at the request of the representatives of the Raj, and I have done my best to maintain law and order and prosperity in my country. That the war so sadly spilled over into Jhansi can at least partly be laid at the British door; had I been Rani when the troubles began none of this would have happened.'

I could see that further argument would be useless, nor was there any point in it. Manu's aim had always been to regain control of her country, and this she had achieved. As she had said, all else, including the odd tragedy, was but a concomitant of regaining and maintaining her powers. But I had to ask one last question. 'Do you condemn what happened?'

She gazed at me for several seconds. Then she said, 'I regret what happened, Emma. I mean that most sincerely.'

I held her hands. 'Then, Manu, I have great news. And you have, without knowing it, granted me absolution.' I told her of my conversation with Tatya Tope.

She listened with a slowly growing expression of supreme confidence. 'Can what you say be true?'

'Have I ever lied to you?'

'Of course you have not. That was unforgiveable of me. I mean, can we trust Tatya?'

'He wishes to fight as much as you.'

'Two thousand men,' she whispered. 'Two thousand warriors!' she shouted 'With my fourteen thousand! I will command the greatest army in Hindustan.'

Thus I became a participant, if only by association, in two of the worst crimes of the Mutiny, at least as seen through British eyes. And here again there had been someone I had known very well. Annie and I had never been friends, but we had certainly, for a while, been intimates, and if it was some years since I had even set eyes on her, I could not think of her being shot down in cold blood without a shudder. No doubt I should have fled Jhansi as rapidly as I could. But that simply was not practical, without Manu's permission and help, and I dared not ask for what she would regard as desertion. Besides, I did not want to leave her, or Jhansi. I had not been lying when I had told the begum, and Colonel Moore, that this was my home. It was the only home I had ever had, as an adult, just as Manu was the only true friend I had ever had, at least amongst women.

And for the moment, at any rate, Jhansi was a haven of peace and prosperity, certainly when compared with Cawnpore. Manu, as she had revealed during the few months when she had enjoyed power following Gangadhar Rao's death, was a born ruler. Owing to the circumstances in the rest of the country, and principally in Delhi, where the British were slowly reinforcing their position outside of the city and the forces commanded by the Mughal – at least in a titular capacity – glowered at them but made little attempt to dislodge them, her debts were at this time uncollectable, and she was able to use all her income as she wished. She had thus embarked on a series of projects, overseen by her father, who was equally revelling in the sudden power, and freedom to use that power, being enjoyed by his daughter, from improving the city's sanitation and general appearance, to beginning the library of which she had long dreamed. This was composed largely of books looted from abandoned British homes, but she was already attempting to correspond with other rulers, seeking volumes of Marathi text.

In addition she was enabled to allow her imagination and her energy full scope. Polo matches were resumed, as well as indoor entertainments; Gangadhar's plays were found and acted and she had new ones written; even I was required to try my hand at this.

But, regardless of the persistent rain, the preparations for war took priority. The recruits were drilled morning and afternoon, the parades overseen by the rani herself; the guns, to which were added those taken from the cantonments, were greased and practised, and the building of the walls continued without cessation. Jhansi was turned into a vast fortress. Manu was in her element, and her energy and bubbling vitality permeated all of her city.

During the early part of these few idyllic but unreal months there was Prince Dignaga to be entertained. I could see that Manu found the young man – he was roughly her own age – every bit as attractive as I did, and even had some hopes that his obvious adoration of the queen might be reciprocated. For all Manu's obvious strength of character and her undoubted talents, I was sure she could only be strengthened by an alliance with a man obviously from the same mould. While the fact that he was a prince, even if far removed from any position of power, would surely negate her determination not to marry beneath her.

But, charming as she obviously found him, she made no move either towards marriage or inviting him to her bed. I could not help but feel that her very odd relationship with her first husband, when every time he sought her she had to know he was doing it out of duty rather than desire, had completely stultified her sexual emotions. Equally I could not help but feel that for these to be reawakened, as mine had been following my equally unsatisfactory relationship with Mr Hammond, might have a profoundly beneficial effect, perhaps not on her innate character, which seemed to me to be everything a queen needed or should possess, but on her happiness

– she had far too little of that, except when actually reviewing her troops or embarking upon some new project.

Her army was certainly her pride and joy, but I worried in this direction as well. The response of her people to her call to arms was immense and gratifying. From a population of not much more than two hundred thousand, men, women and children, and including of course a considerable percentage of the elderly, she had actually created a force of fourteen thousand men, a staggering seven per cent of the population. Had Great Britain, with a population of perhaps thirty million, raised a corresponding force she could have had more than four million men under arms.

The drawbacks to this immense military strength were two-fold. Firstly was the cost, which Manu treated as immaterial in view of her situation in the midst of such a crisis. But the crisis could surely not last forever. The second, and far more important in the short term, was the very simple fact that to have fourteen thousand men, and women, under arms, certainly when the weapons were of every variety from old muskets to simple spears, and the whole is motivated by enthusiasm rather than discipline, is not the same thing as being in command of fourteen thousand professional *soldiers*. When I recalled that Nana's people, a large number of them sepoys and thus possessing at least an acquaintance with disciplined manoeuvring in the face of the enemy, and commanded by a general of repute, had failed on three successive occasions to halt, much less defeat, an infinitely smaller British force, I had to be concerned should the hostilities ever spread to Jhansi. Of course Tatya's promise of two thousand more, and his recognition of the weaknesses of the Indians' capacity for fighting a modern war, was reassuring . . . but would he actually come?

For the moment all was peaceful in the little state. Manu continued to entertain and even flirt with Prince Dignaga, without ever allowing him across the portals of her apartment. She continued to review her troops, and she continued to govern. I resumed my lessons with Damodar, for all my doubts that he would ever really rule, and entertained Alice, who was growing into a most delightful child. And as the monsoon ended Dignaga started playing polo, and displayed great skill and horsemanship, as he did everything in his power to impress the rani, without tangible success.

Like us all, he was intensely interested in what was happening in the outside world. No doubt, like me, he was wondering what success, if any, the begum was having with his cousin, the Scindia. We had no word from Gwalior, but at the end of the year news trickled in from Cawnpore, which had indeed been occupied by the British, and where the horrible relics of the massacre had been discovered.

Manu, Dignaga and I, together with Risaldar and his brother as well as Maropat Tambe and our various ladies, listened in consternation to what the messenger had to tell us.

'It was a terrible thing,' he declared. 'They had been spared nothing. The memsahibs who had not been killed by the musketry, and there were many, were cut to pieces. Their clothes were torn off; every one had been stripped naked, either before or after death. Of many, their breasts were cut away, and then their arms and legs, and then their heads were cut off. Then their bodies were pushed down a well.'

Manu looked at me. 'Did you see this?'

'From a distance. I knew something terrible was happening.'

'At least they were spared rape. What have the British done?' she asked the messenger.

'Terrible things also, Highness. They vowed vengeance, and thus executed every man they could find who ever might have followed Nana. They tied these men to the mouths of cannon and blew them into pieces, laughing as they did so, that their bodies would never be reunited with their souls.'

'And the women?' I asked.

'They were not killed. But most of those of comely appearance were raped.'

Manu was breathing hard. 'And they call themselves civilized men?'

'The British set their women on a pedestal,' Dignaga observed.

'From which Nana's people tumbled them,' I added.

'Nana's men acted in heat,' Manu said. 'The British in cold blood.'

'I would say there was some heat,' Dignaga suggested.

'And what news is there of Nana?' Manu asked.

'No one knows where he is.'

'He should be in Delhi.'

'No one knows, Highness.'

Manu rewarded him and dismissed him, and then looked at Risaldar Khan. 'You had best fight well, if you have to fight, Risaldar,' she said. 'Or they will tie you to the mouth of a cannon.'

His teeth gleamed. 'Will they not tie you to one beside me, Highness?'

Manu snorted, and turned away.

We were all of us considerably affected by the news, not only because of the additional gruesome details the messenger had supplied – although my brain reeled at the thought of Deirdre and her daughter, not to mention Lucy Orr, in the hands of men intent upon mutilating them before they cut off their heads – but by the suggestion that the British could be every bit as savage as any sepoy, and equally capable of acting without reference to any normal judicial procedure.

Yet Manu insisted that what had happened in Cawnpore, on either side, should not affect our lives in Jhansi. She continued to rest her position on her possession of the document given her by Captain Gordon and countersigned by Major Skene, requesting her to resume her rule, and on the confirmation of her status by Major Erskine. Nor could anyone deny that Jhansi was probably the best ruled and most peaceful state in the subcontinent. Had it not been for that massacre on 7 July, however much those events might have been out of her control, even I would have been quite confident of the future.

'Will you spend the rest of your life here?' Dignaga asked.

We walked together in the low hills behind the polo field. This was a place of considerable sentimental importance to me, as it was here that I had consummated my brief romance with James Dickinson. I had continued to come here over the past year, as before with Alice, who was with us now, running around on the grass. And it was even more private now than it had been three years ago; the field, the entire rear of the palace complex, was now surrounded by an embrasured wall. I allowed myself a moment to reflect. I was betrothed to James. Or was I? I had not heard from him in over a year. I understood that with India descending into chaos his letters could well have gone astray, as they had on a previous occasion. But during that year we had, almost insensibly, adopted different sides in a struggle that was far more emotional, and therefore irreconcilable, than mere politics. Could we ever look on life with the same eyes again? In any event, I did not wish to leave Jhansi, even for the prince's company.

'Should I not, as it is my home?' I asked.

'A home is surely a place where one is born and grows to adulthood.'

'Not everyone is fortunate enough to be able to continue such permanency throughout one's life,' I pointed out. But my mind was racing ahead, again.

'I have heard many tales about you.'

'Then I am flattered, although I doubt all the tales are flattering.'

'You could never have been boring,' he assured me. 'Is it true that when your caravan was attacked by thugs you killed them all?'

'That is utterly untrue. When we were attacked by thugs I hid while they killed everyone else.'

'But you executed their leader with your bare hands.'

'That also is not true. Some years later, he was unwise enough to come to Jhansi, unaware that I was now living here. I identified him to the rajah, and Gangadhar Rao had him executed.'

'Then he married you to one of his captains.'

'Abid Kala, yes. That is true. But we are now separated.'

'He never comes to your bed?'

'Never.'

'But yet you are legally married.'

I sighed. 'Yes. I am still his wife.' In Hindu eyes, certainly, I thought, if not in British. 'What is your opinion of the rani?'

'She is the most beautiful and desirable of women.'

'And she is not married.'

'She is a widow. And she is a queen. No man dare approach her until summoned.'

I had no doubt that to bring them together would be an ideal situation, for both of them. But it would have to be carefully planned. Perhaps he might be given a command – the supreme command, in my opinion – in the Jhansi army, and thus make his home here.

I put the idea forward to Manu, but she dismissed it. 'A prince of Scindia would never accept a command under someone like Risaldar Kala,' she pointed out.

'Well . . .'

She wagged her finger at me. 'You have never told me how you found Nana.'

'I did not find him anything. I never went to his bed.'

She raised her eyebrows. 'Is that why he would not send help?'

'He did not send help because he had too many other things on

his mind. I did not go to his bed because I was, shall I say, intercepted, by the begum.'

Manu clapped her hands. 'What sport!'

'You may think so, Manu.'

'Are you not lovers?'

'Not any more. We quarrelled. She felt I was too critical of Nana.'

She frowned. 'It is not your place to be critical of your betters,
Emma.'

'I was desperate because he would not send you help.'

Another stroke. 'Dear Emma. I will consider your proposal. Do
you wish me to speak with the prince?'

'When you consider the time is right.'

'Ah,' she said.

Thus, as usual, we were overtaken by events. Before Manu had made
up her mind what to do, a galloper arrived from the north, from,
indeed, Nana.

'Highness!' he gasped, falling to his knees before the rani. 'Delhi
has fallen.'

We crowded round, unable to believe our ears.

'What did you say?' Manu inquired.

'The British have stormed the walls and taken the city, Highness.'

'But . . . were they not outnumbered, many times?'

'That is true, Highness. Still, they had many men. More than
twenty thousand. And they fought like devils.'

'How were they allowed to concentrate so many men without
being attacked?' Dignaga asked.

'I do not know, Highness.'

'Where is the Mughal?' I asked.

'Captured. He is to be tried.'

'How can a reigning monarch be tried?' Manu demanded.

'He is to be charged with treason, Highness, for breaking certain
agreements he made with the Raj. It is feared that it will go ill with
him.'

'He is a reigning monarch,' Manu repeated. 'There is no way he
can have committed treason. Certainly there is no way he can be
executed.'

I felt she was being optimistic, as I recalled that Charles I had
been charged with treason against the English people – who were
bringing the charge – and beheaded.

The messenger put things in their true context. 'Well, Your Highness, his sons have been executed.'

'What? What did you say?'

'His sons escaped the city, Highness, but were pursued by the British Irregular Horse. They were overtaken and captured, and the British commander, a man named Hodson, had them hanged, without trial and without reference to any higher authority.'

'They hanged two royal princes?' Dignaga asked in a low voice.

'Without trial?' I was aghast.

'The British soldiers are still aflame with a determination to avenge Cawnpore.'

Manu and the prince gazed at each other.

'Well,' Manu said, 'at least I cannot be accused of treason. I have written instructions from the British for everything I have done.'

As usual I felt she was again being optimistic; she had no written instructions regarding the massacre at the City Fort.

'I was at Cawnpore,' Dignaga muttered.

My heart sank. He looked quite dismayed. Was even he now afraid?

'You are safe here,' Manu told him.

'Perhaps, Highness. But my duty clearly lies elsewhere. This has been a great disaster. Who can tell where the British will go next?'

'Have you news of this?' Manu asked the messenger.

'The British are consolidating their position around Delhi, Highness. But they are also trying to relieve Lucknow, which has been under siege for some weeks. They say conditions are desperate, and the British commanding officer, Lawrence, has been killed. But they are still refusing to surrender.'

'Which is hardly surprising,' I remarked, 'after what happened at Cawnpore.'

'Is Nana at Lucknow?' Manu asked.

'No, Highness. He was at Bithur, but now he has left that place, as the British have advanced upon it, and has gone to the west. It is said he will try to rally the Scindia to the cause.'

'I must go to Gwalior,' Dignaga said. 'My cousin may need me.'

'Will you fight with Nana?' Manu asked.

'I will fight with anyone who can use me,' he said.

He came to me to say goodbye.

'What is going to happen?' I asked.

'The British have to be defeated,' he said. 'It must happen. They are not gods.'

'But with the Mughal captured, perhaps to be executed . . .'

'That will only bring more people to our side.'

I wondered if he was right. Hindus and Muslims might be prepared to subdue their religious hatred of each other in the enthusiasm of the revolt, but with things going badly and the Muslim leader a prisoner, I suspected the alliance might well fall apart.

'Will you fight for Nana?'

'If he is prepared to fight. I would rather fight for the Scindia.'

'But if your cousin is not prepared to oppose the Raj . . .'

'We will see,' he said grimly. 'But you . . . you will stay here?'

'My place is beside the rani,' I said.

'You know the British will eventually turn on you.'

'We must hope that they do not.'

'But if they do?'

'We will defend ourselves.'

'That rabble?'

'They will fight, and die, for the rani.'

'As will you.'

He kissed my hand, and next morning he and his two hundred rode out of Jhansi to the north-west, for Gwalior.

The British

I was not the only one sorry to see them go. Quite apart from the prince himself, they had been two hundred trained and disciplined fighting men, each perhaps worth ten of our own people. Manu stood beside me to watch them out of sight.

'I wish they could have stayed,' I remarked.

She glanced at me. 'Yes,' she said.

'What will you do now?'

'There is nothing I can do, save govern my people, and try to prepare them for any eventuality that may occur.'

'Is there not at least some action you can undertake to strengthen your position?'

'You would have me condemn the war? After what happened at the City Fort?'

'You have said you had no part in that, or any wish to see it happen.'

'Will they believe me?'

'I think it is necessary to find out. You have the document signed by Gordon and Skene, virtually begging you to resume your government. You have Major Erskine's letter of approval. But none of these men has, or had, any executive authority. I think you are entitled to have this confirmed by the Calcutta government, or at least require them to inform you what are their plans for Jhansi, when the war is over.'

'And if they say they wish to revert to direct rule by the Raj?'

'Then you will at least know where you stand. But you will never be in a stronger position than this. The Raj is still in a precarious situation. It would surely be most unwise for them to drive Jhansi into the ranks of their enemies, while if they once confirm your position in writing, they will find it very difficult to revoke that confirmation at a future date.'

Manu considered this for some time. But equally on our minds were events in Lucknow, where once again it seemed that the decisive battle would be fought, with the prospect of an Indian victory; we felt certain that a single triumph in the field would be sufficient to unite all Hindustan. Besides, we knew the begum was there, and I had no doubt, knowing her character so well, that she would lead her troops herself. Havelock's force had at last fought its way through immense Indian concentrations to reach the beleaguered fortress, but had suffered so many casualties in so doing that they could do nothing more than reinforce the garrison and accept another siege.

But all the while the mighty Raj was girding its loins, as it were. Troops were being called up from both the Bombay and Madras presidencies. Nana might have been accurate enough when he had claimed that in the beginning the rebels would only be faced by the men of the Bengal Presidency, of whom the vast majority had joined the mutineers, but the beginning was now over. The mutineers had failed to gain a single victory save where, as in Meerut or Delhi, they had taken the British unawares. Now there had been the fiasco of the recapture of Delhi, and as well as the other southern principalities the Sikhs were proving loyal and formidable allies, and even from distant Nepal in the Himalayas, until quite recently a bitter enemy of the British, there came help in the form of a detachment of fearsome warriors known as Ghurkas, anxious to march under the Union Jack. Thus before long a large force commanded by Sir

Colin Campbell finally raised the siege of Lucknow, and the entire state of Oudh was pacified.

I wondered how the begum had fared, and now felt, as her army in turn had melted before the red-coated onslaught. But we had not heard from that lady for some time, and our only certainty was that she had not been taken by the British, or the news would certainly have been circulated the length and breadth of the subcontinent. Rumour had it that she had again gone to Gwalior in search of support from the Scindia. Neither had we heard from Nana, although Manu wrote both of them several times in an endeavour to discover both what they were currently doing, and what they were planning to do.

At the end of the year, by the English calendar, we learned that Sir Robert Hamilton had returned to Lucknow as Commissioner for north-central India, which effectively meant the Bundelkhand. This man had been in office before the mutiny had started, and had been removed to Calcutta for his safety. We regarded his return to office as a promising development. While he had done nothing to assist the rani in her petition against Dalhousie's ruling, he had on more than one occasion written to her on various matters, and revealed an attitude towards her plight that we considered sympathetic. Now he was again in supreme command, as it were. It was to him, therefore, that the rani determined to write, laying out her situation and her achievements, and requesting a ruling as to her future position.

This was a very difficult letter to compose, and the pair of us laboured long over the correct wordage. Obviously we could not allow any suggestion of personal guilt for anything that might have happened to creep into either our words or the sentiments we expressed. At the same time we had no idea what the people she had allowed to leave Jhansi might have said regarding the massacre. We contented ourselves with pointing out that Jhansi had been kept at peace and out of the struggle, entirely by the will of the rani. Our only reference to the events of 7 July were to remind him that this date was before Manu had fully regained her prerogatives, and that while she bitterly regretted the loss of life caused by a riot on the part of her soldiers, of whom she was not then in command, at least part of the blame for the unhappy incident had to lie at the British door for removing her from that command in the first place.

The letter was despatched 1 January 1858, and it may be imagined with what anxiety we awaited the reply, our moods varying from wild optimism to ever wilder despair.

The reply came five weeks later, and was chilling in the extreme. *I have to inform Your Highness*, Hamilton's secretary wrote, *that His Excellency is in possession of accusations against Your Highness which are of the most damning nature, in that they have been made by eyewitnesses to the events of 7 July last year, in which, having accepted the surrender of the British officers and men in the City Fort at Jhansi, and guaranteed the safe removal of themselves, with their wives and children, and the civilians who would accompany them, once these people were in a helpless position you commanded your soldiers to fire into them and continue firing until they were all dead. This evidence has been attested under oath, by Deputy-Collector Thornton and by Mrs Mutlow. His Excellency therefore has charged you with murder and treachery, and commands you to appear before him to stand trial on these charges. Failure to appear will result in your condemnation by default, and your subsequent arrest, following which sentence will be passed.*

Manu stared at the letter for several seconds before passing it to me. 'How can they accuse a ruling queen of murder and treachery?'

'Those are the charges laid against Nana,' observed Maropant Tambe, who was present.

'And Bahadur Shah,' Risaldar Khan put in. 'He is an emperor.'

Manu looked from face to face. 'What will they do to me?' she asked. 'If I am tried, and convicted? Will they shoot me from the mouth of a cannon?'

The messenger looked embarrassed. 'There is talk of hanging, Highness.'

'How may they hang a ruling queen?' she demanded.

'They have sentenced the Mughal to death, Highness.'

'He has been executed?'

'No, Highness. I believe the sentence is to be commuted to life-long exile and imprisonment.'

'But they executed his sons,' Risaldar reminded her, determined to be the voice of doom, 'without a trial.'

I handed the letter back to her, and she glanced at it again. 'Thornton,' she growled. 'He was always my enemy. And this Mutlow. Who is this Mutlow? Have I ever met her? Have I ever *seen* her?'

'I should not think you have, Highness,' I said. 'And here lies the weakness in their case. They were not present when you discussed the surrender with Major Skene. Mrs Mutlow was not even in the fort. Neither was Thornton. This is perjured evidence. Or at best hearsay. That is not permissible in law.'

Manu continued to stare at the paper.

'If they lay hands on Your Highness,' Risaldar said, 'they will find evidence against you. Even if you survive, they will lock you up for the rest of your life. You will never see Jhansi again.'

Manu glared at him, then flung out her arm, finger pointing. 'This is your doing. You are the cause of what is happening.'

'I did what I know was right,' Risaldar insisted. 'The *feringees* are our enemies. They must be destroyed.'

'And when they march against us?' Maropant Tambe asked.

'We shall fight them, and defeat them,' Risaldar declared. 'I have fourteen thousand men under arms.'

'The Mughal had twice that number in Delhi, and was yet defeated.'

'That was Delhi. And the Mughal. This is Jhansi. And our people. We will not be defeated.'

Everyone looked at Manu. Her face was again calm, and I could only guess at the thoughts which must be raging through her mind. The alternatives! Surrender, and a show trial, at which she, one of the most beautiful women in India, and a reigning queen, would face the world, which would be composed almost entirely of her enemies, manacled and humiliated, with death or perpetual imprisonment at the end of it. Flight, to become a perpetual outlaw, dependent upon charity, where she could find it, without power or future, save the certainty that she would eventually be captured, and even more humiliated before execution? Fight, knowing that she must lose, hoping for a miracle, knowing that she could not survive, dared not survive, defeat . . . but that at least she could go out in a blaze of immortal glory?

Suddenly I knew what her decision would be. It was the only decision a descendant of the great Maratha warriors of the past, a worshipper of Sivaji, and a proud and brave woman, *could* make. And besides, this was something she had always wanted to do.

And her handmaiden? Who could do no less than fight and die at her side. But who was also a mother! With a child's future — indeed, her life — to be protected.

Manu turned to the messenger. 'You will take my reply to Sir Robert,' she said. 'You will tell him that I totally reject these charges. That I promised to do what I could to save the *feringees* in Jhansi, but that I could do nothing to prevent the attack upon the British leaving the City Fort, that I bitterly regret what happened but that I cannot accept any responsibility for it as I was not at that time in command of my army. You will tell him further that apart from that incident I have kept Jhansi and the people of Jhansi out of the conflict that now afflicts Hindustan, this in spite of the numerous appeals to me, and threats against my person, made by the so-called mutineers, and in the full knowledge that the fighting men of Jhansi, and there are many, thrown into the balance, would have had a most serious effect upon the determination of the Raj to maintain its power. You will tell him that I and my people desire only to live in peace, with the Raj and with our neighbours. That we will attack nobody . . . but that anyone who attacks us will be resisted with all the power at our command. Tell him those things.'

The messenger bowed, visibly trembling. Manu stood up, and swayed, so that I almost ran to her side, afraid that she would fall. But she regained her balance, and looked round our faces. 'I will retire now,' she said. 'Come with me, Emma.'

She was exhausted, and could barely make her bedroom and throw herself across the bed. I sat beside her and uncoiled her hair, but it was some minutes before she spoke.

'I have condemned my people to death,' she said.

'And glory.'

'Death is still death, however glorious. Will you stay with me, Emma?'

'To the end.'

'Dearest Emma,' she said. 'Well, then . . . I will rest now. And then we will prepare for that end.'

Life in Jhansi during that month of February 1858, and for the first fortnight in March, was curiously unreal. The principality was utterly peaceful, and the people even seemed happy. Yet they were all working like beavers, erecting new walls, strengthening those that were already in place, siting the various cannon to cover the approaches to the city, knowing that their doom was approaching, yet always eager to stop work and cheer their rani when she rode among them. Equally, they brought into the city all the spare grain together with their livestock. As the wells provided all the water we required, we felt we could withstand a siege of several months, probably until the next monsoon.

Manu was herself always in the best of humours. Her momentary weakness was behind her, and she was doing what she had always dreamed of doing: preparing for war, and preparing to lead her people in that war. To this end she drilled her soldiers ceaselessly, had me lecture them on what I had seen of the Raj, reminding them that these were but men, disciplined and experienced and thus confident to be sure, but capable of being opposed by men of similar stature.

Kujula and Vima were no less martial, Kujula taking on the duties of my bodyguard rather than my servant.

Manu was also back to writing letters, to Nana, wherever he might be found, to Gwalior, in search of the begum, although of course she would not have refused help from the Scindia; we had to feel that Dignaga would be doing his best on our behalf. However, the reply from Gwalior was negative in every sense. The Scindia wrote that he had no intention of opposing the Raj in anything, and also to inform us that the begum had spent only a short while in Gwalior before departing again, where to he did not know.

Nana was a different matter; Manu read his letter with a glowing expression. *We are in an increasingly strong position,* he wrote, *and would hope to give the British what they call a bloody nose when they come against us. The begum is only a short distance away and commands ten thousand men; she has been joined by her son. The Moulvie is with me, and he leads two thousand more. Prince Dignaga has joined me with five hundred warriors from Gwalior, determined to fight for Hindustan rather than the Scindia. We are mobilizing to the north-west of Jhansi, and I give you my word that the moment any British soldiers cross the frontier of your country Tatya Tope will march to your support with two thousand men. We shall be with you in a week. So fight well, cousin, and may the great goddess Dirga stand at your side.*

'There speaks a true friend,' Manu declared, handing me the letter. 'Do you know, Emma, I could not bring myself to believe you, when you returned from Cawnpore. Not you, but what Tatya Tope had promised. But now . . . as I said, I will command the greatest army in Hindustan. We cannot lose.'

I could not help remaining sceptical. It was reassuring to think that Tatya Tope was a man of his word; I had no doubt that it was he who had persuaded Nana to at last come to our aid, but I had little faith in the ability of his army to stop the British, unless, as Tatya Tope himself had said, they could fight from behind fortifications. How I wished Dignaga had brought his increased force of five hundred horsemen here, instead of joining Nana, although I had no doubt that there were compelling reasons for his decision. But in his absence, Tatya Tope was the best hope we had, and if he could get here in time to join our people behind our walls all things might be possible.

Was I then not being a traitor to my race? I had done all that I could, almost from the day of my arrival in Jhansi, when I had immediately felt that a conflict with the Raj was looming, to prevent this catastrophe arriving, and I hated the thought of English soldiers dying — amongst them might be James — but I could not argue against my convictions that they were doing so in support of a great crime, which involved the rape and the conquest of the subcontinent, purely for the financial benefits to be gained. Nor could I in any way condemn a people for fighting, and if necessary dying, in defence of their land, their religion, their traditions. Would not the British respond the same way in the event that England were ever to be invaded by an all-conquering foe?

It was in the middle of March that a galloper arrived from our border guards to say that they could see troop movements in the hills to the east. There had been no further communication from Hamilton, no reply to the rani's plea of innocence. At the same time, there had been no definite dismissal of her request for confirmation regarding Erskine's written restoration of her powers. This was important to her, and although I felt this request had in fact been rejected by Hamilton's countercharge of murder, I knew it might be an important legal point. As, for example, King Charles I had remained King of England even after his arrest and charge with treason, and retained his position until he had actually been found guilty. I remained sure that we had a strong defence to the charges brought against her, if it ever came to court.

But now . . .

Risaldar Khan sent out his own officers, led by Abid, to discover what they could, and they were back two days later.

'It is a powerful force, Highness,' my husband reported. 'It moves in several columns, each of perhaps five hundred men. There are six of such columns. Then there is a brigade of cavalry, and a battery of artillery.'

'You are talking of perhaps four thousand men,' Risaldar said.

'That is but a third of our strength. With your permission, Highness, I shall lead our army forth to do battle and defend our frontier.'

'No,' Manu said.

He stared at her, angrily.

'They must fire the first shot,' Manu said.

'But if we do not stop them, the first shot will be fired at this palace, Highness.'

'That will probably happen anyway,' Manu said. 'But we will do better fighting for Jhansi itself, rather than in the open field. Besides, we must wait for the arrival of Tatya Tope and his people. He is surely already on his way.' She looked at me. 'Is this not your opinion, Emma?'

'It is, Highness.'

'Bah!' Risaldar remarked. 'What can she know about warfare?'

'I think she has seen more of it than you, Risaldar Khan,' Manu said.

'Nana's army tried several times to contest the advance of the British on an open field,' I told him, 'and was defeated every time.'

'That was Nana's army,' he said contemptuously. 'But it also could not defend Cawnpore.'

'It *did* not defend Cawnpore,' I reminded him. 'Nana withdrew before the British got there.'

'The Mughal's people could not hold Delhi,' Abid put in, unhelpfully.

Manu refused to be disconcerted. 'As you say – the Mughal's people. His army was composed of many disparate elements, and a large part of it was mutineers, men who had served under the Raj and were afraid of it. We are all people of Jhansi, and we are fighting for our homes and our loved ones. And I tell you more: your loved ones will fight beside you, with me at their head. We shall fight, and we shall conquer. Certainly with the help of Tatya Tope. When he arrives, we will strike a blow for Hindustan which will turn the tide of this war. Meanwhile, command the men on the frontier not to attempt to engage the enemy, but to withdraw here.'

Watching her eyes ablaze, her fists clench, her entire small body trembling with emotion and determination, it was impossible to doubt her. Even Risaldar became infected with her enthusiasm, while the population of Jhansi redoubled their efforts to turn their city into a stronghold.

I worked as hard as anyone, but I cannot say that my personal misgivings were abated. Jhansi had no natural defences, such as mountains or wide rivers. It was situated in the middle of a plain, somewhat undulating to be sure, but nonetheless capable of assault from several different directions. But although I was quite sure that the rani's army, poorly trained and lacking modern cannon and muskets as it was, would stand no chance in a set-piece battle with the British, I still felt that it was morally and politically wrong for us to permit them to invade the country and take up their chosen positions without doing anything about it. This attitude might, indeed, be considered as an acceptance of guilt on our part. Equally, of course, every hour that we could delay their assault gave Tatya Tope more time to come to our aid . . . supposing he truly intended to come at all.

I put these points to Manu. She nodded in agreement. 'I am sure you are right, Emma, and I accept that you have far more experience in these matters than do I. But what would you have me do? My people are certainly not sufficiently trained to mount any kind of guerilla or delaying campaign, nor does the country lend itself to such a plan; there are too few places where a force may lie concealed.'

'I think you are at least entitled to send an envoy to the British, to find out what are their intentions, and by what right they have invaded your country.'

She gave a sad smile. 'They are in the habit of claiming whatever rights take their fancy, the principal one being the sword.'

'They should still be challenged, legally. There is certain to be at least one correspondent with this army. This is the quickest and best way to let your case be placed before the world.'

She was frowning. 'You would have me go to this army?'

'No,' I said. 'I would not trust them to allow you to leave again. You must send an envoy.'

She glanced at me, her frown deepening. 'You would risk so much?'

'I will go as your accredited envoy. I will travel under a flag of truce. As far as I know, I have been charged with nothing. I was not even here when the massacre took place. They can hardly arrest me for being your governess.'

'They will know you were in Cawnpore with Nana.'

'I went to Cawnpore again as your accredited envoy. You sought help to restore order here in Jhansi. Had he sent such help, promptly, the massacre would not have taken place. Manu, we need time for Tatya Tope to reach us. If I can delay them, even for a few hours, that may make all the difference.'

She gazed at me for several seconds. 'Not for the first time, you are revealing yourself to be a woman of great courage,' she said. 'I will eagerly await your return.'

As usual, I took both Kujula and Vima, but no one else. Manu would have provided me with a proper escort, but I declined. I was not proposing to cross our border, and as regards the people of Jhansi, I would be journeying amongst friends, while I considered it as important that when I made contact with the British I should have with me only people who would obey me in everything, to obviate any risk of an incident. And as before, I left Alice in the care of the rani.

As for what I was doing, I found that difficult to explain, even to myself. I still hoped to avert bloodshed, to make the British understand that Manu had only ever done what she had been forced to do, whether by them or her own people, that left to herself she had proved, and would prove in the future, a good and thoughtful ruler. I was also curious to discover just how I was placed in this situation. As Manu had reminded me, I was deeply involved in everything that had happened, but I felt I was entirely innocent of implication in any crime, despite my feelings of guilt over what had happened to the women at Cawnpore, and was anxious to discover if the Raj also felt that.

Additionally, of course, I was in one of my moods of exhilaration at again taking my place upon the centre stage of history, this time hopefully with more success.

We travelled without hindrance throughout the first day. Indeed, we saw very few people, and those we did encounter were following the example of everyone else, and making their way towards the city, driving their flocks in front of them, desperate to get out of the way of the advancing British.

By the time we camped for the night, the country around us appeared to be entirely deserted, but when, after our evening meal, I moved a little distance from the tents Kujula was pitching, I was aware that we were not alone. I could see no one in the gathering dusk, neither people nor lights nor movement, and the poor light precluded any sight of dust, but the wind was from the east, and carried on it a whisper of sound, a rumbling and seething, of men and weapons.

Kujula and Vima, who could also hear the distant sound, were very anxious. I calmed them as best I could, and I think we all slept, but I was awakened by Kujula shaking my shoulder. 'The Raj,' he said.

I was wearing male clothing as I always did for travelling, but the dawn was chill, and I wrapped myself in my cloak and stepped outside. It was just daylight, with the wind still from the east and approaching us over the brow of the next low hill there was a troop of lancers, the first rays of the rising sun glinting from their spearheads.

Vima and Kujula stood beside me as they came closer.

'Do not, under any circumstances, touch your weapons,' I told Kujula. 'But raise the white flag.'

He obeyed, and we watched the horsemen approach, trampling the waving wheat, spreading out as they did so, as if expecting to be fired upon, but also surrounding us.

'Women!' one shouted. Neither Vima nor I had had the time to dress our hair, and although I had pulled the cowl of the cloak over my head, our tresses were floating in the breeze.

'Mutineers' women,' added another, mentally unfastening his breeches.

I reached down to squeeze Vima's hand; she was trembling.

The men halted when some fifty yards from us, and one walked his mount forward. He wore the insignia of a subaltern, and was both young and fresh-faced, if his expression was decidedly hostile.

'We are to take no prisoners,' he announced.

I shrugged the cowl from my head. 'We are not prisoners.'

He stared at my hair and complexion. 'You are the woman Hammond.'

On another occasion I might have been flattered at being so famous as to be instantly recognizable.

'That was once my name,' I conceded.

'You are a renegade. Sergeant, bind her. And her companions.'

'I am here under a flag of truce,' I pointed out.

'You expect me to honour that?'

His sergeant had dismounted, a length of rope in his hands.

'I do,' I said, refusing to reveal any fear, 'as you pretend to be representing a civilized power. I am here with a message from the Rani of Jhansi for your commanding general.'

'Give me this message.'

'I will not. I am to deliver the message personally. Either take me to your commanding officer, now, or kill me. If you ill-treat us, you may be sure that I will report adversely on your conduct.'

The total confidence I projected took him aback. 'Disarm that man,' he told his sergeant.

'Give them your weapons, Kujula,' I said.

He obeyed, reluctantly. Neither the sergeant nor his superior thought to look inside my satchel, where lay my revolver.

'Now bind them and tie them to our horses' tails,' the lieutenant commanded.

'You will do no such thing, sir,' I told him. 'I repeat, I am not your prisoner, and neither are my servants. We are on a mission to your general. We will ride our own horses, with our hands free.'

Once again he was uncertain what to do, and he was well aware that his men were exchanging sly glances as they saw him being ridiculed by a woman. He needed to make a decision, and quickly.

'Very well,' he said. 'Mount up, and I will take you to my colonel.'

'You must give us time to fold our tents,' I told him.

This kept him waiting another half an hour, then finally we mounted. I rode beside him.

'Is your camp far?' I asked, pleasantly enough.

'The regiment will be just beyond that rise,' he said. 'We are the advance guard. I will deliver you to our colonel, and let him deal with you.'

'And this colonel's name?'

'Colonel James Dickinson,' he said.

I drew rein in consternation. 'Colonel James Dickinson?'

'That is correct. Have you heard of him?'

'Yes,' I said. 'I have heard of him.'

This boy was too young even to be aware that James had once been stationed in Jhansi. But of course, with his knowledge of our defences, he would be with this army.

But us! He was the last man I had had sex with. As I had then been married to Abid Kala, I had committed adultery, a crime which in Hindu law gave the husband the right to mutilate the guilty wife, most usually by cutting off her nose. From this ghastly fate Manu had rescued me, but she had been unable so far to negate the law as to absolve me from any punishment, and thus I had been sentenced to a public flogging. From *that* fate I had been saved by Major Skene, supported by the British garrison, under James' command. We had then known each other for six years – he had been the officer who had rescued me from the thugs in 1849 – and our growing regard for each other had climaxed in our carnal encounter, and then a proposal of marriage. Skene having proved that my marriage to Abid had been illegal and therefore did not exist, I had accepted. But I had then shocked him, and the British community in Jhansi – and apparently in all India – by insisting upon returning to Manu's side until he was free to marry me which, as he had just been commanded to lead his regiment on a campaign in the Punjab, could not be possible for at least a year. That was more than two years in the past, and although, as I had informed Skene, we were still betrothed, so far as I knew, we had not corresponded. And now we were on opposite sides, in a war which had degenerated from a political issue to sheer hatred!

We topped the rise and came in sight of the regiment, walking their horses; the rest of the army was still out of sight behind them. The lieutenant urged his mount forward, I followed, and we cantered up to where James rode in the front centre of his people: two officers, a sergeant, and a bugler, as well as the standard bearer, immediately behind him.

'This woman claims to have a communication from the widow Gangadhar for the general, sir,' the lieutenant said.

As I had not replaced my cowl over my head, and my hair was flowing in the breeze, James had obviously recognized me at a distance and got his emotions, supposing he still had had any as regards me, under control. I had spent the last ten minutes busily attempting to do the same; personal feelings apart, I had to determine whether his presence would be to my – considering myself purely as a projection of Manu – advantage or not.

Now he saluted. 'Mrs Hammond.'

'Colonel Dickinson.'

We gazed at each other. There was so much we wanted to say, so much we *needed* to say. But now was not the time.

'You have come from the rani?' he asked, and looked past me to where Kujula still held the white flag. 'Does your mistress then offer her surrender?'

'By no means,' I said. 'Her Highness has sent me to inquire the reason for this invasion of her territory, and to insist that your forces withdraw immediately.'

Another long stare. 'Your mistress is a wanted criminal,' he said. 'And this army has come to enforce the law.'

'Her Highness admits to no crime,' I riposted. 'She rules in Jhansi by virtue of Hindu law and a document signed by the British political agent, and the commander of the garrison, authorizing and requesting her to do so.'

'You expect me to believe that?'

'It happens to be true.'

'But both of those gentlemen are now dead, I understand.'

'Sadly, yes.'

'And was this document ever confirmed from Calcutta?'

'We have never received such confirmation. Possibly it has been lost or delayed in the troubles. It was confirmed by Major Erskine.'

'Major Erskine was not in possession of the full facts when he wrote that letter, Mrs Hammond. Your mistress has no authority to rule, and remains a wanted criminal. My advice to you would be to return to her and convince her that her only course lies in immediate surrender.'

'To be fired from the mouth of a cannon?'

He flushed. 'To stand before the bar of British justice.'

I tossed my head. 'And *then* to be fired from the mouth of a cannon. That will not do, Colonel. Now take me to your commanding officer.'

'Why should I do that? I am entitled to place you under arrest. There is an indictment in your name also.'

'You cannot place me under arrest, Colonel, because I am an accredited envoy from her Highness the Rani of Jhansi, and not to honour my flag of truce would earn you the condemnation of every right-thinking person in the world.'

Once again we stared at each other, but his eyes were the first to lower.

'You'll halt here, Major Lewis,' he told his second-in-command. 'Until I return. Dismount your men. You'll come with me, Mrs Hammond.'

'And my servants?'

'They will be safe here. No one will harm them.'

I had to trust him, at least in that. I reassured Kujula and Vima that I would soon be back, and then rode beside James to the next hillock.

'Why are you doing this?' he asked.

'Doing what?'

'Acting for that black-hearted witch.'

'I beg your pardon. I am acting for my mistress, the Rani of Jhansi. But as she is my dearest female friend, I would willingly act on her behalf even had she no title and no position.'

'She is a murderess. Do you condone that?'

'That charge is unjust and untrue.'

He considered this, as we topped the rise, and I could not prevent myself from drawing a sharp breath. Before me the British army was displayed, six columns of infantry, each of several hundred men – and two of them the fearsome Highlanders in their kilts – several squadrons of cavalry, and in the centre, four batteries of artillery, the guns drawn by oxen. In front and in the centre of this vast array rode the general and his staff, from the number of plumed hats and the various banners flying above them.

'Those are five thousand of the finest fighting men in the world,' James said. 'What can your rani do against them?'

My heart was down in my stomach, but I was not going to let him see that. 'She and her people will defend themselves to the last,' I said. 'And she has fourteen thousand men under arms.'

'If they fight as well as their compatriots,' he said contemptuously, 'this war will be over in a day.' He reined, and turned to me. 'I do not know what your mistress has told you to say to General Rose, but if, having said it, you were to denounce her crimes and throw yourself upon the mercy of the Raj, I am sure you will obtain a sympathetic hearing. I certainly would defend you.'

'I am sure you would, James. Out of a sense of justice?'

'Out of love, Emma.'

'Still?'

'I have no doubt that you acted out of a sense of . . . responsibility for a woman you yourself had educated. But I do not see how you can still feel any respect, much less affection, for a woman who could have you publicly flogged?'

'Lakshmi Bai did what she had to do, by virtue of her laws and her position. She intended to whip me herself, and as lightly as possible, and then raised me higher than ever in her public as well as her private esteem. As she has done.'

'But you are still married to that Indian.'

'Legally, yes. The rani does not recognize divorce. But she recognizes that I am not married according to Christian usage. She has thus annulled my marriage. Abid has no rights, conjugal or otherwise, over me.'

'But you intend to return to him.'

'I intend to return to Jhansi. It is my home. At least until this business is settled.'

'Understanding that, should the rani refuse to surrender and attempt to resist us, our orders are to destroy her and everything she possesses.'

'Understanding that, should you carry out that threat, you would be guilty of a far greater crime than any of which the rani is accused.'

He glared at me, then kicked his horse and we moved forward again.

General Sir Hugh Rose was a splendid-looking man, not all that much older than James, who, while obviously taken aback by my masculine dress and perhaps by my appearance in general, greeted me most courteously, then invited me to dismount and take tea. A table, folding chairs and a large umbrella – the sun was now quite high – were erected, beneath which we could sit in comfort. I observed, however, that although the staff halted to hear what I had to say, the army continued its inexorable advance to every side of us. Equally, to my disappointment, I could discern no one who looked like a newspaper correspondent, certainly in this immediate group.

'I understand that you have a previous acquaintance with Colonel Dickinson,' the general said, sitting beside me.

James had been invited to remain with us.

'The colonel was stationed in Jhansi for a brief while,' I agreed. 'And we are, or were, betrothed to be married.'

Rose raised his eyebrows and glanced at James, who flushed.

'Are you saying that the betrothal is now ended?' the general asked.

'We have not seen each other for more than two years. And now . . .'

'You are, perhaps, on different sides of the political spectrum.'

'That is up to you, your excellency.'

'Not entirely,' he remarked, and himself poured tea from a silver pot. 'I understand that you have lived in Jhansi for some time.'

'For nine years.'

'Nine years. You must regard Jhansi as your home.'

'I do.'

'Then I am sure you would not like to see it destroyed.'

'I would not. Nor can I see the necessity for it.'

'There is none,' he agreed. 'All that we require is that the so-called rani surrender herself, together with those guilty men who actually carried out the massacre of 7 July last year, for trial. It will be a fair trial, I assure you. She and her people will have every opportunity to defend themselves.'

'But she will still be found guilty.'

'That I cannot say. The evidence against her is very strong.'

'May I ask what this evidence is?'

'I do not think I am at liberty to disclose that.'

'Then let me tell you, General. It is the sworn testimony of Mr Thornton, Deputy-Collector of Taxes in Jhansi down to last year, and of a Mrs Mutlow, a former resident of Jhansi.'

The general cleared his throat and glanced at his officers, taken aback by the extent of my knowledge.

'So I would like to put this point to you, General,' I said. 'I presume the evidence of Mr Thornton and Mrs Mutlow was given to your people after they had left Jhansi. It may therefore be assumed that they were not in the group of people who were so unhappily massacred. They were certainly not in the palace when the rani is supposed to have given her safe conduct to the garrison of the City Fort.'

'Their evidence is supported by written testimony, Mrs Hammond.'

'What written testimony?'

'Mrs Mutlow herself saw the document, written in her own hand, by the rani, granting the safe conduct.'

'That is quite impossible, General. There was no such document, nor could there ever have been, because the rani does not write anything in her own hand. She dictates to her secretaries.'

'But she *can* write?'

'Yes, she can write.'

'And am I not correct in saying that you were not in Jhansi when this unhappy event took place?'

'That is correct.'

'You were in Cawnpore. We will talk about that in a moment. The fact is that you have no knowledge of exactly what happened, what was said or what was written, in the palace at Jhansi during your absence.'

'I was in Jhansi when the rani issued a warning to Captain

Gordon that there was to be an attack upon the Europeans, and suggested that they take shelter. That is hardly the act of a woman who wished them killed. As for what happened in my absence, I know what the rani told me.'

'Well, she would defend herself, would she not? No, no, Mrs Hammond, we are acting on written and sworn testimony . . .'

I refused to admit defeat. 'I should like to see this testimony.'

'Well, I can show you a copy of it, certainly. Maitland.'

One of his aides opened a satchel and took out the sheet of foolscap paper, which was handed to me. Mrs Mutlow had written: *I saw this paper with my own eyes. The queen had written, I, Lakshmi Bai, Rani of Jhansi, do hereby grant permission to the inhabitants of the fort known as the City Fort in my city of Jhansi to leave the fort and depart my country, and I further guarantee their safety to the boundaries of my country. She signed it herself.*

I laid down the paper. 'This is an utter fabrication.'

'Because you say it is, Mrs Hammond?'

'You have agreed that I have lived in Jhansi, in the royal palace, for nine years.'

'I am prepared to accept that.'

'Then will you accept that for almost all of those nine years I have been an intimate companion of the rani?'

Rose looked at James, who nodded.

'Very well,' the general said. 'I accept that.'

'Then you must accept what I know of her procedures. I am quite certain that Mrs Mutlow could not have gained access to any paper given by the rani to Major Skene, simply because there is no way she can have been present. However, I understand that I cannot prove this. May I ask what language this document is supposed to have been written in?'

'I believe it was written in English, as it was for the use of English people.'

'The rani does not write English. Had she written such a document it would have been in Marathi. Then let us consider the style. The rani is a reigning queen. As such she does not use the first person singular. I have seen innumerable letters written by her, and in every case the style is the third person and the royal we. Nor does the rani ever sign anything; she affixes her seal. To suppose any document such as has been described by Mrs Mutlow can have been dictated, much less written, by the rani is an absurdity.'

General Rose studied me for several seconds. As he was an honest and intelligent man I had no doubt he knew I was speaking the truth. But he was also a soldier, intent upon carrying out his duty.

'You make an able advocate, Mrs Hammond. However, there is one certain fact which you cannot deny: more than fifty British subjects were murdered by the rani's people.'

'At a time when she had no authority.'

'You have just said that she did have that authority, conferred upon her by Major Skene.'

'Conferring authority is not the same thing as also conferring the means by which that authority may be carried out. At the beginning of July last year the rani, thanks to the invocation, by the Raj, of the Doctrine of Lapse, had actual authority only within the walls of her palace, and when the palace guards determined to join in the mutiny, she was helpless.'

'Do you deny that, as testified by Mr Thornton, the rani gave her soldiers five elephants and several horses from her own stables? As well as a considerable sum of money?'

'Those animals were taken, General, and the money was stolen. Lakshmi Bai had no means of stopping it.'

Another long consideration. Then he said, 'Now let us talk about you, Mrs Hammond. You are, I understand, in Hindu eyes, married to a captain in the rani's guard.'

'I was. We have been separated for several years.'

'But you remain close to the rani. It is established that you were not in Jhansi when that massacre took place. You were in Cawnpore. Are you aware that several British officers escaped the initial massacre there, by swimming down the river? Their names are Lieutenants Mowbray, Thomson, Delafosse and Sullivan. There was another, but he drowned in the river. The other four gallantly got ashore, were given shelter by some loyal natives, and eventually regained our ranks. They were thus able to give us a full report as to what happened there, as regards the first massacre. I may say that your name was prominently mentioned.'

'I was there,' I acknowledged.

'Do you deny that you persuaded General Wheeler to abandon his entrenchments and take to the boats, trusting in the promise of Nana Sahib that he and his people would be safe?'

'I acknowledge that I accompanied Nana's envoy, Azimullah Khan, into the British position. I did this to assist in case there were any language difficulties during the negotiations.'

'You offered General Wheeler a safe evacuation.'

'I offered General Wheeler what Nana was offering. If any of your surviving officers were actually present when I was speaking with Colonel Moore, they should recall that I refused to guarantee their safety, or to guarantee anything. But I did express my opinion that to remain in the entrenchment would mean certain death for everyone, while to take advantage of Nana's offer might be to save their lives.'

'You did this in full awareness that a British relief column was approaching Cawnpore.'

'I was aware that a small British force was endeavouring to reach the city. But I also knew that it was several days away, and I was informed by Nana that it would certainly be defeated. I believed him.'

'Would I be right in assuming that this gentleman is a friend of yours?'

'He is no friend of mine, General. I was sent to Cawnpore on a mission for my mistress, and he took advantage of my presence.'

'Ah! Then you admit he is a friend of your mistress.'

'They have known each other a long time. They were children together, and the rani's father worked for Nana's uncle.'

'And so she sent you to him. No doubt with a message of support.'

'No, General. The rani sent me to him seeking support for herself.'

'To attack the Raj.'

'To assist her in regaining complete control of Jhansi, and thus *preventing* an attack on the Raj. Sadly, I could not obtain that support.'

He stroked his chin. 'Tell me, Mrs Hammond, do you condemn Nana's actions?'

'Without reservation, sir. I left Cawnpore as soon as I could afterwards.'

'Hm. Well, your actions and attitudes will have to be investigated in due course. I'm afraid you will have to be placed under arrest for the time being.'

'You cannot arrest me,' I said.

His brows drew together. 'Cannot? My dear Mrs Hammond, you are in the midst of my army.'

'I came to you under a flag of truce as an envoy of the rani. You are bound, by international law, to honour that flag, and permit me to return to her with your answer.'

'My answer? Let me tell you, madam, that if you insist upon leaving this camp, under your flag of truce, I will be forced to regard you as an enemy of the Raj. As I am bound so to regard your mistress. And when my troops enter Jhansi, you will be treated as such an enemy, regardless of the colour of your skin, or of your religious affiliations, if you have any.'

I drew a deep breath. 'But you intend to enter Jhansi as commander of a conquering army. If you can.'

'I intend to enter Jhansi as a representative of Great Britain, in order to arrest all of those guilty of the murders at the City Fort on 7 July 1857. If I am resisted, then I will indeed enter as the commander of a conquering army, and I will say to you, again, woe to the vanquished.'

I stood up.

He did also. 'I would most earnestly beg you to reconsider your position, Mrs Hammond. If everything you have told me is true, and can be proved, you have nothing to fear from British justice.'

'And the rani?'

'She must take responsibility for what happened in her country, whether or not she actually commanded the deed.'

'Then, sir,' I said, 'we have nothing more to say to each other.'

The Battle for Jhansi

James accompanied me back to where Kujula and Vima waited.

'There is still time to change your mind,' he remarked.

'And desert the rani?'

'And look to yourself. This business could turn out very badly. The general has been very patient and understanding in listening to what you had to say. But if he is forced to order an assault upon Jhansi, there will be no quarter permitted. Our troops have developed a deep hatred for any Indians who have killed white women and children.'

'Do you suppose men are the only sex with a sense of honour?'

'By no means. But men are better able to defend their honour.'

I was so angry, and indeed, despairing, that I performed a childish trick. I drew rein, and opened my satchel to take out my revolver.

'Good God!' he exclaimed. 'Where did you get that?'

'I have had it for some time,' I said.

'You mean you had it with you when you were taking tea with the general?'

'Of course I did. '

'And what do you intend to do with it now?' he asked, somewhat anxiously, even if we were surrounded by the entire British army.

'I am going to demonstrate something.' I looked left and right to find what I sought. Some seventy yards away there was a peculiar rock formation, a large boulder with a much smaller stone resting on top of it. The smaller stone was in fact not much larger than a man's fist. 'Do you see that rock?'

'Yes.' He was frowning.

'I am speaking of the little one.'

'Yes,' he said again.

'Then watch.' I levelled the Colt, drew a deep breath, and squeezed the trigger. Heads turned at the somewhat flat sound, but I was pleased enough; the little rock had disintegrated.

Several men rode towards us. James waved them away, while I restored the revolver to my satchel.

'Where did you learn to shoot like that?' he asked.

'I practise. So does the rani. So do all our people.'

This was not true, but I wished to make my point.

'I wish you to have no doubt that taking Jhansi by force will be a costly business,' I said. I had, of course, no intention of telling him of the approach of Tatya Tope's two thousand warriors.

'I think we all understand that.'

'But you will still assault.'

'We will still carry out our orders.'

We had come up to Vima and Kujula. James made one last attempt to suborn me. 'If we say goodbye now,' he said. 'I fear we shall not meet again.'

'I am sorry.'

'So am I. So very sorry. But . . . you will return to the rani.'

'Like you, James, I will carry out my duty.' I reached across to squeeze his hand. 'But James, dear James, take care of yourself, I beg of you.'

Knowing that the British army was following us, we made all possible speed, not camping for the night, and reached Jhansi the following dawn. I went immediately to the rani and told her of my meeting with General Rose.

'They are very polite,' she commented. 'I am sure they will be very polite as they fit the noose around my neck.' Then she smiled. 'But they are not going to do that. We will hold them, until Tatya Tope arrives.'

There was nothing left for us to do. Our flags and banners were hoisted above the palace. Every gun was emplaced, every man or woman for whom a musket could be found was in position. The remaining women still worked, some making sure their children were safely sheltered, others continuing to bring up supplies of food so that no man would need to leave his post; still others baked all the bread of which they were capable. With the wells in the city, we were confident we could stand a lengthy siege, and we knew Tatya Tope was on his way.

I took Alice down to the underground stream beneath the palace, and placed her in the care of Vima, arranged for food to be taken down to them, and told her not to move until I came for her. Then I joined Manu on the high tower, beneath the standard, to look out beyond the city at the east.

We were joined by Risaldar and Abid. 'This will be a great day, Highness,' Risaldar said.

'It is good to be alive at such a time,' Manu agreed.

She was glowing with excited confidence. If I knew her sole ambition was to rule Jhansi in peace, I also knew that all her life she had been preparing for this moment, when she would lead her people into battle. And certainly she looked the part, dressed as a man with a gold tunic over her green jodhpurs, her hair wrapped up in a gold turban, with her revolvers as well as two pistols tucked into her gold cummerband and her jewel-hilted tulwar hanging at her side. Incongruously, she still wore her diamond rings and her gold bangles. As I knew nothing of swords, I was armed only with my revolver, and as I regarded myself as being in a purely defensive and supportive capacity, I continued to wear the sari, although I chose my best cloth of silver.

Thus we waited, and at dusk we saw horsemen on the nearest rise. Having come into sight, they remained there for some time, no doubt studying us through their telescopes, although the distance was so great I doubt they could have determined much about our defences. We studied them in turn.

'Shall I take our cavalry and disperse them, Highness?' Risaldar Khan asked, all martial ardour.

'No,' Manu said. 'You would not be able to drive them very far. The battle must be fought here.'

She was quite unafraid. This was the moment of her destiny.

She even slept soundly. I spent a sleepless night, Alice in my arms. But I was soon recalled to reality, just after dawn, by the shouts from the battlements. I gave Alice to Vima to return to their refuge, and went up to the tower to watch the whole of Rose's army slowly come into sight. They advanced to about a mile from our walls, a lengthy operation which took them the entire day. Then they began to emplace their batteries, while a group of horsemen advanced towards us beneath a white flag.

Manu herself went to the east gate, standing on the battlements to look down at them.

'I would speak with Lakshmi Bai, widow of the late Rajah Gangadhar Rao,' the envoy called.

'I am Lakshmi Bai, Rani of Jhansi,' Manu replied.

The envoy studied her for several seconds, no doubt taking in her warlike, and masculine, dress. Then he said, 'General Sir Hugh Rose, commanding the forces of Her Britannic Majesty, requires entry into your city.'

'General Rose is welcome to enter my city,' Manu said. 'By himself, or with his staff. But not with his army.'

'If you defy him, Your Highness, he will, in accordance with his orders, take the city by storm.'

'If he is determined upon an act of war, then so be it,' Manu said.

'He is prepared to give you time to consider,' the envoy said.

'I need no time,' Manu told him. 'I have already considered.'

The envoy hesitated, then saluted, and turned his horse. His two companions did likewise, and they trotted back towards the British camp.

'Wait until that flag is lowered,' Manu said. 'Then you may open fire, Risaldar Khan.'

Ten minutes later the first cannon roared.

The range was extreme, and I doubt we did much damage with those opening shots. But with the explosion of the guns the whole of Jhansi seemed to erupt into a series of cheers and huzzas, and there was a good deal of musketry, although no one had as yet a target at which to aim.

There was little reply from the British forces, who were still taking up their positions, and soon enough our own guns fell silent as it became dark. But at first light the British cannonade began, to which we replied with vigour. Now the enemy had approached to within a mile, and we could see our balls bounding amidst them, and knocking over some of them, to be sure.

But then, their balls were bounding amongst us, and they had more to aim at. We were surrounded by the crash and smash of shattered and collapsing masonry, the whish of flying splinters, and the cries of those struck by these missiles. The British were also using red-hot shot, and soon large parts of the city were in flames. For the moment the gunners were concentrating more on the town than the palace, which was situated in the rear of the houses and at a distance, but that they would eventually turn their attention to us was certain.

Manu was of course not content to remain in this temporary safety, and she was also furious at the destruction being wrought, principally by the fires, which were reignited by the flying shot as quickly as they were doused.

'The devils seek to destroy my Jhansi,' she growled, and insisted upon going down into the town itself, riding her white mare that all might see her and know that their queen was in their midst. Thankfully she excused me from accompanying her, but I watched her progress with a painful anxiety. Both the distinctive horse and the cheers that greeted her wherever she appeared soon alerted the British as to who she was, and I learned afterwards that one of the gunners told Sir Hugh that he was sure he could hit her. Fortunately the general, however determined he might be to hang Manu after due process of law, was also an old-fashioned gentleman, and told his artilleryman that it was not his purpose deliberately to aim at either women or enemy commanders.

I also heard, at a later date, that in attempting to inform his superiors in England as to whom he had been fighting, he referred to Manu as a 'kind of Indian Joan of Arc'. This did not go down very well with that large portion of the English public who continued to regard the rani as a vicious murderess, and of course it should be remembered that however the English eventually came to regret the deed, when they finally managed to lay hands upon the original they burned her at the stake, again revealing the hatred of fear.

So the rani was not fired upon, deliberately, although as she constantly exposed herself, earning the praise of the British for doing so, she was often nearly hit anyway. And whatever Rose's consideration for her, she was not disposed to have any for him. She returned to the palace that night thoroughly exhilarated at being at last really under fire, as opposed to the few shots from the Star Fort the previous year, and well pleased with the way her people were standing up to the bombardment, and we were just settling down to our evening meal when there was an alarm. We hurried on to the porch, looking to our left, where the defensive wall extending from the town joined that now surrounding the palace, close to. Just beyond this wall, at a distance of not more than two hundred yards, was a group of mounted British officers, studying our position through their glasses.

'What impudence!' Manu exclaimed. 'Do you know any of these men, Emma?'

I pointed at the plumed hat in the centre of the group. 'That is General Rose himself.'

Manu levelled her glass. 'He treats us with contempt,' she said. 'Well, I will give him what he came for. Fetch my musket.'

Her maids scurried off, and returned a moment later with the gun. As was her custom, she loaded it herself, and took careful aim, then squeezed the trigger. 'Confound it.'

She had clearly missed, although there was considerable agitation amongst the British group.

'Oh, to have one of those Enfield rifles,' she said. 'I could have ended the war there and then.'

I felt she was being optimistic; the British had lost generals before and continued the war. But at least they were retiring at some speed.

Despite having missed her target, Manu was again exhilarated. 'How soon do you think Tatya Tope will get here?' she asked.

'Did not Nana promise in a week?'

'And that was five days ago. *Then* we shall sally forth and catch the *feringees* between two fires.'

But it will be in the open, I thought, remembering Tatya Tope's own analysis. We needed him here in the city, and he had already missed that opportunity. Supposing he was actually coming!

★   ★   ★

The bombardment was kept up for two more days, while the British slowly edged forward, using the hours of darkness to dig trenches and throw up redoubts. Our casualties so far had been light although, distressingly, they had been evenly shared between men and women, but everyone's spirits were still high.

'They are preparing for an assault,' I warned Manu.

'Let them come,' she said. 'How may five thousand attack fourteen, especially when the fourteen hold a strong position?'

It did not seem logical, but I had to remember how the British had assaulted, and taken, Delhi at even greater odds.

The assault came the next day, at dawn. Bugles blew, the cannon ceased firing, and with a series of cheers lines of redcoats left their entrenchments and rushed at the walls. They were headed by a forlorn hope of six men, who advanced to the east gate to place a petard intended to blow it open. Our people fired at them with everything they had, Manu mounting her horse and galloping down to the scene. Four of the British soldiers were killed, but still the explosive went off and the gate was left sagging on its hinges. Manu and Risaldar Khan summoned every man that could be spared to block the breach, and the fighting, hand-to-hand, was fierce in the extreme. To my consternation I saw Manu in the thick of the battle, waving her tulwar. But there was a great deal going on elsewhere, as scaling ladders were set against the walls to enable the redcoats to clamber up. Our people threw them and their ladders down again and casualties on both sides were heavy, while a squadron of horse, happily not the lancers, galloped round the wall to approach the palace. Even I joined in the fighting, taking my place with the guards – and so too did the court ladies, all trained in wepons by Manu – firing my revolver. I don't know if I hit anyone.

It was an odd and yet exhilarating experience to be taking part in a battle, especially alongside my estranged husband, for Abid was in command of our small force. But we saw off the assailants, and listened to a series of bugle calls which brought the fight to an end. The redcoats trudged sullenly back to their lines, while our people cheered themselves hoarse at this initial victory. I reloaded my revolver, wiped sweat from my brow, and was touched on the arm by Kujula, who, faithful as ever, had remained at my side through the battle.

'Your husband asks for you, Memsahib.'

I frowned at him, and then looked across the porch at Abid, who lay on the floor between two of his men and, distressingly, three of the girls, all bleeding profusely, moaning, and calling for water. They were being attended by their fellows, so I hurried to Abid, and knelt beside him. This was the first time I had ever been close to a man who had been shot through the chest. Abid gasped for breath, but each gasp was accompanied by a froth of blood to join that already staining his tunic.

'He has been shot through the lungs,' Maropant Tambe said. Like me, he had prudently remained in the palace during the battle; unlike me, he had taken no part in any of the fighting.

'Will he survive?'

'I do not think that is possible.'

'Where is Bhumaka?'

'The surgeon is in the city, tending the wounded there.'

When he could be here, I thought.

Fingers closed on my hand, and I looked down. Abid was trying to speak, but could not. And I? What does one say to a man of whom one has seen the best and the worst, and is now breathing his last? But that he had asked for me, and now sought my hand, seemed to indicate that despite all he still felt a considerable affection for me. I squeezed his fingers back, and continued to hold them tightly until, only a few minutes later, his grip relaxed.

For the second time in my life, I was a widow.

Manu hugged me and kissed me when she returned later that evening, but her shared sorrow over Abid's death and also those of two of her girls, was tempered by her elation at the success of our day. 'They came, they saw and they were conquered,' she declared, paraphrasing one of the events of Caesar's life that I had taught her.

'They will come again,' I warned. 'The first attack on Delhi also failed.'

'Let them come again,' she said. 'I am not some senile old man. We shall beat them again, and if necessary, again. But first, we will give Abid and my girls an honourable burial.'

As we could no longer reach the river, the pyre was erected in the palace courtyard. Risaldar stood with Manu and me, and the rest of his family, while the flames were lit and the bodies consumed.

Risaldar regarded me speculatively throughout the ceremony, no doubt harking back to his youth when I would have been on the pyre beside my dead husband. Indeed, I felt quite nervous, because, as we were with such determination defying the Raj, should we not also be defying all of the Raj's laws, including the outlawing of *suttee*? But Manu would never have permitted my immolation, as Risaldar well knew, and the matter was not raised.

Then it was a business of attending to the other dead, as well as the wounded. This consumed most of the night. And before we could retire for a few hours' sleep, we were aware of a great stealthy movement out on the plain. It was still dark, and we could not tell exactly what was happening, but the noise was definitely receding rather than coming closer.

'Can they be leaving?' Manu asked in wonderment.

The British camp fires were still burning, but this was the oldest trick in the world when an army was making a secret withdrawal. Suppose they were? It would mean we had won. Jhansi would have secured its independence, at least in the short term.

We could hardly wait for dawn, and then we saw, to our disappointment, that the British were still very much in evidence, their guns still pointing at us, their people already taking up their positions. Although this time they were not advancing, but merely standing their ground.

We were busy with our telescopes, attempting to determine what our enemies were about.

'They wish us to attack them,' Risaldar suggested. 'They know we are too strong, behind our defences.'

I doubted that, as I continued to study the British encampment.

'Well, we are not going to fall into that trap,' Manu said. 'We can survive better in here than they can out there. And every day brings Tatya Tope closer.'

'I think Tatya Tope is already here, Highness,' I said.

'What? You see him?' She swung her glass to and fro.

'No, Highness. But I think that noise we heard in the night was the British withdrawing part of their force to meet him. I can see no lancers in their camp, and yesterday there was a regiment. There are some Highland regiments missing too, as well as a battery of guns.'

Manu studied the camp. 'You are right,' she said.

'Well then, perhaps we *should* attack,' Risaldar said, 'if their numbers have been reduced.'

Manu chewed her lip. 'No,' she said at last. 'We will remain here.

When Tatya Tope has defeated the force sent against him, these men will have to withdraw. I will not sacrifice my people unnecessarily.' She turned to me. 'Am I right, Emma?'

'I think you are right, Highness.' I could not doubt that even the two thousand or so men left in front of us would destroy the Jhansi army if it could get us into the open. Whereas if Tatya Tope did indeed gain the victory we hoped, all things were possible. But he also would be fighting in the open.

It was a very long day. The British kept up a desultory firing, to which we replied, but for the most part it was quite peaceful, so much so that I was encouraged to bring Alice up from her hiding place and give her some fresh air and sunlight.

Manu spent the day walking up and down the porch, and mounting to the battlements to peer to the north-west. 'Oh, to be out there,' she said, 'with Tatya Tope, beating the British.'

The next day was no less peaceable. It was difficult to be sure that we were at war. Some of our horsemen were so restless as to gallop right up to the British lines, waving their tulwars. They were driven away by musketry, but no attempt was made to attack them.

It was in the middle of the following morning that we heard the skirl of the pipes. We looked at each other in dismay, then hurried up to the tower with our telescopes, and saw, winding over the hills, not the victorious warriors of Tatya Tope, but the red coats of the British, the glittering lanceheads and the fluttering pennons of the lancers, the flaring banners of the various regiments; in their midst walked a considerable body of dejected, manacled men.

'It cannot be,' Manu said. 'It cannot be!' she shouted.

Soon enough the envoy was again before our gates.

'Sir Hugh Rose wishes to inform Your Highness that a Hindu army, commanded by one Tatya Tope, and representing, he understands, the forces of the so-called Nana Sahib, has been encountered as it endeavoured to cross the Betwa River, and put to flight. From the prisoners he has taken, General Rose has learned that this force was intended for the relief of Jhansi. There is now, therefore, no hope of relief, and General Rose once again calls upon Your Highness to surrender and save the lives of your subjects.'

'He is lying,' Manu said. She looked over our anxious faces. 'Tell me he is lying.'

'Those are victorious troops, Highness,' Risaldar said, grimly.

'Begone!' Manu shouted at the envoy. 'Away with you. I will

recognize no more flags of truce. Tell your master either to attack me or leave my country.'

An hour later the assault began in earnest. The British artillery kept up a steady fire, concentrating now entirely upon the east gate and the wall to either side. Soon several of our guns were dismounted, rolling over to lie on their backs like dead animals, feet pointing at the sky. Around them lay our gunners. Dust swirled over the doomed city, but at least we were for the moment spared the attention of the vultures; the cannonade frightened them away.

We replied as best we could, but with so many of our guns lost we were naturally less effective. And behind their barrage the redcoats moved steadily closer, digging their trenches but not yet attempting another attack, while their horsemen rode round our defences and inspected the palace from the sides and rear. They included the lancers on this occasion, but they kept a respectable distance so that it was impossible to identify any one man.

'They are closing in for the kill,' Risaldar growled. 'We must sortie, Highness.'

Manu looked at me. She was still depressed from the realization that Nana's people had been defeated, that there was going to be no relief. It occurred to me that we were in roughly the same position as General Wheeler and his people in Cawnpore. But at least we, or certainly Manu and her principal officers – and that included me – could be under no illusions as to *our* fates should we surrender.

'I think we must, Highness,' I said regretfully. 'But it would be best to wait until midday, when the sun is at its hottest.'

I had observed that the British fire usually slackened during the heat of the day, and there was far less activity in their camp.

'Yes,' Manu said. 'That is when they are at their weakest. Muster a force, Risaldar Khan. Three thousand men, armed with muskets and bayonets.'

'And tulwars, Highness,' Risaldar recommended. He knew his men were not trained to use the bayonet.

'And tulwars, to be sure.'

'Am I to lead them, Highness?'

'I will lead them.'

'No,' I said.

She looked at me.

'We are talking about an assault, a hand-to-hand conflict. That is man's work. If you were to fall, or be captured, Highness, we would all be lost.'

Manu looked at Risaldar, who nodded. 'My sister-in-law is correct, Highness. Your place is here. I will lead the sortie.'

'Be sure you come back,' Manu told him.

The rest of the morning was spent assembling the men, behind the crumbled wall and gate, which the British continued to pound. But as I had anticipated, as the sun climbed to its apogee in a cloudless sky, the enemy fire slackened, and we could hear bugle calls, no doubt summoning the various regiments to mess. We waved the flag we had chosen as a signal, Risaldar Khan waved his tulwar in turn, and his men gave a great shout and swarmed over the debris to charge the British line. For a few minutes they were obscured by the smoke which drifted across the burning houses and the dust which continued to swirl around the breech, then they were in the open air and streaming forwards. Now bugles again rang out, and red coats rushed to take up their positions. But it was a good minute before the first guns were fired, and by then our people were almost upon them. The British met the attack with musket and bayonet, checking it with furious vigour. But yet they were being forced back, and Manu was jumping up and down in excitement, when there were more bugle calls and we saw the lancers, supported by a regiment of irregular horse, coming round the side of the British lines. Risaldar apparently did not see these troops, for he made no attempt to detach any of his people to guard his flank, although, given the lack of training and discipline in our ranks, I doubt he would have been able to carry out such a manoeuvre in the heat of battle even had he thought of it.

'Oh, Kali, come to my rescue!' Manu screamed, as she anticipated the catastrophe to her arms.

Another bugle call, and the cavalry surged forward, lances lowered, sabres flashing. Those of our people closest to the onslaught broke and fled. Their comrades were struck as by an immense sledge-hammer, and disintegrated. Men fled in every direction, many throwing away their weapons as they tried to get back to the shelter of the city. Manu covered her face with her hands while I stared in horror, realizing that we were lost.

The British did not immediately pursue; they knew they had gained a sizeable victory, but then, they regarded sizeable victories as their due whenever they were opposed to an Indian army. But they were not content with even the many mounds of disintegrating flesh which covered the plain between their lines and the walls. For now the cannon were reformed in a close line pointing at us.

'Where is Risaldar Khan?' Maropant Tambe demanded of a dust-covered captain who came to the palace.

'Dead, Sahib. Dead. His head was blown off.'

Maropant looked at his daughter in consternation.

She at last raised her head. 'How many men are lost?'

'Many men, Highness. Many. Many hundreds of men.'

'What are we to do?' Maropant asked.

'We can fight,' Manu said, beginning to regain her energy. 'We can . . .' She was interrupted by a great wail from the city. We levelled our telescopes, and I felt my stomach roll.

From the British lines there came several files of red-coated infantry. Between each file there was an Indian prisoner, stripped to his dhoti, his hands bound behind his back. While we watched in horror, each man was placed before a cannon, his back against the muzzle. His arms and legs were carried behind him and secured to the wheels, as tightly as possible, so that he could move no part of his body save for his head. The prisoners were certainly moving their heads, to and fro, and although we could not hear them, from their movements we could guess that they were shrieking their fear of the coming moments.

'Kali give me strength,' Manu whispered.

When all the men were in place, their guards retired behind the cannon, and then the guns were fired, one after the other, each explosion spewing the shattered remnants of a man into the afternoon air.

Manu burst into tears.

By the time the last man had been executed, it was nearly dusk. The city was a vast moan of anger and despair. It did not appear that any of the mangled men was from Jhansi; they had all seemed to be prisoners taken from Tatya Tope's army, and as such I could suppose they were all considered by the British to be part of the army at Cawnpore responsible for the massacre.

But what had happened was a sombre indication of what was likely to happen when the British took Jhansi. Because now it was a matter of when.

That evening a deputation of the city elders came to see us. 'You must leave this place,' Maropant Tambe, acting as their spokesman, told his daughter.

'Leave? How can I leave?'

'You have still your cavalry, two thousand strong. Muster them, quietly, place yourself in their midst, and ride out of here to the north-west. If it is done tonight, the British will not be able to stop you or catch you. Then you ride with all haste to Nana.'

'You expect me to desert my people?'

'You can do nothing more for them, Manu. You have been defeated. And it is you the British want. Risaldar Khan is dead. So is his brother. There is only one person left alive who they regard as responsible for the massacre at the City Fort, and that is you. Will you allow yourself to be tied to a cannon and blown to bits? You?'

Manu's shoulders were hunched. 'And you suppose they will cease their assault if they know I have left?'

'No. They will not cease their assault. But if you are not here, we may then surrender. They have no cause to punish us. We fought for you, and for our country. With you gone, we can make an honourable surrender.'

'We?'

'I will remain here and take charge.'

Manu regarded her father for several seconds, and then looked around the other faces perhaps wondering if she was being deposed, by the back door, as it were. 'My people will execrate my memory,' she said.

'They will honour you, for all time, because of your resistance, and because this war is not finished yet. You will go to Nana, and you will rally his people, and lead them back here again, to defeat the British and regain your throne.'

Once again Manu considered for several seconds. But he was making a telling point. She was only twenty-two years old. She did not wish to die, certainly in so ghastly and humiliating a manner as to be fired from the mouth of a cannon. Or even to be publicly hanged. While she certainly wished to continue the war, and gain that elusive victory, she was enough of a soldier to know that it could not be gained here, in these circumstances.

She squared her shoulders. 'I will go, but only in order to come back, as you suggest, my father, with all of Nana's power. You will accompany me, Emma.'

'With my child, Highness.' I certainly was not going to leave Alice behind.

'Of course. And Damodar. And your servants.'

I told Vima and Kujula what we were planning, and they packed up what we could take with us, which was not very much, although I packed two saddlebags with my accumulated wealth, now amounting to more than two lacs, and the priceless bracelet Hazrat had given me. Manu's people were also packing up; everything they felt she could carry. She was especially concerned about her correspondence, with the various Indian rulers as well as people like Erskine, and of course her letter from Gordon, countersigned by Skene. All of this together with her available money and her prize pieces of jewellery, were placed in four large satchels.

Meanwhile, the British had advanced their lines to within little more than a hundred yards of the walls, and obviously intended to launch their final assault at first light. As soon as it was dark, Manu went down to the city and walked about her people, smiling at them and talking to almost every man crouching beside his musket, while their womenfolk served them food and water. I accompanied her, knowing that she was deeply grieved at having to abandon them, however sensible the strategic reasons for her doing so. What made her feelings more acute was that she could not tell them what she was planning to do, had to leave them with the impression that she meant to fight and die in their midst. I was hardly less unhappy. These people *were* preparing to die for her. I could only reflect that there was not a great deal of point in dying for someone who was also going to die, especially if, her father had said, by leaving she could actually save their lives. Her business *was* to live, with the intention of fighting again, and avenging the dead.

It was utterly dark when we returned to the palace. On the polo park the cavalry had been assembled under their commander, Mansur Khan. They had no idea for what purpose they were waiting, could only assume it was for some midnight sortie; they were both anxious and excited. With them was the five-hundred-strong regiment of women.

'Have you sent out scouts?' Manu asked.

'Yes, Highness. They report that there is a screen of horsemen to the north-west, but no cannon.'

'How numerous is this screen?'

'Hardly more than a hundred men, Highness.'

'And no infantry?'

'They believe there are some infantry, Highness. But again, not very many.'

'Do you suppose this is a trap?' Manu asked her father. 'To leave so obvious an escape route for me to take?'

'I think that is a risk you must accept.'

She looked at me.

'I think they are inviting you to escape, Highness,' I said. 'Because they feel that if you do, Jhansi will be theirs the more easily. Which is true.'

'They do not fear me,' Manu said regretfully. 'Well, I shall make them fear me. But listen, my father. Our magazine must not fall into their hands.'

Maropant Tambe nodded. 'I will lay the train with my own fingers.'

She gazed at him for several seconds. 'We will ride to victory together.'

'I know it.'

She embraced him, then turned away. 'Mount your men, General.'

'Our destination, Highness?'

'We are going to unite our forces with those of Nana Sahib, that we may return and beat the redcoats.'

He gulped, but saluted, and went down to his people.

'Well, then,' Manu said, and looked around her personal party, which was very small. She would be accompanied by her two favourite maids, Mandar and Kashi, by Damodar and his nurse, by myself – I was carrying Alice in my arms – and by Vima and Kujula, as well as the two pack animals carrying her valuables. She had no other personal escort, and as she was armed to the teeth I did not suppose she needed one. Besides, there was her cavalry corps.

She embraced her father again. 'Stay well until I return,' she told him.

'I shall be here, waiting for you,' he assured her.

Another embrace, then she led us down the stairs to where our horses waited.

It was now past midnight, and we needed to make haste, but at the same time, we did not wish to alert the British camp to what we were doing. We walked our horses across the polo field and into the low hills beyond, where we mounted. As we knew where the enemy was, there was no point in using a screen of our own, which could only alert them. Manu rode in front, beside Mansur Khan, with us following. I would have preferred her to be some ranks back, for her own safety, but she was again aglow with the desire, and the determination, to fight. The rest of our command followed.

It took us half an hour to reach our defensive line where our people gazed at us in consternation, but stood aside to allow us through. Presumably they also assumed that we were on our way to carry out an attack, and indeed they would have cheered us had not Mansur signalled them to silence. Thus we passed through with only the clop of our horses' hooves and the occasional clink of our weapons.

Still we walked our horses, for perhaps another mile, before we were challenged. The voice spoke Marathi, but it was not Indian.

'Ride!' Mansur called, and we urged our horses forward.

There was another challenge, and then a shot, followed by some more. Mansur and his people relied upon their tulwars to clear the way, and there was indeed only a light screen in front of us. These were mostly dismounted for the night, and by the time they were in any sort of order we were through them; I doubt either side suffered any casualties in the brief encounter.

But the whole area had been alerted. Bugles blew and shots had been fired. Yet these were now far behind us, as we slowed to a canter, the night air playing about our faces, our mood one of total exhilaration. We were therefore the more disconcerted when, about half-an-hour later, we were greeted by a volley of shots out of the darkness. Several men fell, and the rest of us pulled our horses back.

'Manu!' I shouted, forgetting my rank in my agitation.

'I am here,' she replied. 'The swine have trapped us after all.'

That seemed evident. The cavalry screen had been intended merely to draw us on. Rose had calculated correctly: that if the rani left Jhansi, she would have nowhere to go, save towards Nana's camp. However, he had *mis*calculated as to the force she would have with her when she fled. Mansur had been counting the musket flashes, which were now dotting the night as the obstructing force fired as fast as they could reload. The bullets were whistling about our ears, but we had withdrawn to extreme range and they did little harm. Not that I, at the least, felt comfortable. I had been shot at a few days previously when we had engaged the cavalry at the palace, and had had no fear on that occasion. But now I was holding Alice in front of me on the saddle. She was awake, and interested in what was going on, not realizing that she could be hit at any moment.

'They are not more than a few hundred men, Highness,' Mansur said, 'we must either ride through them or turn back.'

'We will ride through them,' Manu decided. There was certainly no other sensible alternative. She understood my apprehensions, and called four men to ride immediately in front of me. 'Now remember,' she told us all. 'We stop for no one and no reason. I place the rajah in your care,' she said to me.

I drew my revolver, and hugged Alice closer yet. Damodar was riding his own horse, and this he brought in to be between Vima and Kujula, his nurse behind him. Mansur took his place at our head, Manu immediately behind him. He waved his tulwar, shouted 'Charge!' and we galloped into the night.

I kept my eyes fixed on the four men in front of me, and tried to ignore the flashes and the explosions from all around me. We came to a low ditch, narrow enough for most of our horses to leap. Mine did not, and slid down the embankment with a flurry of snorts and whinnies, so that it was all I could do to keep my seat. Then he was scrabbling at the far side. But now I was surrounded by men, their red coats visible even in the gloom. I shot one who reached for my bridle, deemed myself lost as another lunged at me with his bayonet at the end of his musket, but he went down before he could reach me, shot by Kujula. Then we were up the far side of the ditch and galloping into the darkness.

I discovered I was both shouting and weeping. I had killed a man.

We were not yet out of danger. Mansur brought us to a halt when he reckoned we were beyond musket range, and we could determine how we had fared. Damodar, panting with excitement, was still close to me, as were the women and Kujula, and to my immense relief Manu was unhurt. There was no way of telling how many of us, if indeed any, had fallen; behind us there was a confused melee of sound and flashing lights. And now too we could hear the drumming of hooves; there was a large body of cavalry in pursuit.

'Ride, Highness, ride,' Mansur shouted. 'My people will hold them off.'

Manu hesitated only a moment, then called out, 'Stay close, Emma, with the children.'

We kicked our horses forward and rode into the night, while behind us the noise swelled to a crescendo, and a few minutes later we heard the clash of arms.

'Brave Mansur,' Manu said. 'Brave Mansur.'

Our horses were now blown, and we had to slow to a walk, listening always to the sounds of battle from behind us. We had a long way to go, and the ground was uneven. It was also rising. With the first light we halted to look back.

We were now some five miles from Jhansi, and we could hear no new sounds of pursuit. Disturbingly, there was no sign of Mansur and his cavalry. But for the moment we appeared to be safe; no doubt because, not being informed of our flight until it was too late, Rose had carried out his intended dawn attack. Even at this distance we could hear the rumble of the guns, and supposed we could even hear the shrieks of the participants, while the smoke pall rising above the burning houses was visible for miles.

We could certainly imagine what was happening back there. 'My poor people,' Manu said. 'Oh, my poor people.'

'We must get on, Highness,' Kujula said, well aware that he was the only man left in our party.

Manu remained staring back at her city for several seconds, then she nodded. We continued to walk our horses over the uneven ground, now descending into valleys and then emerging on to hillocks again. It was the middle of the morning, and we were perhaps ten miles distant from the battle. By now all sounds of the conflict had died, but at this moment we were brought up by a huge rumbling roar, as of a thunderclap immediately above us.

We drew rein, and looked back, and saw a vast pillar of smoke rising into the morning sky, high above even the cloud that had been there before.

'They have fired the magazine,' Kujula said.

'Then Jhansi is no more,' Manu said. Tears were rolling down her cheeks.

The General

It was still nearly a hundred miles to Calpi and, hopefully, Nana and his army. An hour after the explosion we rode into the village of Bhander, where the locals turned out to gape at us, and where we stopped for a hasty breakfast and to water our horses.

We were in the middle of this scanty meal when the headman came to us. 'Horsemen,' he said tersely.

We scrambled to our feet, and saw, not a hundred yards away, several mounted men. My first reaction was that they were part of Mansur's command, but then we made out the blue uniforms.

'How did they get there?' Kujula complained.

'Haste,' I told Manu. 'Mount.'

But we were too late. The British horsemen had identified us, principally I would say through sighting Manu's white mare, and now charged, waving their sabres. It was the most desperate situation of my life, to that time. 'Mount and ride,' I shouted at Vima, more concerned for the safety of Alice, and thus Damodar, than the queen herself.

Vima gathered Alice into her arms, called for Damodar, and ran for the horses. Mandar and Kashi ran behind her.

'Highness!' I addressed Manu.

But she had drawn her tulwar. 'We must give them time to escape,' she said.

I could do nothing less than support her, and drew my revolver. Kujula also drew his tulwar.

I was first into action, as it were. As the horsemen galloped into the village, I aimed and fired my revolver and brought one down. Another shot had his companions separating to avoid being hit.

But their commander, a lieutenant whose name, I later learned, was Bowker, continued to ride straight at us, and before I could shoot him was upon the rani, sword held at the end of his extended arm like a lance. Now at last Manu's years of practice and training came into use. She threw up her own weapon and brushed his aside, and then continued her thrust, gouging him in the thigh and throwing him from the saddle. He fell heavily, and his men gave shouts of dismay. I further discouraged them from approaching by emptying the remaining chambers of my revolver.

Meanwhile the rani stood above her stricken foe, sword raised, eyes blazing, so that he and I both felt his last moment had come. But Manu, however warlike her training and dreams, however eagerly she had fired at General Rose, had never yet killed a man face to face. And she could not do it now.

She lowered her sword. 'Let us leave this place,' she said, and went to her horse.

A few minutes later we were galloping away from the houses. Some desultory shots were fired behind us, but the Britishers were more anxious to discover how badly hurt their officer was, and there was no further pursuit.

We kept going for the rest of the day, the adults occasionally walking beside our horses to rest them. Nor did we stop at dusk. That evening we reached the town of Konch, where, happiest of sights, we found Mansur and the main part of his cavalry. They had fought their way through the British forces, and having no idea what had happened to their queen, had correctly ridden for the nearest town in the hopes of finding us there. Instead we found them, just as they were giving us up for lost.

At dawn the following morning we rode into Calpi, having covered a hundred miles in little over twenty-four hours. Behind us we left several outposts, pickets to look out for any move towards us by the British.

There had been a detachment of Nana's people at Konch, where we were welcomed with open arms. A galloper was sent ahead of us to Calpi and outside of the town we were greeted by Tatya Tope and Nana's nephew, Pandurang Rao, known as Rao Sahib, who turned out a large portion of their troops to give the queen a royal greeting. Best of all, however, certainly from my point of view, was the sight of Dignaga.

'Highness!' he cried. 'Is Jhansi held?'

'Jhansi is destroyed,' Manu said bitterly, and looked at Tatya Tope. 'You did not come.'

'I was defeated,' he acknowledged. 'I would have tried again, but my men would not follow me.'

'It is a serious situation,' Rao Sahib remarked.

'What are you doing here?' I asked Dignaga, who had brought his horse alongside mine.

'My brigade forms the garrison at Calpi,' he said. 'I command two thousand men.'

'And we have nearly two thousand more. What of the Sahib?'

'He has at least three thousand.'

'Then can we not again take the field?'

'I see no reason why not.'

'Where is Nana?' Manu asked.

'Not far,' Tatya Tope said.

'The Moulvie is close too,' Rao Sahib said. 'With two thousand men.'

'And the begum and Birgiz Kudr are also near,' Tatya said. 'She has ten thousand more.'

'Then we have an army,' Manu said. 'We shall concentrate, and then return to Jhansi. And deal with this man Rose.'

'I suspect this man Rose may well be coming to you,' Dignaga said, watching one of our own cavalry pickets approaching at the gallop.

'Redcoats, Highness,' this fellow panted. 'Only a few miles from Konch, and marching this way.'

'We must retire,' Rao declared.

'Again?' Manu demanded. 'And again and again? When will we concentrate?'

'When Nana tells us to,' Tatya Tope said.

'I am telling you to, now,' Manu said. 'I and my people will return to Konch and defend it. Tatya Tope, you will send to Nana requesting him, in my name, to join us here with all his power. It would be wise for him in turn to send messengers to the Moulvie and the begum.'

Tatya Tope and Rao Sahib exchanged glances; they were not used to being commanded by a woman.

'I will place my brigade at your disposal, Highness,' Dignaga volunteered.

That convinced the others that they had better do something, and various messengers were despatched.

'You will serve at my right hand,' Manu told the young prince.

They made a splendid couple, both young, strong, in the best of health, and brimming with enthusiasm. Once again I allowed my thoughts to drift towards a marriage between them, but once again the rani was clearly interested only in military matters.

'Will you go to safety?' she asked me. 'I would put Damodar in your care.'

'Where is safety?' I asked. 'If you perish, then our cause is lost in any event.'

She nodded. 'I was but thinking of the children. But this time we are going to win. You will stay with me.'

When we reached Konch, no redcoats were to be seen, and indeed the village looked utterly peaceful. It was also clearly going to be difficult to defend, for it lay in the midst of utterly flat country, covered in waving wheat, and the houses themselves straggled for something like a mile rather than forming a cohesive group which could be used as a strong point. But despite not having had any sleep, Manu was as usual filled with energy, and the moment we arrived she had her men, and those from Gwalior, hard at work building earthworks and digging trenches.

'Their cannon will have less to aim at than a walled city,' she pointed out.

Yet would they have cannon, I reflected. Well, so did we, but ours were only half-a-dozen light field pieces.

However, we were here, and they were not, yet, for all the alarm given by the horseman. And every moment would be bringing Nana closer.

But we had thought that about Tatya's army approaching Jhansi.

Still too exhilarated at the night's events, and especially at her part in them and her fight with Lieutenant Bowker, to consider sleep, Manu wished to go out and see what was happening, and I wished to accompany her. I left the children in Vima's care, and then the queen and Dignaga and I, accompanied by a small escort, rode to the south-east. A few miles from the town we came upon our first picket, who agreed that some British cavalry had been seen earlier that day, but the enemy had withdrawn when fired upon. We went further, and reached our outer picket, who told us roughly the same tale.

Dignaga had spotted a knoll to our right and so we went to this, and from the top inspected the country through our telescopes. I thought I saw the sun glinting from some lanceheads. But they were a long way away, and not coming any closer.

'What can it mean?' Manu asked.

'That they were only a patrol, sent to ascertain where you had gone,' Dignaga said. 'Encountering resistance, they have withdrawn to join their army, which I would say has not yet left Jhansi.'

'But they were in the city yesterday morning,' I said.

'They will have a great deal to do, especially if your magazine was indeed exploded. There will have been heavy casualties to be dealt with, and the city to be made secure. They will also be waiting for reinforcements and reserves of powder and ball. They will now be sure where you are, Highness, and thus that you have linked up with Nana, and perhaps the begum as well. They will know that they need to advance in strength.'

'And we shall meet them with strength,' Manu said with some satisfaction.

'Over there.' I pointed, and we saw the glint of metal amidst the wheat, some fifty yards to our right.

'An assassin,' Dignaga snapped. 'You and you, follow me.' He galloped off, followed by two of the troopers. The rest gathered round their queen, protectively.

My fear was more for the prince, but a few minutes later Dignaga was returning towards us, at a walk, shepherding a shambling figure.

'That is Mankad!' Manu exclaimed.

I recognized him also, even if with difficulty. He was one of the palace guardsmen, but he had lost his turban and his uniform was torn and slashed and stained with blood, although he did not appear to be wounded.

'Highness!' he cried. 'Highness.' He fell to his knees beside her horse.

Manu dismounted and herself held a canteen to his parched lips. 'You are from Jhansi?'

He gulped water, and swallowed, and gulped again. 'I escaped, yes, Highness.'

'Alone?'

'There were some others. But we became separated.'

I also dismounted. 'You have walked, all the way from Jhansi?' A hundred miles!

'I found a horse, Memsahib. He carried me most of the way. But then he died, and I have walked the rest.'

'Tell me what happened,' Manu said. 'After we left.'

'We fought as hard as we could, Highness. But the redcoats would not be stopped. They stormed into the city, and then they came up to the palace.'

'It has been destroyed?'

'No, no, Highness.'

'We heard the explosion. The magazine.'

'Oh, yes, Highness. The explosion was very great. The train was laid by your father himself, and he waited to fire it until the redcoats were inside the Star Fort. When it went up it took more than a hundred of the *feringees* with it. Oh, it was a very great explosion. It even stopped the fighting for a few minutes. Then the redcoats came on again.'

'But . . . my father was going to surrender when he blew the magazine.'

'I think he tried, Highness. But they would not accept surrender. They wanted only to kill.'

'They killed my father?'

'They surrounded him, and forced him to throw down his weapons. Then they hanged Maropant Tambe, Highness.'

Slowly Manu sank to her knees.

'They hanged Maropant Tambe?' Dignaga asked. 'After he surrendered? Was there no trial?'

'No, Highness. He was held by two of the redcoats, and a British officer came up to him and asked him, "Are you the commander of these people?" And Maropant Tambe drew himself up and said, "I am the father of the Rani of Jhansi." And the officer said, "Hang him." There was another officer present, a cavalry officer, and he protested, but he was overruled. So they put a rope around Maropant Tambe's neck, threw it over a beam, and they hoisted him from the very floor of the palace.'

A cavalry officer, I thought. Oh, my God, a cavalry officer. But at least he had protested.

Manu remained kneeling, her head bowed.

'You saw this happen?' Dignaga asked.

'I was there, Highness.'

'But they did not hang you.'

'I was lying in a pile of the dead, Highness, and they thought I was dead also. I was covered in blood. Here you see, it still stains my clothes. They thought I was dead, and they were in a hurry to loot the palace.'

'The women?' I asked.

'They threw them to the floor and raped them, Memsahib. Then they chased about the palace like madmen, tearing the furniture apart to get at the silver. But I believe it was worse in the town, the rape and the murder and the looting. And the bayonetting, men, women and children.'

'But you survived,' Dignaga said, grimly. 'How?'

'Like I said, I lay with the dead, Highness. For a long time I lay with the dead. Then the British general came into the palace and said that the dead must be buried. His people had dug a big pit, into which the bodies were to be thrown. But when they carried me outside I managed to roll away, and was overlooked. So I got out of the palace and came to seek her Highness.'

'She will honour you for that,' Dignaga said, perhaps optimistically, as Manu remained kneeling, head bowed. Dignaga looked at me, but I did not know if I dare interrupt her at that moment.

'I have not eaten for two days,' Mankad said.

Manu raised her head. 'Then you must be fed.' She herself helped him to his feet, and gave him into the care of the soldiers.

'Kali give me strength,' she said. 'Kali give me power. Kali give me the will, to kill every *feringee* in Hindustan.'

Dignaga and I said nothing. There was nothing we could say.

Manu mounted, and led us back to where the picket was camped. 'Send word the moment you see any movement out there,' she said.

We cantered back to Konch. On the way we met Mansur. 'My people are ready, Highness,' he said.

'Stand them down,' she said. 'We will wait.'

'Will the *feringees* come, Highness?'

'They will come,' she said. 'And we will meet them, at Konch.'

We regained the town, and the rani retired to the house that had been prepared for her. She summoned Mandar and Kashi to be with her, but did not call for me.

'I think, at this moment, she hates even me,' I suggested.

'She will recover,' Dignaga said.

I looked at him.

'Surely you condemn what they have done?' he asked.

'Yes,' I said. 'I condemn what they have done.'

That afternoon, having rested, Manu sent for me. She dismissed her women, and we were alone.

'Do you wish to leave us?' she asked.

I had also had some sleep. 'Leave you, Highness?'

Now was not the time for the intimacy of Manu.

'There is only death to be found here.'

'Do you not believe you, we, can defeat them?'

'Perhaps,' she said.

It was the first time I had ever heard her express a doubt.

Then she actually smiled. 'Perhaps, if I were in command.'

'Then you should take command.'

She sighed. 'They would not accept it. Nana, the begum, the Moulvie, they are all older than I, and consider themselves experienced. I have done nothing but attempt to defend Jhansi, and failed. I should have stayed, and died beside my father.'

'Never,' I said. 'You have too much to do with your life.'

'Must I then devote it to fighting the Raj?'

'Have you not always known this was your karma? Were you not devoted to weapons and warfare from your girlhood?'

'Why, that is true,' she said. 'You are a great comfort to me, Emma, but yet, the most probable fate of those who live at war is to die in war. This is not your war. If you wish to leave, I give you that permission.'

'Leave to go where, Highness?'

'I know it will be difficult. You cannot fall into the hands of the British; they would probably hang you as they hanged my father. As they would hang me, if they can lay hands on me. But you could go north, to Afghanistan. Beyond Afghanistan lies Russia. They hate the British as much as we do. If you could cross Russia, or get into Persia, it might be possible for you to regain your home.'

'My home was Jhansi, Highness. And if Jhansi has fallen, then my home is at your side.'

She squeezed my hands. 'Faithful Emma. If you stay at my side, you may well die at my side.'

'If that is my karma, Highness.'

'And Alice?'

'Only she concerns me. But . . . I can only protect her to the last.'

'As we both must protect Damodar. Well, then, Emma, so be it. We will fight and die, together.'

The events of the last year had had a profound effect on me, even if I had not realized that it was happening. But down to last June, and even after the beginning of the rebellion in Jhansi, I had always regarded myself as an observer of life rather than a participant; even my forced involvement in the execution of Zavildar Khan, the leader of the thugs who had murdered my husband and who I had denounced when he had incautiously visited Jhansi, unaware that I was now living there, had cast me in the role of judge rather than executioner. Even when I had left Jhansi for Cawnpore as the rani's envoy I had considered myself as an irrelevance, a pawn being moved hither and thither on the chessboard at the behest of my mistress. I had conceived my role as being essentially passive, an orderly progression through life. There might from time to time be crises, and even indignities, but these would never involve others to any great extent, and would never personally endanger me.

Cawnpore had changed that. Perhaps I had only personally known two of the women, but I felt as if I had known them all. I could have been one of them, but for that Thug attack so long ago which had so dramatically and irrevocably changed my life; but for that attack, Mr Hammond could well have returned to Cawnpore in the course of time, to resume his preaching there, and been caught up in events beyond his control. Not that he had ever been in control of anything.

But had he returned there, with me, I would have been herded into those dreadful barracks with the others when Nana had taken the town. To share their misery and their terror . . . and their fate. What thoughts had tumbled through their minds, their so protected and restricted minds, as they had realized that all those unmentionable words, humiliation and rape, mutilation and murder, were about to become realities, inflicted upon them? How would I have responded? How, indeed, had they responded?

Even all of these unhappy events could be considered from the point of view of a spectator. I had been there, I had seen them happen, I had realized that I could have been one of the victims, yet I had been standing to one side. It was as if I had been riding in a carriage, behind another, which had suddenly left the road in a precipitous place and gone tumbling down the hillside, shattering all inside. It could have been me, had I been in the lead carriage. But it had not.

Jhansi had been different. At Jhansi I had been on the inside looking out, rather than the reverse. I had been under fire for several continuous days. When we had fled, I had killed a man, in defence of a principal rather than my own life – and equally I could not now doubt what would have been my own fate had I remained in the palace and been taken by the British. If Mankad was to be believed, rape at the least. And then . . . what had been Maropant Tambe's thoughts when he had realized he, a high-ranking Brahmin and the father of a queen, was about to die, in a most ignominious and humiliating manner, without the benefit of a trial at which he might have defended himself, and with the certainty that far from being returned to the life cycle via cremation, his naked body would be thrown into a common pit? That could have been my fate! And still could be were we to lose the coming battle. We had lost so often that even the rani was beginning to have doubts. And I had more than ever compounded my guilt, in British eyes, by taking so active a part in the fight at Bhander!

I might have only a few days to live. And my child! Alice, being bayoneted to death!

It was a tense fortnight, overlaid as it was by the sense of impending crisis. But we felt ready, even if we were not being as fully supported as we had hoped. The begum had led her people back to Oudh; she was still hopeful of regaining her country. With her went the Moulvie. While Nana did not hurry to our aid, I no longer had any doubt that he was a coward who had no intention of risking his precious person in battle against the British. That he remained the leader of his people had to be simply because he was the son of the last peshwa, and was considered of that rank himself. Not even the rani would denounce him. 'He will come when he is ready,' she said.

Having made up her mind this time to fight and die, if need be, she was in a much calmer frame of mind. She had the sense to know that we could lose the coming battle, however, and thus sent her precious satchels of money and letters back to Calpi for safe-keeping; Tatya Tope placed them in his magazine, a vast store of powder and shot, which he regarded as making Calpi impregnable. But he came up to Konch with the majority of his people, leaving Rao Sahib in command of the rear.

With his reinforcements, we mustered some four thousand men, a far cry from the fourteen thousand who had attempted to defend the walls of Jhansi, and there were no walls save for our hastily erected earthworks around Konch. There was a difference, however: every man of our little army was a professional soldier – Tatya Tope's men still wore the red coats and shakoes of the sepoys they had once been – and were looking forward to the fight.

The same could be said of us women.

It was at the beginning of May that word reached us that a body of the enemy horse had crossed the Betwa, thus leaving Jhansi territory. This heralded the British advance, and sure enough the next day our scouts brought us word that General Rose and part of his army, numbering perhaps a thousand men, had reached Poona, which was only a couple of marches away. The following day his second brigade came up to him, and there could be no doubt that he would soon attack us. In fact, he did so the very next day.

Knowing that he was on his way, we made our dispositions. As usual, the rani had every intention of being as much in the middle of the fight as she could, and again as usual I was resolved to be at her side. We sent the children, together with the three women, and Kujula as their bodyguard, back to Calpi. Kujula was reluctant to leave, considering as he did that my safety was his prime responsibility, but I persuaded him that he would protect me far more efficiently by enabling my mind to be at rest regarding the safety of Alice and Damodar than by merely firing a pistol beside me.

Our loved ones sent to safety, we prepared to meet the assault. Most of our people were behind the earthworks Manu had had erected outside the town, but she had also sent several small detachments to occupy some outlying plantations so as to harass the British advance. Tatya Tope tugged his moustache in agitation, but conceded the ultimate command to Manu, as her people provided the bulk of our force. At her request, Dignaga kept his cavalry in reserve, hopefully to deliver the *coup de grâce* when we had repulsed the initial attack.

Konch contained a fort, long ruined, but still rising above the houses, and here Manu took her position, having had hoisted the flag of Jhansi, which fluttered bravely in the breeze. The town itself was half hidden behind a considerable stand of trees, which did much to conceal our dispositions, but from our tower we looked beyond these and across the wheatfields for a considerable distance. It was still early in the morning, just after seven, when we saw the gleam of the bayonets and heard the skirl of the bagpipes, and within a few minutes the whole of the British strength came into view, their banners flying and their red coats as always glowing.

Having come within sight of our position, and no doubt they could see us as clearly as we could see them, or at least our flags and the gleam of the sabres of Dignaga's horse, for they had all drawn their weapons and had them resting on their shoulders, they halted, and to our consternation, as we could see through our telescopes, sat down to breakfast.

'They must have commenced their march before daybreak,' Manu said. 'They must be both tired and clearly hungry. Should we not launch an attack on them while they are thus disarrayed?'

'That is what they would like you to do, Highness,' Tatya Tope objected. 'If you will look closely you will see that every man has his musket close to hand, and that their cavalry are eating in the saddle. Also that they have stopped virtually in order of battle. We would do better to wait behind our defences.'

I began to suspect that, like his cowardly master, his main idea was not to come within range of a British bayonet. Manu undoubtedly shared my opinion, but she bowed to his supposedly greater experience and judgement; I watched Dignaga walking his horse up and down impatiently, but he was waiting orders from us, and none went to him.

And now . . . 'Look there,' I said, and they turned their glasses to study the cloud of dust coming down from the north. The Union Jack was clearly visible above it.

'That will be the force from the Betwa,' Tatya Tope said. 'It is not very great.'

I reckoned there were several hundred of them, quite sufficient to make a difference.

'They are attacking,' Manu said.

The British had finished their breakfast and were advancing, but in skirmishing order, while their cannon, placed on the right, opened fire and began dropping their shells amidst our entrenchments. They did not appear to be doing much damage, and our own guns were replying vigorously, again without much effect.

'There!' Tatya Tope pointed to our right, and we saw that a considerable British detachment had peeled off from the main body and was moving at a very rapid pace to approach our position from the side.

'Quickly,' Manu shouted. 'Go down there and face your people about.'

For the sepoys in our entrenchments would be unable to discern the flanking movement.

Tatya Tope scrambled down the steps.

'I must go down too,' Manu said.

'To do what?' I asked.

'Well . . . Dignaga must launch an attack with his cavalry.'

'I can give him that order as well as you, Highness,' I said.

She bit her lip, then nodded. 'Come back to me, Emma.'

I went down the steps as fast as I could – in places the stone had crumbled – reached the ground, and hurried through the trees. Now the British were also aiming at the town, and all around me there was a seethe of noise, people shouting, shells exploding . . . I saw women and children peering at me from doorways, and several of the houses were already burning.

I reached the edge of the tree screen, and saw the British skirmishers very close. Around me were several casualties, but now Dignaga rode up to me. 'This is no good,' he said.

'I know. The rani would have you charge those men. Is this possible?'

'Willingly.' He kicked his horse.

'My lord,' I shouted, 'take care.'

In reply he waved his tulwar, and a moment later rode out from the trees, his Gwalior warriors behind him. But almost immediately they came within range of the British rifles, and received a volley which tumbled a good score of his men from their saddles. I did not see if the prince had been hit, and before I could look more closely I was overwhelmed by a great cheer from almost beside me, and I saw the flank attack, composed in the main of kilted Highlanders, charging at the trees.

What Tatya Tope had been able to achieve it was impossible to say. There certainly were only a few sepoys facing the onslaught, and these now turned and fled, some even throwing away their weapons. I looked over my shoulder and saw our people streaming out of their entrenchments and running as hard as they could for the rear of the town.

I could only go with them, or be bayoneted myself. I sobbed as I ran through the houses for the fort. I had sent Dignaga to his death, to no purpose. But at least I could save the queen.

Manu was already coming down the steps, tulwar in her hand. 'What has happened?' she demanded.

'We have been beaten,' I told her, and had to restrain myself from adding, *again.*

'I will rally them,' she said, and went into the street, into the midst of the running sepoys. 'Wait!' she shouted. 'Wait! We are not beaten. We outnumber the *feringees*. Wait, and I will lead you back to battle, and victory.'

They ignored her, and one now gave her a push that tumbled her to the ground. I feared she would be trampled, and dashed into the midst of the fleeing army. I was buffeted and thrown down, but managed to reach her side and help her to her feet.

'Cowards,' she moaned. 'Oh, the cowards. Well, let us show them how to die.'

'That is useless,' I shouted. 'Let us fight another day.'

I held her arm and forced her out of the throng and back to the tower, where our horses were tethered. We were both covered in dust and bruised and battered, and I doubt anyone would have recognized the Rani of Jhansi at that moment, for as we mounted the first of the Scots appeared at the head of the street. They gave a whoop, but recognizing me at least as a woman because my hair was unwinding from my turban, preferred to run at us rather than shoot, in the hopes of having us to themselves for a while before their officers came up. That gave us the opportunity we wanted. We both fired our revolvers at them, and then kicked our horses into a gallop.

Outside of the town the road to Calpi was clogged with fleeing sepoys, many throwing away their red jackets as well as their muskets. We turned our horses aside and went into the wheat. Now the British had trained their cannon to fire at the road itself, and the plunging shot was bursting amidst the fleeing men, causing them to shriek their fear and pain as they were tossed about, losing arms and legs in the process. And now there came a fresh series of bugle calls, and we saw the cavalry charging, lance heads gleaming in the sunlight. Fortunately this was on the far side of the road from ourselves, but even so our progress through the wheat was slow, and when we heard the drumming of hooves close by we thought we were finished. But, happiest of sights, it was Dignaga, although with only a few men at his back.

'Highness!' he panted. 'Emma! Thank the gods you are safe.'

'Are we safe?' I asked.

'You are now. We will take you to Calpi.'

And what then? I wanted to ask, looking back at Konch. The

town was now well alight and, judging by the racket arising from there, those who had not been killed were suffering all the agonies of helpless people at the hands of an angry and merciless foe.

I looked at Manu. Her shoulders were hunched; indeed her whole body seemed to be hunched on the back of her horse.

I could not blame her. The battle had lasted hardly an hour.

Fortunately, the sun was now high and the British, having marched for several hours to launch their assault, were suffering from both exhaustion and the heat. The pursuit soon ended, and the remnants of the sepoy army were able to gain Calpi, if not in safety, at least alive.

Here Rao waited, pacing anxiously up and down. He had heard the gunfire and seen the first fugitives who had got there before us. Now he was all boldness. 'Let them come,' he declared. 'My people are ready.'

'Is there word from Nana?' Dignaga asked.

'No. No, but I am sure he is coming.'

'I would send another messenger,' the prince said. 'We need him here, now.'

Rao looked at Manu, who was suffering the exhaustion of utter dispiritedness. Indeed, she sank to the ground. I fetched her water to drink.

'Are you hurt?' Rao asked anxiously.

She raised her head. 'Did you hear the firing?'

He nodded.

'But you did not come?'

'My duty was to defend Calpi.'

'Your duty, our duty,' she said hotly, 'is to defeat the British. This will not be done by waiting on events. Had you led but a thousand men to attack the British flank, once their assault was launched on my position, we would have routed them.'

Rao chewed his lip, and looked from face to face. There could be no doubt that both Dignaga and I agreed with the rani. Tatya Tope, as Rao's uncle was his employer, was less obviously certain.

'They will come here next,' Rao said. 'Then we shall see.'

Exhausted as she was, Manu went amongst her people, making sure they had food and water, and that their ammunition stocks were replenished. Of the two thousand horses who had accompanied our escape, and the thousand or so who had managed to flee Jhansi, more than two hundred had fallen, but even if they had been unable to face the bayonets they remained full of fight, the cavalry in particular; they had not actually been defeated. 'You have but to point your sword, Highness,' Mansur said.

'Brave men and women,' she replied. 'You will have your chance.'

Once again we were awaiting attack. We sent small cavalry patrols up the road towards Konch, and although they were usually met and sent off by the British cavalry, they were able to report that our enemies had pitched camp, in and around the town, and were there resting, tending to their wounded, and no doubt, as was usual, awaiting reinforcements.

'They treat us with contempt,' Manu complained. 'They move when they are ready, attack when they are ready. They have no interest in what we may be doing. Do they not know we have summoned Nana to join us with all his force? Do they not know that then they will be outnumbered by two to one?'

There was not really a diplomatic answer to that, either with regards to Nana's coming or any superiority we might hope to have in numbers. We had outnumbered Rose's army by more than two to one at Jhansi.

'We cannot just sit here and wait for them to choose their own time and their own place,' she insisted.

'I agree with you,' Dignaga said. 'But our scouts report that they are firmly entrenched, and they have a number of guns.'

Needless to say, our six pieces had been lost in the rout at Konch.

'Are you saying there is nothing we can do?'

'No, Highness. I am not saying that. But I think it will require careful timing.'

She gazed at him. 'If we are driven out of Calpi, where do we then go?'

He stroked his beard. 'To Nana.'

'To what end? Every time we fight the British we lose more men, and more materiel. Mansur tells me we lost seven hundred men at Konch.'

'Sadly, yes.' Dignaga's tone was sombre; about half that number had been his own people.

'And all our guns.'

'Nana has many guns.'

'Even if he will not use them,' Manu said bitterly. 'If only your cousin would fight with us . . .' She paused, again gazing at him.

Dignaga sighed. 'That is a faint hope.'

'Because he is afraid?'

'No,' Dignaga said sharply. 'I have told you, because he has given his word.'

'But he will not fight for the Raj, either.'

'His word was never to fight against them, not to fight for them. He will not willingly fight his own people.'

'Do all his people feel as he does?' Manu spoke quietly.

'I think most of his people feel as I do,' Dignaga said.

They gazed at each other, understanding each other without actually saying the words.

In the days that followed, Manu was entirely bound up with military matters, revealing an energy and determination which obviously terrified both Rao and Tatya Tope. 'It seems obvious,' she said, 'that Nana is not coming.'

'Well, you see, he has to be concerned with a possible attack from Gwalior,' Rao said.

Manu tossed her head. She knew the Scindia would not lead his people in battle against fellow Hindus, unless forced to it, and at the moment there was no evidence of that happening; the British were just happy to have Gwalior neutral.

'Whatever the reason,' she said, 'we must prepare to fight with what we have, here. We have sufficient men.'

'Indeed,' Rao said. 'Let them come. We shall smash them.'

Manu's glance was at once tired and contemptuous. 'As we have smashed them before,' she commented.

'It has been difficult,' Tatya Tope objected. 'They charge with such speed and fury. And they come at us from all sides at once.'

'But we *know* this is how they fight,' Manu pointed out. 'So we must take steps to counter it.'

'How do we do this?' Rao asked.

'They come at us, with such speed and fury,' Manu said, 'because they hold us in contempt. They know we are afraid of the bayonets.'

'Well . . .' Rao pulled his moustache. 'Have you even seen a man pierced by a bayonet?'

'Have you ever *heard* one?' Tatya Tope asked.

'It can be no worse than being cut or pierced by a lance or a tulwar,' Manu said. 'And if you are afraid to face the bayonets then you may as well throw down your weapons now, walk out of here, and place yourself in front of their cannon to save them the trouble of arranging you.'

More tugging of moustaches; her contempt was getting to them.

'Let me tell you something,' Manu said. 'It is my certain belief that if we can deliver *one* check to the British forces in the open field, we will win this war. All Hindustan will rise behind us, instead of waiting, as now, to see what will happen.'

'If it were possible,' Rao muttered.

'It can only be possible by meeting the British as equals, matching elan with elan, speed and fury with speed and fury. Now, as I have said, we know what they will do. They will come down the road from Konch, emplace their cannon, bombard our position, and then advance to make a frontal attack. As they do this, they will send a force either to the left or the right to attack us in the flank, and we know this will be their main attack; the frontal assault will be intended merely to pin us in our positions. On the opposite side to the flank attack they will maintain a body of cavalry, to charge the moment we show signs of retreating. It is very simple, is it not? How to beat an enemy in one easy lesson.'

Once again she looked round the faces of her officers, which remained glum. There could be no argument with her masterly exposition of the British tactics; they simply had no idea how to deal with them.

'So this is what we are going to do,' the rani said. 'Simply to march out from our defences and line up opposite them will not do. It will not alter their tactics, and they will simply cut us to pieces with their rifle and cannon fire. So we wait behind our defences, as usual, while they position themselves and start shooting their cannon. Everything will appear as normal, from their point of view. We wait, until the flanking body is detached, and is committed to its march. Then we attack in turn. We will have a picked body of men, a thousand strong, waiting behind our lines. And as soon as the British divide their force, this body will attack, frontally, the British position. This will put an end to their tactics. We will still have sufficient men to repel the flank attack, because that is all they will have to do, instead of having to fight both at the front and at the side, as in the past. The British frontal attack will be taken by surprise and driven back. The flank attack will be distracted and repelled. It is the British who will retreat, not us. It is the British guns we will capture. It is we who will gain the victory.'

There was a brief silence.

Then Tatya Tope asked, 'Who will command this counter-attack?'

It was clear that he was not going to.

'I will command it,' Dignaga said.

'No,' Manu said.

'But Highness . . .'

'I need you to lead our cavalry, and deliver the *coup de grâce* when the British are broken.'

He hesitated, then bowed.

And we also need you, I thought, just in case something goes wrong, because you are the man who can unlock the gates of Gwalior, as a last refuge.

'I must command my people, here,' Rao said. 'It is my sacred duty to my uncle.'

'Of course,' Manu said, her voice loaded with contempt. 'No one should attempt to deflect you from your sacred duty. Well, then . . .'

I held my breath. I could not believe she would lead the assault herself; that would mean her death.

'I will lead the attack, with your permission, Highness.' Mansur spoke quietly, but with enormous dignity.

Queen of Glory

Manu embraced Mansur, to his delight. 'You will bring great honour and glory to your name and that of the people of Jhansi,' she said. Her gaze swept the other officers, all of whom were looking distinctly embarrassed. 'And if everyone else fights as bravely as you will do, then victory will be ours.'

We made our preparations immediately. Mansur recruited his people, looking mainly to the Jhansi contingent, who were still eager for a fight, and drilled them in the tactics of advance and assault, in which they were quite inexperienced. Manu and I sat on our horses and watched them, Manu swelling with pride, and even I was feeling an increase in confidence.

But the other commanders were also working with a will, Dignaga drilling his horse and explaining their role, and Rao and Tatya Tope busy with creating a strong defensive position. Calpi was in fact very defensible, being a mass of walls, low to be sure when compared with Jhansi, but yet capable of holding up an attacking force, if resolutely held. That indeed was the question.

I, as usual, had the children to worry about. However confident I might be in our coming victory – and I was still not *that* confident – I could not bear the thought of the British, in their present bestial mood, breaking into the town and finding my daughter and the boy Rajah at the point of their bayonets. I therefore sent them off, with, as usual, Kujula as escort, to the village of Indurkee. This was selected by the rani herself, a clear indication of how her thoughts and plans for the immediate future were hardening, for Indurkee was not on the way towards Nana's last reported position, but was on the road to Gwalior itself. She also despatched letters to other rebel leaders she knew to be in the vicinity, such as Rahim Ali and Kugar Daulap Singh, requesting them to rendezvous at Indurkee, where there would be word – she dared not use the term instructions to two very masculine leaders – of her plans and whereabouts.

By the time they assembled, she anticipated having gained the victory which would turn the tide of the war – and establish her own credentials as a leader of men.

Konch had fallen on 7 May. Our dispositions at Calpi were in place three days later, and then, as before, we waited. This time the British did not delay so long, although our scouts told us that they had, as usual, suffered severely from the heat, most of the men being absolutely exhausted, and needing several days of rest before they could proceed. The scouts also told us, however, that reinforcements had come up, commanded by a General Maxwell. This brought their numbers up to very nearly our own, and Rao and Tatya Tope grew correspondingly nervous. But Dignaga and Mansur were still anxious to get at the enemy.

Too anxious, as it turned out.

The British cavalry appeared on the afternoon of 16 May, surveying our position through their glasses, as was their habit. We sent one or two shots after them, and they withdrew. But over the next few days the rest of the army came in sight, moving slowly to lessen the effects of the heat exhaustion to which the *feringees* were prone.

As they pitched their camp, within clear sight of us, Mansur became eager to launch his attack, his theory being that we could defeat them piecemeal. But Manu was against this. Her theory, equally arguable, was that if we did overrun the first, or even the second, limited camp, the survivors would simply withdraw to join the main body, and from then on would anticipate our changed tactics. She felt, and I agreed with her, that this had to be an all or nothing and decisive victory, not a series of skirmishes.

So we continued to wait, our people in a state of growing excitement. On the morning of 22 May the guns began to boom and the shells to fall amongst our houses. We replied in kind, and the twin cannonades continued throughout the day. We anticipated that, as before, the British would attack after an hour's bombardment, certainly before it got too hot. But they did not, and by mid afternoon the firing had become desultory.

'They will not attack today,' Tatya Tope said with some satisfaction.

'They will come at first light tomorrow,' Rao said. 'This is what they always do.'

'If they have definitely determined not to attack until then,' Dignaga said. 'Well . . .'

'I agree with the prince,' Mansur said. 'They expect nothing. Now is the time to attack *them*. We will take them by surprise.'

Manu looked from face to face, and then at me. No, I wanted to say. No, no, no. This is not our plan. We were to attack them when they were already committed to attacking us, when they had divided their forces. I also remembered too well the sortie led by Risaldar Khan outside of Jhansi, which had ended in disaster.

But I said nothing, not wishing to cause any discord between Manu and her officers.

'It might work,' Tatya Tope said. 'Surprise. That is the secret of success. And the men are ready for it.'

I wanted to point out that the British had never relied on surprise. They had always, as now, made their dispositions in full view of our people. Their victories had been won because of their discipline, their fire power . . . and the dreaded bayonets. I could also have pointed out that there could *be* no element of surprise in an attack at this moment, as the British would certainly see us coming long before we could get to them.

But again, I did not speak. My natural reluctance to do so was reinforced by Tatya's last words. Manu's people had spent the entire day under bombardment, but sustained by the expectation of an imminent attack. To leave them sitting behind their fortifications for another night would certainly have a diminishing effect upon morale.

Rao added his argument. 'Yes,' he said. 'Now is the hour. I feel it in my bones.'

Neither he nor Tatya had any intention of taking part in the coming assault, of course.

Manu drew a deep breath. 'Very well,' she said. 'When?'

'As soon as we hear their bugle, calling the men to their evening meal,' Mansur said.

He assembled his people, and they crouched behind the walls, glaring up the road at the British position. They would have about a mile to cross before they came to grips, and it would have to be done at speed if they were going to gain the British lines before our enemy could form ranks against them. Manu went amidst them talking to every man, encouraging them, promising victory.

Then came the bugle call. The time was six o'clock, but as it was late May it was still bright, and there were a couple of hours of daylight left, ample time to carry out the assault. Mansur waved his tulwar, and his men gave a great shout and ran forward.

Manu had returned to where I and the generals were waiting in the house we had appropriated as our headquarters. We levelled our telescopes to watch the advance, which began as a charge but slowed as the men ran out of breath. Yet they had covered more than half the distance separating the two armies before the first shot was fired from the British side. There were a plethora of bugle calls, and we could see men running to and fro, but yet only a scanty line had been formed before our people were upon them. Now there was for several minutes a general melee.

'Kill them, kill them!' Manu shouted, in a state of high excitement. I continued to peer through my glass, and felt a lump of lead starting to form in my stomach. The British were being driven back, but slowly, and as yet less than half their force was engaged. While behind the battle I saw more and more redcoats forming up, and I also saw the glint of bayonets in the setting sun.

'We are winning,' Tatya Tope said. He was concentrating on the conflict itself.

'There!' Manu shouted. 'They are broken.'

Yet another bugle call had rung out, and the defenders had indeed disengaged themselves and were running as fast as they could. Our men gave a great cheer and surged forward, and then saw what I had earlier observed. Facing them, and advancing towards them, was a glittering wall of bayonets, the men not running, but moving at a steady pace to the beat of their drums. Our people were already exhausted by their efforts, and this, together with their fear of the bayonet, caused them to check and perhaps insensibly move backwards.

'On!' Manu shouted. 'On! Kali, give them strength!'

They could not of course hear her, but it would have accomplished little had they been able to do so. The bayonets were now close, and Mansur's men broke and fled, streaming down the road towards us. Manu gasped, and clutched her left breast as if she would hold her very heart.

Dignaga ran down the steps and called for his horse. But there was nothing he could do to stem the rout. 'The plan was ill conceived from the outset,' Rao remarked.

I glared at him. Manu was still staring at her fleeing troops.

'They will come at us first thing in the morning,' Tatya Tope said. 'Do we retire, or do we try to hold them here?'

'If we retire, where can we go?' Rao asked. It was obviously what he wanted to do.

I turned away from them in anger at the way they had suddenly reduced Manu to a cipher, and stared along the road, once again feeling the lead filling my stomach. For again I was observing what they had not yet noticed. Their minds were so clouded with fighting in the leisurely, pre-conceived Indian fashion, that it had not occurred to them that the British, having gained this initial victory, and with darkness only an hour away, would not rest on their laurels, to resume the contest the next morning. But, having repulsed the Indian attack, the British were now advancing down the road, quickly, without running, while their horsemen covered their flanks and their guns again boomed.

Tatya Tope had at last looked. 'By the great god Rama!' he shouted. 'They are coming now.'

Rao also looked up. 'We must evacuate while there is time.'

Manu awoke from her reverie. 'Evacuate?' she cried. 'If they repulsed our attack, why should we not repulse theirs?'

The two generals looked at each other, so Manu decided to ignore them. She went down the stairs, with me at her shoulder. We ran out into the street, where all was confusion as the first of the defeated assault force returned.

'The British are coming,' they gasped. 'The British are coming.'

'Then we will stop them, here,' Manu said. 'Where is General Mansur?'

'Taken, Highness. He fell, wounded, and they dragged him away.'

Manu bit her lip, then drew her tulwar. 'Follow me,' she said.

Some of them did so, but not all. We ran up the street to the first line of defence. The sepoys crouched behind the wall, some firing their muskets, but most staring at the advancing British line. Thus far the enemy had not fired a shot, and they were not even shouting or cheering; the only sound was the tramp of their boots and the steady rhythm of their drums, for the guns had also fallen silent as the redcoats neared our position. The silent intensity of their advance was the more terrifying, and already some men were leaving their posts.

Manu stared at the bayonets, perhaps anticipating her last moment on earth. I certainly was, and could only hope that the first thrust would kill me instantly. But then, what of Alice? No doubt Vima would bring her up as her own, but what sort of a life would that be?

The redcoats stopped, at a distance of hardly more than fifty yards. For all of our firing, only a few of them had fallen. Now we watched as with great deliberateness they checked their priming and levelled their muskets. I threw my arms round Manu and forced her to the ground as the evening exploded into flame and smoke and noise. Men shrieked as the bullets crashed and tore their way into the masonry of the walls; these began to crumble before the onslaught.

It was too much for the already terrified sepoys. To a man those that remained standing turned and fled. We could do nothing else. I grasped Manu's arm, dragged her to her feet, and then pulled her down the street. The British had remained motionless for perhaps thirty seconds after they had delivered their volley, to see what, if anything, was left to face them. Now they gave a cheer and charged.

But the thirty seconds had given us a respite. We ducked down a side alley, gasping and panting as we ran, and encountered horsemen, with Dignaga at their head. Wihout a word he leaned from his saddle and scooped the rani up behind him. One of his men did the same for me, and we galloped out of the stricken town.

It was now growing dark, and although there was a crescendo of sound all around us, much of the firing was wild. Outside of the town, as outside Konch, we found ourselves in the midst of fleeing men, throwing away their weapons, and more significantly, again discarding their red tunics in a vain attempt not to be identified as sepoys.

'We must go back,' Manu shouted. 'We must go back.'

'To go back is to die,' Dignaga said.

'You do not understand. My belongings are there.'

He drew rein, as did his people; there were only a score of them left.

'In the magazine. I placed them there for safekeeping. My correspondence,' Manu said. 'My jewels. My money.'

But it was the correspondence that mattered. Not only did that include the precious letters from Gordon and Skene and Erskine, but from the other point of view, Manu's letters to and from – copies were kept of all her letters – other Hindu rulers, which could be used to implicate them in the rebellion.

Dignaga understood the gravity of the situation, and I know he would dearly have liked to return and see what could be rescued, or at least if the magazine could be blown up. But it was too late. Even in the gloom it could be seen that the redcoats had completely overrun the town and were forming ranks on the other side of it, while their cavalry were commencing to charge the fugitives. To attempt to return would be to die on the instant.

He turned his horse again. 'At least we have our lives.'

We reached Indurkee two days later, the British as usual being too exhausted to mount a prolonged pursuit. But that we were a shattered army could not be doubted. We were exhausted, hungry, thirsty, dirty . . . and utterly dispirited. Manu had to be helped from her horse, was half carried into the house chosen for her headquarters, and fell into a deep sleep. I only wanted to do the same, but could not until I had located Vima and Kujula and the children, then I too went to sleep, with Alice in my arms.

When I awoke, it was to a sense of panic. The town bustled . . . with panic. Manu continued to stay in bed. I don't think she wanted to get up. 'What am I to do, Emma?' she asked. 'They will not fight. They just will not stand and fight.'

'Perhaps, if you were in total command . . .'

'Can pigs fly?' She buried her face in her pillow.

I had to see to the children, and was breakfasting with them when Dignaga arrived. I gathered he had already been up for some hours.

'What is happening?' I asked him.

'There is no sign of the British.'

'But they will come. They always do. What of our people?'

'They were dispirited. But now they are much better. Rahim Ali is close, and with him Kugar Daulap Singh. They have fifteen hundred men, and some cannon.'

'Is that enough?'

'For our purpose. There is also news of Nana.'

I snorted.

'He is marching to join us with five thousand men and six guns.'

'Now,' I said. 'When it is too late.'

'It is never too late. I have been corresponding with Nana for some time.'

'Does the rani know this?'

'I did not wish to raise her hopes without certainty. But Nana will join with us to carry out his plan.'

'He has a plan?'

'Yes,' Dignaga said. 'It is my plan also. It has always been my plan.'

Now I was interested.

'Nana knows, as do I, that we have suffered from not possessing an impregnable base from which to carry on this war.'

'Did he not once have Cawnpore? Or Delhi? And what of Jhansi? Had he come to our aid in the defence of Jhansi we would not be here now, beaten and despondent.'

'None of those were impregnable. Delhi was too large, Cawnpore was a wreck, and Jhansi was really indefensible. It is our intention to take Gwalior.'

I stared at him in consternation. 'Just like that? Will not your cousin have something to say about it?'

'The Scindia must either join us or surrender to us.'

'Does he not have an army of several thousand men? And Gwalior?'

'I have been at work for the past year and more, sending my agents amongst his people, reminding them of where the paths of honour and glory lead. I do not think he can count on this army of his.'

I was completely surprised at what had been going on in the background while Manu and I had been fighting for our lives.

'And the rani's place in this?' I asked.

'We would be honoured to have her ride with us, leading her people.'

I dared take it no further than that. Here was at last a positive and concerted plan of action, however I might suspect that the man who really intended to profit from this manoeuvre was Dignaga himself. I could not blame him for that.

I went into the rani's room and sat beside her on her bed. She stirred, opened her eyes, saw who it was, and closed them again.

'Are the British here?' she asked.

'The British have not come. And perhaps they never will.'

Her eyes opened again, suspiciously.

I told her what Dignaga had said. She sat up. 'Can it be possible? That all our people will come together?'

'Better late than never,' I agreed.

'Is there news of the begum?'

'No, and I do not think we should count on her. She is only interested in Oudh. But if we can take Gwalior, and secure the allegiance of the Scindia's army, we should not need her.'

'Yes,' she said. She clapped her hands, and Mandar and Kashi, who had as usual been sleeping in a corner of the room, hurried forward. 'Help me dress.'

Miraculously – some might consider it an omen – her white mare had been amongst the horses brought to Indurkee, and this she was now able to mount. I mounted also, and we rode out, with Dignaga, to welcome the approaching troops. Manu embraced the princes from the saddle, and then led them in an inspection of her people. These were dusty and unwashed, lacked uniforms, and had a variety of weapons, regained from the dead and dying, but they were men who had fought the Raj, and were the more respected for that.

The next day Nana's outriders reached us, and that afternoon he arrived himself, seated on his elephant, surrounded by his lancers, his men marching behind him. They raised a cloud of dust that must have been visible for miles, and I had no doubt was reported to General Rose; he would certainly have sent scouts out to keep an eye on the situation.

When all were assembled, we mustered four thousand cavalry, seven thousand infantry, and twelve guns. Now this was an army, I felt, which could successfully oppose Rose, who as far as we knew had less than half this number. On the other hand, if we could secure Gwalior, we might dispose of an even larger army, and victory over the Raj could become a probability.

Certainly our leaders thought so. The next day they held a great parade of their troops, in which horses, elephants, infantry and guns marched past Nana, who stood on a hastily erected rostrum, Rao on his right and the rani on his left, with Tatya Tope, Jowalla Pershad, Balla Sahib and the other princes behind. Dignaga rode in the parade, commanding the Gwalior cavalry.

I stood behind the dignitaries, holding Damodar by the hand. Vima stood behind me with Alice.

'Are these soldiers all mine, Emma?' Damodar asked.

'Some of them, Highness,' I assured him. 'But they all mean to fight for your cause.'

Even if in a roundabout manner, I supposed. But how I wished news would now arrive that Rose's army was a march away. Then would this formidable force be turned against the proper foe. Needless to say, it did not happen.

The army moved out the next morning, the last day of May. Scouts had ranged behind us, and brought no news of any British movement towards us. I would have liked to see some kind of a rearguard, but Nana, who had taken full command, bristling with martial ardour now he did not have to face British bayonets, ordered his entire force to move on Gwalior. He invited me to ride in his howdah with him. Fortunately he also invited the rani, and even more fortunately, she accepted the invitation, so I was protected from any importunities.

Would you believe that after fourteen years in India this was the first time I had ever ridden on an elephant? It was not at all comfortable, the undulating movements being rather like in a small boat in a choppy sea, but my stomach eventually got used to it.

There was a lot to see. The cavalry were out in front and to either side, their blue and gold and green uniforms brilliant in the sunshine, their guidons floating proudly in the breeze. To either side of us marched the infantry, no less brilliant. Nana's men were mostly sepoys, and retained their red tunics. Their drill remained good, and they marched with great elan. Those who had fought at Konch and Calpi were no longer as well dressed, and were more ragged in their drill, but every man had been found a musket and a tulwar; there could be no doubt that they too were relieved that they would not again be facing the bayonets, at least for a while. The artillery brought up the rear, immediately in front of the baggage wagons, in which rode Vima and the children with Nana's harem. I had nowhere to leave them, and even I did not contemplate the possibility of a defeat on this occasion.

The march was made the more dramatic by the backdrop of mountains that surrounded our route. I could not believe there were not men on those peaks overseeing our advance, but no effort was made to interfere with our progress.

Our camp that night might have been the scene of a holiday, as our people danced and sang and played their instruments, and great quantities of food and drink were consumed. No one seemed the least interested in sleep, nor were any adequate sentries posted.

'Will these men fight, tomorrow?' I asked Dignaga.

'They will fight,' he assured me.

Manu came with me when I went to see the children to sleep. 'Tomorrow will be the greatest day of our lives,' she told Damodar.

'May I ride with you, Mother? Into battle?'

She was clearly tempted, but when she raised her head to look at me I gave a quick shake of the head.

'You will ride with me, in triumph, *after* the battle,' she said.

We went outside, and she held my hand. 'You have come a long way with me, Emma,' she said. 'Perhaps it has not always been the direction I would have chosen, but I would like to have you beside me, always, for the rest of my life.'

I did not tell her that Dignaga had the same idea. In any event, there could be only one reply. 'That is my desire also, Manu.'

'Well, then,' she said. 'Let us sleep in each other's arms, one last time, before we fight.'

Amazingly, to me at least, for all the drunken debauchery of the night, the army was astir with the first light, and there was a great rustling and clinking of armour and weapons.

'What will happen?' I asked Dignaga, when he joined me for breakfast. I did not know if he had sought me during the night, but I had been unavailable, and he did not look put out.

'We will assault and take the fortress,' he said.

'Just like that? An impregnable fortress?'

He tapped his nose. 'Did I not once tell you that I could unlock the secrets of Gwalior?'

I remembered our conversation on the road to Cawnpore, and felt a glow of confidence. I saw the children to their wagon, then mounted, and accompanied Manu to the front of the army, which was already moving out. It was 1 June 1858.

As usual we made a splendid array, Nana as ever on top of his elephant, his troops spread out to every side behind their cavalry screen. Although it was still early in the morning, it was already hot, and promised to be much more so before the end of this day. We marched for little more than an hour before coming in sight of the city, glowing in the still rising sun, the immense fortress perched on its hill above the houses. And, to our consternation, an army forming up, directly in front of us.

Nana leaned out of his howdah. 'What is this?' he shouted. 'What is happening?' Dignaga galloped up. 'It is the Scindia,' he said. 'He has come out to do battle.'

'Is he mad?' Nana asked, somewhat querulously.

'He is noble,' Dignaga replied, with dignity. 'He would spare his people the savagery of a siege and an assault.'

We watched the opposing forces wheeling into position.

'What are we to do?' Nana asked.

'Begin the battle, Great Sahib,' Dignaga said.

'How many people do you suppose he has?' Nana inquired.

'He is about equal to us in infantry,' Dignaga said. 'But he has only a few squadrons of cavalry. And we are equal in guns. The day is ours, Sahib.'

Nana chewed his lip, and the Scindia's guns opened fire. Nana hastily commanded his mahout to withdraw the elephant. This made sense, as regards the beast, for these huge animals not only present an easy target but are also prone to panic and can wreck a general's dispositions. But the manoeuvre also effectively ended Nana's control of the battle.

Although this was no doubt to the good. Our own guns opened in reply, and for a brief while there was an exchange of cannon balls, which did no great damage to either side, although I felt the rani was exposing herself needlessly as she insisted upon staying close to Dignaga, who was in front of his troops. Naturally I had to stay with her.

'With your permission, Your Highness,' Dignaga said, 'I would put an end to this.'

'Can you?' Manu asked.

Dignaga pointed. 'His guns are inadequately protected. If we can take them, the day is ours.'

'Can you do this?'

'Give the word. You are a commanding general.'

Manu looked left and right, as if uncertain of her exact position. But Nana was now behind his forces and had quite lost touch with them, Tatya Tope, Rao and Jowalla Pershad were with the main body in the centre of the field, and Rahim Ali and Kugar Daulap Singh were commanding their own contingents, and no doubt, like everyone else, awaiting orders.

'Then take those guns, Prince Dignaga,' Manu said. 'If you can.'

She and I pulled our horses to one side, and Dignaga led his men, now once again recruited up to two thousand sabres, including the Jhansi contingent, out from our ranks and across the open space, not much more than half a mile, that separated the two armies.

I doubt there can be a more inspiring sight in war that that of a full blown cavalry charge. The horses galloped along, nostrils flaring, tails streaming behind them, bodies heaving, while their riders shouted their determination to destroy the foe. Certainly both the enemy and our own people were taken aback by this unexpected manoeuvre, and stared at the hurtling cavalry for some seconds. Then the Gwalior gunners realized what the horsemen were after, and attempted to turn their pieces to confront the foe. But there was no time for that; the cannon had all been directed to the centre of our position, and before they could be adjusted Dignaga and his men were upon them.

The tulwars flashed as they were swung, blood flew, visible even at a distance, and those of the gunners who were not cut down fled. Bugles blew, and a body of Gwalior horse galloped into a counter attack. With their horses blown, Dignaga's men could only await the coming shock, and my heart pounded most painfully as I watched the two forces come together with a huge clash of arms. That battle might have gone either way, had not at that moment, a division of infantry, some two thousand strong, left the Gwalior ranks and advanced towards us on the double. There was a tremendous stir in our army, and several shots were fired, but then our own bugles rang out to stop the shooting as it was observed that the Gwalior men had thrown away their banners and were advancing beneath white flags.

As this became apparent, a burst of cheering rose from our people, and equally a moan of anger and despair escaped the Scindia's ranks. A few moments later his headquarters staff, which undoubtedly included himself, could be seen spurring from the field. The horsemen fighting Dignaga now disengaged to follow their king, and the rest of the army was close behind, streaming away from the field, and not back to the citadel, which could still have been held by determined men, but into the open country to the north-west.

'A victory,' Manu said. 'A victory!' she shouted, and rode towards the disintegrating enemy.

I could not help but wish that it could have been gained over the British army, but it was undeniably a victory. I rode behind her, and Dignaga came back to us.

Manu embraced him from the saddle. 'You are a man amongst men. But yet, you were fortunate, in that those people deserted just as you were attacked.'

'Fortunate, Highness?' Dignaga asked. 'Did I not arrange it, that the desertion would take place the moment I charged with my cavalry?' He smiled. 'They were a little late, to be sure.'

We laughed with him, our triumph complete.

Needless to say, the battle won, Nana returned to the front of his troops. He inquired who had given the command for the cavalry to charge, and being told it had been the rani, embraced her enthusiastically while the army cheered. He then led us in triumph into the city. Fortunately, as there were no Europeans left in Gwalior, and no scores to settle – our quarrel had been with the Scindia, not his people – there was no looting and no massacre. Besides, by now a good third of our army was composed of Gwalior men. Their families lined the streets to cheer them, and us, as we marched through with flags flying and drums beating.

The gates of the fortress were thrown wide, and once again, to my great relief, there were only servants left; the Scindia had sent his family to safety the moment he had learned of our approach – no doubt he had had some inkling that his camp was rife with treachery.

Thus we entered unopposed into one of the great palaces of India. A grim fortress from without, inside it made the palace at Jhansi look like a hovel, not only in its size, for the ceilings were higher, the corridors wider, the rooms larger, than anything we had seen before – the centre courtyard, littered with fountains and carved representations of the tiger, was very nearly as large as all of Jhansi itself – but the appointments were of an opulence none of us, save perhaps Dignaga, had ever previously encountered. Apart from the palace itself, its surroundings were of unimaginble splendour, with endless brilliant gardens, a menagerie of tigers and other wild bears, and a perfect army of elephants. Manu, whose experience was actually very limited – she had known only Benares and Jhansi – was quite overwhelmed, and wandered through the rooms and apartments with her mouth open.

Nana and his officers pretended to take it all very much in their stride, but they were principally interested in the treasury. Here we beheld riches beyond our wildest dreams, stacks of golden ingots, silver arms and armour, inlaid swords and pistols, and chests filled with jewels and precious stones.

'With these riches you can finance the greatest army in the world, Sahib,' Jowalla Pershad said.

'You mean the new maharajah can do that,' Nana said, jovially.

All our heads turned towards Dignaga; I was the first to observe that Nana was not looking in this direction, but was instead regarding his nephew.

Rao realized that not everyone was in his uncle's confidence, and determined at once to seize the initiative and distract us all from the real issue. He went to one of the huge chests, where his eye had alighted on what he sought. 'Then,' he announced loudly, 'my first act will be to reward the great lady whose command for the cavalry to charge gave us the victory. Her Highness, the Rani of Jhansi.'

Manu looked quite embarrassed as Nana held her arm and escorted her forward, while Rao took from the chest quite the largest pearl I think any of us had ever seen, suspended from a golden chain. This chain he now placed over her head and settled it on to her neck, the pearl itself resting on her tunic between her breasts, while all around, myself included, cheered and clapped.

Dignaga cheered as loudly as anyone, but his eyes were watchful, and when the applause died down, he stepped forward. 'A fitting reward for a gallant lady,' he said. 'But should not I have made the presentation?'

'You?' Nana asked. 'You are not the maharajah.'

'I am the Scindia,' Dignaga said.

'It is my decision that the honour be given to my nephew.'

'You have no right to do this.'

'I have every right. As of this moment I am the peshwa. This title, this authority, is mine by lineage, as I am the son of the last peshwa, and by the right of arms, as I am commander of the armies of Hindustan.'

I thought that a bit rich, coming from a man who had never actually led his armies into battle. But the other generals were applauding.

Save for Dignaga. 'And this gives you the right to place an usurper on the throne of Gwalior?' he demanded.

'This gives me the right to do whatever I choose. But my decision has been taken on the soundest of grounds. Rao Sahib is related to the House of Scindia by marriage.'

'And I am a prince of that house, by birth.'

'You have never been recognized as being in the line of succession,' Nana said. 'More, you have defied your cousin in leading your men against him. To the Scindia, you are an outlaw.'

'I did this to fight for Hindustan. To fight for you.'

'And you will be honoured for it, by the new maharajah. But for you to sit on the throne would cause dissent amongst your people, between those who will regard you as a patriot, and those who will regard you as a traitor to your cousin, a rebel against his rule. Come now, Your Highness . . .' he spoke to Rao, 'what post of honour will you give Prince Dignaga?'

Rao looked around the expectant faces, and drew a deep breath. 'In view of the events of today, it is my intention to give the command of my cavalry to her Highness the Rani of Jhansi.'

There was a moment of stunned silence; this was a man's world being invaded by a twenty-two-year-old girl. Then a storm of cheering again broke out.

Dignaga looked at their faces, while I could read his mind. He had been completely outmanoeuvred, and his position was now totally undermined as Manu, all beaming smiles said, 'Let me embrace you, great prince; you will be my right hand and together we shall ride to victory!'

Dignaga looked as if he might have protested further, but decided against it. Again, I could follow his reasoning. He was, at this moment, at a considerable disadvantage, simply in terms of numbers, and he knew there was a certain amount of truth in what Nana had said, in that he could not be sure of the support of a majority of the Gwalior people. He also understood that Rao was right when he said that the British had still to be defeated. In this regard, and most important, he had been given a vital role, and he had to feel that if he could distinguish himself, and protect Gwalior from conquest by the common enemy, he might receive sufficient support from his own people to make his claim to the throne irresistible.

I would also like to feel that he realized he and his allies could only defeat the British by standing shoulder to shoulder; now was not the time to introduce dissent into the Indian command. Besides his acceptance meant that he would be working closely with the woman he adored.

All of these conflicting emotions were well understood by the rani. When he went to her, she embraced him most tenderly.

'I and my Jhansi people, will fight the more bravely knowing you will be at their head,' she told him.

She had entirely regained her spirits since the defeat of the Scindia, just as I could see that she was taking in her new surroundings, appreciating them and allowing them to spark her own imagination.

'If what we hear is true,' she said, when we had left the other princes, 'and Jhansi has been destroyed, it will have to be rebuilt.'

Clearly she had Gwalior in mind as a model.

She ruffled Damodar's hair. 'I will build you a palace fit for a maharajah,' she promised. 'When we have beaten the British.'

To this end all of her energies were now concentrated, far more so than Nana's entourage, who seemed to be intent upon enjoying the pleasures of Gwalior as long as possible, without caring much about the immediate future. And indeed for some days we were left in peace, were content to let her make her own arrangements, in conjunction with Dignaga.

This euphoria did not last very long, as the British were determined to restore the Scindia to his throne, and the following week we learned of a significant development. It appeared that Sir Hugh Rose, whose health, like that of so many Britishers, had suffered due to his constant campaigning in such a debilitating climate, had been intending to retire after his victories at Jhansi, Konch and Calpi, but had been requested to stay on and finish the job, as it were — Calcutta was well aware that all of the eggs they wanted, Nana, Rao Sahib, Tatya Tope and the rani, were in the one basket of Gwalior, and assumed that a victory here could end the war at one stroke.

'If he dies, so much the better,' Nana declared.

To our surprise, and relief, Rao, now in effective command of the Hindu army, proved a much more energetic and determined leader than his uncle had ever done. He recruited every available man, including most of the Scindia forces who had fled the battle but now returned, to virtually double the size of his army, and then summoned his principal officers to a conference, 'Our spies tell us that Rose commands some fifteen thousand men. That is a formidable army, but as we now number thirty thousand the advantage is still with us. However, I am aware that our numbers count for little in the open field when opposed to British discipline and firepower. We will therefore fight behind the barricades we have erected around the city.' He looked around our faces; he well knew that both the rani and Tatya Tope would have preferred a more active defence.

'That way,' he went on, 'if we were to be defeated, we have the fortress at our backs as a last resort. But it is not my intention to fight a purely defensive battle. I shall command the centre, with fifteen thousand men and twenty-four cannon. Jowalla Pershad, you will be my chief of staff. We will stand on the defensive behind our barricades and draw the British on to us. You, Tatya Tope, will command the right wing with ten thousand men. You will maintain your position until the British are fully committed to their attack on the centre. Then you will advance your people to assault their flank. You, Queen Lakshmi Bai, with your five thousand horsemen, will form our left wing. You will have two batteries; twelve cannon. You will keep your men . . .' he smiled, 'and your women, in hand and out of sight, but you will position your guns to enfilade the British advance. Only after Tatya Tope has launched his counter-attack, will you charge to take the fully committed British in their right flank. Your Highness, I would remind you that your business is to command, not to die at the head of your people. Prince Dignaga will lead the charge. Please remember this.'

Manu snorted. 'Because I am a woman.'

'Because you are a general. Your business is directing your people into battle, but you must be there to extricate them if things go badly, or if there has to be a change of plan.'

Manu glared at him, but she knew he was speaking sense. In any event, there was a great deal to be done. We went down to inspect the ground that was to be our position. We had no desire to station our people in the city itself, as close packed houses were no place for cavalry, but beyond the walls there were the cantonments used by the British army when it had been stationed there. These were deserted now, but were made up both of solid walls and open spaces, ideal for cavalry to manoeuvre, charge from, and then use as a base to regroup. Here we did our training, for the rani still held to the opinion, valid enough, that if the British could once be made to lose their discipline, they could be defeated. This had in fact happened on more than one occasion during the Sikh War ten years earlier, and she was confident of making it happen again here, now that she was in command of at least one wing of the army.

Thus we placed our people, practised, and trained, and prepared. Our morale was high, partly certainly from the easy victory gained over the Scindia forces, in circumstances and against foes we could hardly hope to have repeated against the redcoats, to be sure, but also partly from a feeling that we were at last going to win.

As usual, it took just under a fortnight for the British to arrive. It was the afternoon of 15 June when our scouts rode in to say that the enemy were within ten miles of us. Instantly all was put into readiness, the men issued with additional supplies of bullets and powder, the horses groomed a last time.

In our cantonment we were even visited by Nana, in a highly nervous state. 'When will you come into the fortress?' he asked.

'Our business is here,' Manu said. 'If we succeed in throwing their attack into disorder, will you come out?'

He pulled his beard.

'The gods ride with you, Highness,' Tatya Tope said.

'But if you need to withdraw,' Nana said. 'We shall be waiting for you.'

Which entirely convinced me that he had already made up his mind to flee the moment he felt matters were going badly. But as the rani seemed to be prepared to trust him, and embraced him most tenderly, I said nothing. Manu was, however, fully aware that tomorrow might be the most important day of her life, and she became quite agitated when, just before dusk, we saw a group of plumed officers sitting their horses on a hillock perhaps a mile away from our position, surveying us through their telescopes.

She levelled her own glass in reply. 'That man in the middle,' she said. 'Is that not Rose?'

I focussed my own telescope. 'Yes.'

'He haunts me,' she said. 'He hanged my father.'

'We don't know that, Highness,' I protested. 'As I understand what Mankad told us, the general was not present when Maropant Tambe was killed.'

'He was in command,' Manu said bitterly. 'The British say I am responsible for the massacre at the City Fort, because I was the rani, and must take the blame for anything done by my people. He is the commanding general, thus he must take the blame for anything done by his people. Tomorrow he must die. But . . .' She looked from me to Dignaga, on her other side. 'In case something goes wrong, under no circumstances must I be captured. If this happens, I command you both to shoot me dead.'

I swallowed, but Dignaga nodded. 'You will not be captured, Highness.'

'Neither must the British ever lay hands upon my body,' she said. 'Dead or alive. Swear this.'

'I swear this,' Dignaga said.

'And you, Emma.'

I took a deep breath. 'I swear, Highness.'

'Good. Now let us eat.'

After the meal, she seemed calmer, but yet made every preparation for any eventuality. She spent some time at her devotions, then allowed Damodar to help her clean her weapons, a chore she always undertook herself. Then she sat with me. 'In a few months time, we will have known each other for nine years. Tell me truly, Emma, what was your first impression of me? Truly, mind.'

'I thought you were the most beautiful girl I had ever seen,' I said. 'But I was afraid of the intensity of your personality.'

She smiled. 'I think my husband was, too.'

'And many others. Many still are, afraid of you.'

'It is necessary, for a queen to instil fear in her subjects,' she said. 'But I wish also to be loved. When this war is over, I will make my people love me.'

'I think they already do,' I said. 'Will you tell me what was your first impression of me?'

She laughed. 'I was afraid of you, too. I thought you were too close to a goddess, with your height and body and your hair.' She took some of the auburn strands and sifted them through her fingers. 'Such hair. I never thought that I would be able to love you. But I do.'

'Do you regret anything about your life?'

She sighed. 'That my husband could not love me, and could not give me children. Had I had a son of my own loins, we might not be here now.'

'The rebellion would still have happened,' I suggested.

'Yes,' she said. 'Yes. That is karma. There is no good in attempting to resist it. We are here because fate has willed it. Thus we must make the best of it. We must win. But Emma, I wish you to remain here.'

'I cannot do that,' I protested. 'Save only for your first campaign, against the Pathans, I have been at your side in every battle.'

'And acquitted yourself nobly. But don't you see, you have to be responsible for the children. Should anything happen to me, you have to care for Damodar until he is old enough to rule.'

'And should, which God forbid, anything happen to you, have you not made me promise to . . . attend to your body?'

'To cremate me, immediately. Make no mistake about that. Yes, you must be there. But you must not take part in the battle. You must survive.'

'Your life is more important than mine.'

'My life is dedicated to my people. If they are to fight tomorrow, I must lead them.' She squeezed my hands.

In my nine years at Manu's side, and for all her immediate indications of physical happiness, I had never known her in so sombre a mood. Even when she had contracted the dread disease of smallpox she had never lost her zest for life, her determination that there were so many things to be done, and that she was the woman to do them. Certainly over the past few weeks I had observed a certain pessimism in her moods, but I had put this down, very reasonably, to the murder of her father, and the inability of her army to check the British advance. But the pessimism had been accompanied by a growing streak of steel, a determination that one day she would win her struggle. Now it seemed that she was accepting the possibility, perhaps even the probability, of another defeat, and this would be the final one; the princes had no hope of ever concentrating a larger or better army than this one. Thus it was a defeat she was determined not to survive, as there would be nothing left for her.

I slept with Alice in my arms. She was now four years old, an enchantingly lovely child. I felt I had never had the opportunity really to know her; her life, and mine, had been in a constant turmoil since she had been a year old. But for all the comings and goings of the past few months, she remained a happy child, basking in the love of both Manu and myself, and relying upon the loyal strength of Vima.

At dawn, as was my custom, I sent both of the children, and Vima, to safety, in this case the fortress. Again as usual, I deputed Kujula to go with them, but for the first time that I could remember he refused to obey me.

'I would fight this day at your side, Memsahib,' he said. 'Your daughter and the rajah will be safe in the fortress. They have the whole army to protect them.'

I embraced him, and then Vima, and waved Alice and Damodar out of sight.

To my surprise, I found that both Mandar and Kashi had also refused to seek safety and, dressed like their mistress as men and bearing weapons, were mounted immediately behind Manu. She herself was fully accoutred but, incongruously, if strikingly, wore her pearl necklace, as well as all her jewellery, her gold bangles and her diamond rings. With her gold coloured tunic, her green jodhpurs and turban, and carrying as always her tulwar and two revolvers, she made a spectacular sight. But also, I was afraid, a most obvious target, especially as she was riding her white mare.

Also mounted and waiting was Dignaga. 'What are your orders, Highness?' he asked.

For the guns were already firing, and the British were advancing. The guns from the fortress were replying in a desultory fashion. Manu levelled her glass at the enemy position, and then touched Dignaga on the arm. 'Is that not your cousin's standard?'

Dignaga looked. 'Yes. It is. He has come back to reclaim his city.'

'Or been brought back by the British to lend his name to their enterprise. He will have to be brought to trial after the battle. But for now, we must be patient.'

The red-coated infantry were advancing in close order, in their usual inexorable fashion, firing their volleys, reloading, and then advancing again. Regularly one of them fell, but the forward march never slackened. The bayonets were fixed, and even at a distance we could almost see the tremor rippling through the Indian ranks. But the redcoats had not yet reached the earthworks when, to our consternation, Tatya Tope launched his attack, his men moving forward with huge shouts.

'The fool!' Dignaga cried. 'He has compromised our position!'

For with the utmost coolness and discipline a detachment of redcoats turned away from the main battle and formed up to deliver a succession of devastating volleys.

'This will turn out badly,' Dignaga observed, and looked at Manu, who chewed her lip. Her orders had been to hold her position until the British attack had been met and held and was beginning to waver. But the attack was not being held, and there was no sign of any wavering. 'Yes, she said. 'It is up to us to save the day. Prince Dignaga, leave me my Jhansi horse as a reserve in case you have to retreat. Take the remainder of our command and charge the enemy.'

'Yes, Highness.' Dignaga's eyes glowed. He drew his tulwar, presented it to the queen, then raised it to his lips and kissed it. A quick glance at my petrified features, then he raised his sword above his head. 'To me!' he shouted, and cantered out from our shelter. 'Colonel Kapoor, you will hold your men until further orders.'

Actually, half of the surviving Jhansi contingent, some seven hundred strong, were women, and they as well as their commander, who had succeeded Mansur, looked extremely put out to be left behind, as the other four thousand horsemen trotted out and formed up behind the prince. He pointed his tulwar at the battle, and they gave a great shout and rode forward.

Manu raised her tulwar to them as they passed us, and they gave another cheer.

At this moment we were joined by Balla Sahib, who had ridden across from the main battle. 'The Rao wishes your people to charge,' he said.

'That is what they are doing,' the rani replied, but she was not to be distracted from the situation. 'The batteries!' she snapped. 'We need to resite those guns, or they will be firing into our own people.' Her only immediate aides were myself, Kujula and the two maids, and she understood that none of us knew anything about siting artillery, so she wheeled her horse and rode away from the cantonments to where our twelve guns were waiting, in a row, and firing at the British forces, but ceasing now as our own cavalry rode in front of them. Indeed, the gunners were craning their necks to watch the approaching clash.

I knew there was no use trying to restrain her, and so tried to see what was happening. Dignaga's horsemen broke into the enemy ranks, waving their tulwars but as they did so, I heard a bugle call, and turning to my left saw, debouching from behind the original British line, a large body of cavalry, perhaps two thousand strong. Half of these were the lancers, weapons already couched. The other half was composed of those light horsemen known as hussars, from their bright uniforms, flowing capes, and tasseled busbies. These carried sabres, but also carbines.

I realized that Rose had anticipated our manoeuvre, no doubt from the fact that our cavalry had been conspicuously absent during the early part of the battle, and had kept his own horse back to await events. Now they were charging towards the rear of Dignaga's people, and I could not doubt that the arrival of the lancers, mounted on powerful horses and armed with so fearful a weapon, would be decisive.

I was in a quandary. I had no military experience and no command. But I knew our people had to launch a counter charge. I looked for Balla for the necessary authority, but he had ridden off. Then, to my great relief, Colonel Kapoor came to me. 'We must charge those men, Memsahib. Her Highness . . .'

Manu was still resiting the guns some two hundred yards away, unaware of what was happening behind her.

'Yes,' I said. 'Please charge, Colonel Kapoor. I know the rani would wish it.'

He saluted and rode off, and a moment later the Jhansi horse gave a cheer as they received their orders, and moved forward in a body, men and women stirrup to stirrup. Manu heard the shouts and turned towards us. She took in the situation at a glance, and spurred her mare to join her people, waving her tulwar.

The enemy had actually ignored us as they hurtled by, but those hussars nearest to us could not help but see the slight figure on the white mare, at that moment isolated. Undoubtedly, they knew who it had to be although for the most part they ignored her to continue their charge. But now several of them broke away from their ranks and galloped across the front of our people, still some distance behind them and unable to stop them from a distance because they were armed only with tulwars, while to my horror I saw one of the hussars sheathing his sword and drawing his carbine from its scabbard behind his saddle.

'Haste!' I shouted at Kujula, and we kicked our horses forward, followed by the two girls. 'Manu!' I screamed.

She turned towards me, then saw the approaching horsemen and

drew her tulwar. But they were very close and their leader levelled
his carbine. He was still at a full gallop, but my heart constricted as
I saw Manu jerk in the saddle, and a splodge of red appear on the
gold of her tunic.

'Manu!' I screamed again.

Manu's face was twisting in pain, as the horsemen reached her.
She drew her revolver and with a single shot brought down the man
who had wounded her. But now the rest were up to her, surrounding
her, and one of the hussars drove his sword into her back with such
force that the blade emerged beside her pearl.

The Rani of Jhansi fell from the saddle.

The Eternal Legend

I reached the scene. By now our charging cavalry were up to us,
and the hussars hastily made off. But the man who had struck the
fatal blow was slow to turn, preferring to draw his carbine as he
saw me. I levelled my revolver; at thirty yards I could not miss, and
he went down. Then I leapt from the saddle, fearing the worst.
Kujula also dismounted, and between us we reached Manu's body
and raised it up. She had fallen on her face, blood welling from the
dreadful wound in her back. We withdrew the embedded sword and
turned her over. Her eyes were open, but blood was also dribbling
from her mouth.

'Damodar,' she whispered. 'Damodar is your charge.'

Then her eyes became sightless.

I was utterly paralysed, with grief and a sense of the world having
come to an end. That it should, or could, end so suddenly and like
this had never occurred to me.

Hooves drummed, and Kapoor joined us, but I waved him away.
'Win the battle,' I told him. 'I will attend the queen.'

Kujula lifted Manu's lifeless body and carried it to the shade of
a mango tree just outside the wall. The battle continued to rage
around us, but none of us took the least heed of it.

'It is here,' Kashi said, and to my consternation I saw that there
was already a pyre of branches and straw. 'Her Highness had us build
it last night,' she explained. 'And soak it in thin oil.'

I suddenly realized that she had resolved not to survive a defeat. But surely she had not anticipated dying while the result of the battle was undecided. Now . . .

Tears rolled down my cheeks as Kujula laid Manu's body, as tenderly as if she were still living, on the wood and straw, and stepped back.

'Her jewellery?' Mandar asked.

'Dies with her. Kujula!'

A camp fire still glowed. He thrust a branch into it to create a flaming a torch. This he handed to me. I drew a long breath, then thrust it beneath Manu's body. The fire burned so fiercely that in only a few minutes it was consumed. The pearl, lying between her breasts, glowed to the end.

I think that, as the flames licked around that so beautiful body, that unforgettable face, we all went a little mad. My brain continued to be paralysed, and I was only dimly aware of much movement about me. I raised my head and looked at Dignaga, blood stained and dishevelled. 'The battle is lost,' he said. 'The queen . . .'

I gestured at the flames. He stared at them, Then at me. Then he left my side, without a word or a touch, mounted his horse, and dashed back into the fray. I never saw him again, or his body. I know that Mandar and Kashi, screaming angry defiance, found swords and ran at the enemy, Kashi, a girl hardly less beautiful than her mistress, stripping off her clothes as she did so, that she died, naked.

I was surrounded by shots and shouts, and finally was able to tear my gaze away from the now almost totally disintegrated corpse, and stood up, just in time to see Kujula fall, shot through the chest as he tried to defend me. Then I was surrounded by white-skinned, red-jacketed men, whooping their triumph. I expected to die, and only slowly realized that I would be forced to undergo another trial first. But this was prevented by the arrival of an officer.

'The widow Hammond!' he announced, no less triumphantly.

I raised my head.

'I am she.'

'And where is your foul mistress?'

I pointed at the pyre. 'If you mean the Rani of Jhansi, she lies there.'

I was manacled, and led to the rear.

'My children,' I said. 'I wish to see my children.'

'What you wish, and what you shall have, are two different things,' the officer told me.

There were no other prisoners, and I was left to myself for several hours, being fed in that time some water and a crust of bread. At least I was not ill-treated; indeed my guards, a couple of brawny Scots lads, seemed to hold me in some awe. My concern for what might have happened, or be happening, to Alice was all but unbearable, and in fact I attribute the fact that I did not actually go mad during that day mainly to the state of shock I was in from the thought that so beautiful, so energetic, so confident, so *vital* a piece of humanity could be in an instant reduced to a lump of lifeless flesh, and then within another few minutes to a heap of ashes, left my senses absolutely bereft of the power to think, and almost of the power to feel.

Added to which was the almost certain death of Dignaga, no less beautiful, no less talented, no less *vital*. The two most splendid people I had ever known, both gone in a few minutes.

The battle continued most of the day, the firing only dying down towards afternoon. I was surrounded by bustling movement, but none of it seemed directed at me, and it was dusk before General Rose stood above me.

'Well, Mrs Hammond,' he said. 'The end, eh?'

I raised my head. 'The prince, and my child . . .'

'Your daughter is safe. As is the young rajah.'

'Thank God for that. May I see them, please?'

'Not at this time. They are being taken care of.'

I sighed. But I supposed I could have expected nothing better. 'My maid was with them. Is she . . .?'

'She is in custody.'

I licked my lips. 'Was she . . .?'

'No,' he said.

Another sigh, this time of relief.

'This was an altogether more orderly affair than at Jhansi,' he said. 'A restoration rather than a revenge, I suppose one could say. The Scindia once again sits on his throne. It is only sad that he has lost all his treasure.'

'You don't mean . . .'

He gave a grim smile. 'Oh, yes, Mrs Hammond. Your friend Nana made his escape, as usual, taking with him the contents of the Scindia's treasury. But he won't get far.'

The bastard, I thought. How easily could Manu also have escaped, and lived to fight another day. But she had chosen to fight this day, like the heroine she was.

'Tell me what happened to your mistress,' Rose invited.

'She was attempting to resite her artillery when she was killed by one of your hussars.'

'No one has claimed that honour.'

'I should think not. I shot him, immediately.'

'You admit to this?'

'I was endeavouring to save my mistress's life. Unfortunately . . .'

'What have you done with her body?'

'I cremated her, in accordance with her instructions. She did not wish it to fall into your hands.'

'Did she suppose I would desecrate her body?'

'She could only make her judgement on the evidence of recent events.'

He flushed.

'And at the very least,' I added, 'you would have been required to exhibit it, probably naked, if only to prove that she was dead.'

'And now it shall never be certain.' He sighed. 'I would have given much to see her, just once. Was she as beautiful as is claimed?'

'She was far more beautiful that you can possibly imagine.'

'And she had the seeds of genius, as well as the steadfast perseverance necessary for success. Do you know, it is my opinion, that had she been placed in overall command of the rebel forces from the beginning, we might well have lost this war.'

'Why, Sir Hugh,' I said. 'I do believe that, after all, you are an honest man.'

Another flush. 'I am told that she was quite young.'

'Lakshmi Bai was twenty-two years old.'

'Twenty-two? My God! What a waste.'

'The rani did not consider it so. She was a queen, fighting aggression with her people, in the best traditions of Hindu royal womanhood. It was her karma.'

'Karma,' he mused. 'I had forgotten that you have become a subscriber to the Hindu beliefs yourself.'

'Sir Hugh, after what I have seen these last nine years, and especially this last year, I have no desire to subscribe, as you put it, to any belief at all, save that of common humanity.' We gazed at each other, and I asked, 'What is going to happen to me?'

'Ah,' he said. 'Do you know, you are the only prominent member of the rebels we have managed to capture? So far.'

'And thus, I assume, I am to be fired from the mouth of a cannon?'

'My dear lady, the images you conjure up. Do you truly suppose that we, your own people, are barbarians?'

'I am afraid, sir, that in view of everything I have seen and heard during this past year, you will have to persuade me that you are not. When in the mood.'

'And I am afraid that I can only say, touché. But we can be generous in victory. However . . . you will have to stand trial, I am afraid.'

'And my child?'

'She will be taken into care, until after the trial. Then . . . well, we shall have to see.'

Because then, I thought, she may well be an orphan.

It was fashionable, on the British side, to adopt Rose's point of view and assume that the rebellion effectively ended with the recapture of Gwalior. This was quite untrue. The rebellion dragged on for another year, while Tatya Tope conducted a guerilla campaign with a skill and a determination which if he had shown earlier might have changed the course of history. It was not until May 1859 that he was finally cornered and executed.

The British never did capture Nana. In fact, neither they nor anyone else has the faintest idea what happened to him. He went north, and disappeared. The British naturally have put it about that he perished in miserable solitude on some mountain side, but if indeed he had the Scindia's treasure with him, he very probably found refuge in Nepal and is probably still existing, as always, in the lap of luxury.

His relatives vanished with him.

The Moulvie got himself killed in some minor engagement. But the indestructible begum triumphed in a manner none of us was able to achieve. She was unable to regain the throne of Oudh, but she made her peace with the Raj and also retired to Nepal with all her fortune, still referring to her son as the Nawab.

And me? For several months I languished in a Calcutta gaol, seeing hardly a soul except gaolers, and being allowed no visit even from Alice.

The exception was Mr Lang, who was able to assure me that my child was well, although missing me, that Vima was still her nurse, and that Damodar would be granted a pension, although there was no question of his ever being allowed to rule Jhansi. For the time being they were in the care of one of the few English families prepared to be sympathetic.

Sadly, Mr Lang told me that although tempers had largely cooled, the rani was still execrated as the wickedest of women in England.

'She was a heroine,' I protested, 'who fought for her people. And died for them.'

He nodded. 'I believe that in the course of time she will be recognized as such. She already is, here in India. In fact, I suspect a great deal of the emotion with which she is regarded arises from sheer fear; she was the most formidable of all the antagonists of the Raj. I happen to know that General Rose, in his report, suggests very strongly that had the other, male, rebel leaders had the sense to place her in overall command of their forces, the rebellion would not have ended so quickly or so successfully, if it ended at all.'

'He said the same thing to me. But I am glad he has made it official.'

'Yes. I wish he were still here to appear in court, but unfortunately he has been invalided home. However, although the charges against you are severe, you have friends, amongst whom I am proud to count myself, who are working on your behalf, and are not pessimistic about your prospects. I can assure you, for a start, that there is no question of you being executed. Mr Canning has determined that the bloodshed has to stop, and every sentence of death has been commuted. They are calling him Clemency Canning. Unfortunately there is a considerable body of what appears to be irrefutable evidence to your wholehearted support of the rani, and your role in the massacres at Jhansi and Cawnpore.'

'The first I will always be proud of, the other two are calumnies. I was not present when the Jhansi massacre took place. I was in Cawnpore.'

'That is it.'

'Where I did everything in my power to save the lives of the women and children.'

He sighed. 'Unfortunately, all those who might testify to the truth of your claim are either dead or fled. However, we may, I'm sure, place our trust in the innate British sense of justice and fair play.'

He meant well, but I had not seen a great deal of British justice and fair play over the past few years, and in my position, and the conditions in which I was being forced to live, I found it very difficult to be anything other *than* pessimistic. While my loneliness at being separated from Alice, and my continued worry as to how she was faring, added to my grief over the deaths of Manu and Dignaga, was all but unbearable.

I feared the worst, for both of us, and when, a week later, the door of my cell was opened, and a man stood there, a sheet of paper in his hand, I started to my feet, supposing my last moment had come.

Then I realized that it was Mr Lang.

'Is my trial to begin?' I asked.

'No, no.' He advanced into the room. 'There is to be no trial, Mrs Hammond. This paper is my authority to remove you from this place.'

I could not believe my ears. 'But . . . the charges against me . . .'

'Have all been dropped.'

'But how? Why?'

'Simply that the Begum of Oudh, approached to appear as a Crown witness at your trial, has refused to do so and has entirely exonerated you from any guilt. Not only does she support your story of your part in the Cawnpore business, but she adds that she was aware of how your only concern was for the safety and well-being of the prisoners, and how devastated you were at what happened.'

Again I could not believe my ears: that Hazrat, from whom I had parted so acrimoniously, should have come to my aid.

'And,' Mr Lang went on, 'her evidence, given in writing and under seal, establishes that you could not have been in Jhansi when that massacre took place. Therefore your only crime is that of being governess to the rani and then to the rajah-elect Damodar, and of acting as an emissary for the rani when she required it. None of those can be considered treasonable offences.'

I sat down; my knees would not support me. 'I have killed,' I muttered, 'at least two British soldiers. I confessed as much to General Rose.'

'The general has made no mention of that in his report, and I would not shout it too loudly,' he advised. 'There are no witnesses, and in any event, as I understand it, you killed them in battle when they were trying to kill you. Again, that can hardly be considered a criminal offence. I cannot pretend that you are the most popular woman in India, at least amongst the white population, but it has been determined that you will not be charged with any crime. On the other hand, you are to be deported as an undesirable alien. On the *other* hand, I assume you would wish to leave anyway. Your daughter will of course be returned to you.'

Leave India? I thought. To go where? 'I am penniless,' I said.

'That will be taken care of. If you would care to come outside.'

I hesitated, then followed him. There was a guard on the outer side of the door, standing rigidly to attention. But I had eyes only for the man who waited in the antechamber.

Colonel Dickinson!

For a moment I could not believe my eyes, much as I had been unable to believe my ears a few minutes before, for he wore civilian clothes; this was the first time I had seen him out of uniform.

He stepped towards me. 'Emma?'

I remained speechless.

'I wanted you to know,' he said, 'that I have resigned from the army.'

'But why?'

He shrugged. 'Perhaps I'm getting a little old. Actually . . . sheer disgust. I believed in what we were doing here. I even believed that the mutiny had to be put down as quickly and ruthlessly as possible. I know that what Nana did was one of the most horrible crimes in history. I won't pass judgement on the rani. But I do know that the bestiality of the British troops has been quite equal to anything inflicted by the Indians. I was sickened by the idea of firing men from the mouths of cannon. But that was as nothing with what I saw in Jhansi when our people took the city.'

'Was everyone slaughtered?' No one had thought to tell me.

'No, thank God. Rose managed to regain control after a couple of days, and after that the troops actually tried to help the people burned out of their homes. But that does not excuse the raping and murdering of unarmed people that happened before. Perhaps it was the blowing up of the magazine which took so many of our lives . . . but blowing up magazines to prevent them falling into the hands of the enemy is a legitimate act of war. Our people blew up the magazine in Delhi, taking with it something like a thousand Indians, and are honoured as heroes for what they did. Then the hanging

of Maropant Tambe. That was another act of cold-blooded vengeance. I could stand no more of it.'

'What will you do?'

'I shall return to England, and join my father's business. He has
assured me I shall be welcome.'

'Oh,' I said. 'Then I will wish you every good fortune.'

He hesitated, biting his lip for a moment. Then he asked, 'Would
you regard it as an insult if I were to ask you to accompany me?'

'An insult?' My heart was pounding.

'Well . . . we have so often found ourselves on opposite sides in
the past.'

'But you have just said that we are on the same side, now.'

'Yes,' he said. 'Yes. We cannot turn back the tide of history. But
I think, after what we have both experienced, that we are better
human beings, and that we are entitled to seek some happiness.
Together.'

He held out his hand, and I took it.

'With Alice and Vima,' I said.

'Of course.'

We both looked at Mr Lang.

'If you will come with me,' he said, 'I will take you to Alice.
And Vima.'

'And will we honour Manu?'

'The rani,' James said, 'will be remembered, and honoured, until
the end of time. Her fame shall be sung long after the Raj has
disappeared into history.'

> '*How valiantly like a man fought she,*
> *The Rani of Jhansi*
> *On every parapet a gun she set*
> *Raining fire of hell,*
> *How well like a man fought the Rani of Jhansi*
> *How valiantly and well!*'
>
> Indian folk song